POSSESS ME

POSSESS ME

R. G. ALEXANDER

HEAT | NEW YORK

THE BERKLEY PUBLISHING GROUP
Published by the Penguin Group
Penguin Group (USA) Inc.
375 Hudson Street, New York, New York 10014, USA
Penguin Group (Canada), 90 Eglinton Avenue East, Suite 700, Toronto, Ontario M4P 2Y3, Canada
(a division of Pearson Penguin Canada Inc.)
Penguin Books Ltd., 80 Strand, London WC2R 0RL, England
Penguin Group Ireland, 25 St. Stephen's Green, Dublin 2, Ireland (a division of Penguin Books Ltd.)
Penguin Group (Australia), 250 Camberwell Road, Camberwell, Victoria 3124, Australia
(a division of Pearson Australia Group Pty. Ltd.)
Penguin Books India Pvt. Ltd., 11 Community Centre, Panchsheel Park, New Delhi—110 017, India
Penguin Group (NZ), 67 Apollo Drive, Rosedale, North Shore 0632, New Zealand
(a division of Pearson New Zealand Ltd.)
Penguin Books (South Africa) (Pty.) Ltd., 24 Sturdee Avenue, Rosebank, Johannesburg 2196,
South Africa

Penguin Books Ltd., Registered Offices: 80 Strand, London WC2R 0RL, England

This book is an original publication of The Berkley Publishing Group.

This is a work of fiction. Names, characters, places, and incidents either are the product of the author's imagination or are used fictitiously, and any resemblance to actual persons, living or dead, business establishments, events, or locales is entirely coincidental. The publisher does not have any control over and does not assume any responsibility for author or third-party websites or their content.

PRINTING HISTORY
Heat trade paperback edition / August 2010

Library of Congress Cataloging-in-Publication Data

Alexander, R. G., (date)
    Possess me / R. G. Alexander. — Heat trade pbk. ed.
        p.   cm.
    ISBN 978-0-425-23528-7 (trade pbk.)
    I. Title.
    PS3601.L3545P67 2010
    813'.6—dc22   2010006715

PRINTED IN THE UNITED STATES OF AMERICA

10   9   8   7   6   5   4   3   2   1

To Cookie: Love is the reason. This is *all* because of you. To Mom and Kelly: You have always been the kind of women I aspire to be—strong, courageous, and beautiful. To all the Romance Divas and my Smutketeers—Eden Bradley, Crystal Jordan, and Lilli Feisty—who kept me sane, or at least let me know that crazy was okay. And a special thank-you to Beth, Robin, and Eden for your red pens; to Lacy for giving me inspiration; to my editor Kate for her support and encouragement; to Roberta for believing in me; and to the city of New Orleans—may your magic never die. Thank you all.

❦ RELEASE ME ❦

CHAPTER 1

"*HIM?* OH, BABY GIRL, ARE YOU SURE? HAVEN'T YOU HEARD the stories? What they call him? The man is trouble. By that I mean *I'd* do him, and you know what bad taste *I* have in men."

A few curious tourists eating at the table beside them raised their eyebrows at Michelle's overloud reaction to her plan, and Allegra grinned in spite of her nerves. She probably shouldn't have invited Michelle out to lunch at their favorite po'boy shop to explain it.

Witnesses wouldn't save her from her roommate's vocal, if humorous, disapproval. At least the food was comforting. And filling. She pushed away from the table, half of the giant seafood sandwich left uneaten. "Personally, I can't believe you haven't."

"What? Done him?" Michelle held her hands up and shook her head, chocolate curls bouncing with her vehemence. "He's easy on the eyes, true enough, but that man has a monkey on his back. A giant, climb-the-Empire-State-Building-and-swat-at-airplanes kinda monkey."

Allegra snorted, her sweet tea nearly going up her nose while Michelle shuddered dramatically. "No. He's not for me. And I don't think he's for you either, Allegra. No matter how big a risk taker you are."

Allegra smiled again. This was one of the reasons she'd moved to New Orleans. She needed her friend, even if they disagreed. She needed a little laughter in her life. Someone to tell all her secrets to. Okay. *Most* of her secrets to.

Since the accident, her family back in Houston acted as though she were an invalid with one foot in the grave. She wasn't *their* Allegra anymore. To her it seemed they could barely look at her, and they spoke in those hushed tones reserved for terminal patients and funeral homes. It was like a never-ending wake.

Michelle, on the other hand, treated her the same way she had when they'd shared a dorm at the University of Texas. Back when Allegra was a wild, carefree youth who wasn't afraid to take chances, to live. Back when she was whole. So when Michelle called and mentioned her roommate had moved out and taken a job in North Carolina, Allegra jumped at the chance to start again. Before she let her family's concern overtake her determination to heal. To have a life again.

Michelle was right about one thing; he *did* look like trouble. Lucifer the fallen angel himself. Too beautiful not to be a sin. Celestin Dias Rousseau. It was a mouthful of a name for the mouthwatering man who owned the small coffee shop across the street from her and Michelle's apartment.

The man she was going to seduce.

Luring men into having sex had never been one of her pastimes, even before the accident. But for the last few months Rousseau had become Allegra's obsession.

Who was she kidding? She'd been hooked from the first morning she'd laid eyes on the man.

Her physical therapist in Houston had left her with strict instructions not to overdo, but not to let her leg muscles weaken any further from disuse either. So as soon as she'd arrived in town she'd taken to walking through the French Quarter early in the morning. Oh there were still people milling about, there always were, but in the morning it was a different crowd.

Workers unloaded trucks to replenish the bars and restaurants that had been drained dry by the influx of tourists and businessmen. Artists, psychics, and performers staked out their places on the sidewalk, ready for the crowds that were their bread and butter. Crowds that, according to Michelle, were finally coming back after the nightmare of Hurricane Katrina.

Allegra had pushed too hard that morning—had it only been six weeks ago?—leaning heavily on her ridiculous cane, her skin covered in sweat as if she'd run a marathon rather than walked a few simple blocks. She could see the apartment. She only had to cross one narrow street and climb one steep flight of stairs. It might as well have been Mount Everest.

She'd lowered herself carefully onto the curb in front of a shop that smelled of espresso beans and chocolate. It was as good a place to live as any, she'd thought, closing her eyes and focusing on slowing her heart rate. All she needed was a cold drink and a pillow, and she'd pay whatever curbs were going for these days.

"I have an extra iced coffee with your name on it."

The voice had slid down her spine like a rough tongue, instantly making her think of late nights and sweat-soaked sex.

Sultry, with just enough edge to put her hibernating libido on red alert.

Allegra fanned herself dramatically. "Don't lie to a dying woman."

They'd laughed softly together and she shielded her eyes with her hand, looking up with a friendly smile at the warrior god who was handing her a coffee.

He was perfect.

Light cocoa skin and full lips framed by a closely trimmed goatee that saved his face from being too pretty. His body, however, was all male; thick thighs, lean arms roped with muscle and tribal tattoos, the hand holding the to-go cup so big she actually shivered. And those eyes. Hazel, heavy-lidded, long-lashed. The writer in her was inspired. *Smoky eyes. Bedroom eyes. Brooding.* Unless you wrote romance, how often did you get to use *those words*?

His hair fell in thick dreadlocks to his waist, tied back loosely with what looked like an extra apron tie. Allegra nearly melted into the concrete at the sight.

In high school, when her friends had all gone insane for the rock-and-roll hair bands, she'd never understood it. No male should have prettier or longer hair than she did. But he'd done it. This stranger had made long hair—knotted hair—sexy. She'd wanted to grip it and pull his lean, broad-shouldered body closer, to study every line of his face and the tattoo she noticed peeking out from the neckline of his white T-shirt. To kiss him, before he'd even told her his name.

He'd handed her the coffee, free of charge, and they exchanged a few sentiments about the weather before he abruptly left her to go back inside, the line at the cash register grabbing his attention.

The next day there'd been a small table and chair beside the café, just for her. It had quickly become a ritual between them.

She, sweaty and wrung out from her morning workout; he, cool and devastatingly attractive, if distant. But every day she came back, hoping for more. For conversation. For flirting. For something. She'd never drunk so much coffee in her life.

Like Michelle said, she'd heard the talk. Noticed that his morning crowd was mostly made up of women. And those women would speak in loud, giggling whispers about him as they walked by her table. They would say he knew the right words to heal, and his touch could melt even the coldest heart. And sex with him? Sex with him was a blessing from Marie Laveau herself. According to them, he was the love doctor of the Big Easy.

Bone Daddy.

That's what they called him. A walking, talking, well-hung pleasure factory who, with a few easy orgasms, could bring you whatever your heart desired. Your boyfriend would propose, your boss would give you a raise. Rumor had it he could even heal your scars, inside and out. *If* you satisfied his lust.

The conversations were confusing, since they didn't seem to jibe with her own observations of Rousseau. With her, Rousseau was solicitous but shy. And always respectful. Maybe she wasn't his type, though sometimes she thought she saw something in his eyes. Lust. For her. And it gave her hope.

She could be mistaking pity or heartburn for desire, but she didn't think so. She couldn't be wrong. Her feelings were far too intense to be one-sided.

Yes. He was trouble. But it was exactly the kind of trouble she wanted. After a year of being resigned to the life of a shut-in, the wild thing in her wanted to come out and play. And it only wanted to play with him.

"Earth to Allegra, come in loony lady. You haven't heard a word I've said, have you?"

Allegra blinked, coming back to the present. "Probably not. Chelle, you know what this last year's been like for me. I thought you told me it was time to take some chances again. To jump off a few new cliffs."

"Baby cliffs, hon. You don't just go straight for the Grand Canyon. If I hadn't seen Stacy make such a fool of herself over him, maybe I'd be singing the 'I saw him first' tune. Unfortunately I had a front row seat to the crazy show."

"You told me. She followed him around like a groupie."

Michelle huffed. "Worse. She did everything short of throwing herself on his counter and spreading her legs. When she finally crossed that line as well, he took her up on her offer." She shrugged. "But maybe he's not the stud the gossips make him out to be. I mean, if he was, would she really leave the state less than a week after landing him?"

"It *was* the job of her dreams." Allegra mentally chalked another one up for Bone Daddy Rousseau. That man had some heavy-duty mojo. Occasionally it struck her as odd that she wasn't jealous, hearing about all these ladies and the lengths they were willing to go for his attention. She didn't like the thought of him with other women, but that in no way deterred her from going after him. Was Michelle right? Was she begging for more heartbreak?

Michelle reached for her hand. "That isn't the point. Look, instead of deciding to go after Rousseau, why don't you let me introduce you to one of the teachers from my school? Then at least I'd know you'd be safe."

"Is she in danger? Sounds exciting. What have you gotten yourself into now, darlin'?" A tall, muscular blond with a sexy smile twirled an empty chair around and straddled it to sit beside them, setting two plates of cheesecake drizzled in praline sauce down on the table in front of the wide-eyed women. "I stole these from that sweet little waitress with the big . . . personality. Your favorite, isn't it, Mimi?"

Michelle didn't look like she appreciated the interruption. "I don't know why I thought you'd listen to me. You didn't take my advice when I told you to stay away from Benjamin Adair."

Allegra covered her mouth to hide her grin. "Hi, Ben."

"Afternoon, Legs. I don't think Mimi is too happy to see me." He dipped his finger in the whipped topping on Michelle's plate, popping it into his mouth with a moan. "It's not as good as the chocolate caramel rolls at Café Bwe, but still decadent enough to tempt anyone with a pulse."

"I'd rather be undead, thank you very much. I've got to get back to work, Allegra. We'll talk about this later." Michelle slid her purse over her shoulder and stood to leave. "Don't do anything crazy until then. In other words, don't listen to a word he says."

Ben leaned back to watch her walk away and let out a low whistle. "She's feistier than usual today. You told her, huh?"

"Not that you were helping me. She'd lock me in the apartment for the next millennium if she knew."

Ben had told her that he and Michelle had been friends when they were children, but they'd grown apart. Allegra was sure there was more to the story. The two of them avoided each other whenever possible, and snapped at each other incessantly each time they met. Well, Michelle snapped at Ben. He just scared her away with sexual innuendo.

He pulled Michelle's dessert closer, dipping his finger in the creamy concoction once more before holding it up to Allegra's lips. "We can't have that, can we, Legs? Can't let the mean ol' teacher ruin all our fun."

Her lips tingled and she opened her mouth, tongue flicking the pad of his finger. His thick lashes fluttered in surprise, and he smiled in approval.

She rolled her eyes. "You're a big tease, Ben Adair."

But she had to admit, he was infinitely charming. He'd just shown up at her special table at Café Bwe one day, acting as though they'd know each other for years. When she'd told him her name, he decided to call her Legs for short. From anyone else she'd think it insulting. After all, she walked with a distinctive limp, and beneath her sweat pants her left knee was riddled with scar tissue from multiple surgeries. But Ben's green eyes had been full of mischief, free from judgment. And he'd also been a fount of information on her favorite subject. Rousseau.

From Ben, she'd discovered the unique looks she'd been salivating over came from Rousseau's unusual ancestry. His father was of Haitian descent, and his mother was half Irish, half Portuguese. It was a breathtaking combination.

She'd also learned he'd basically raised himself and taken care of his mother and sisters since he was very young. His father wasn't exactly a model citizen. But Rousseau hadn't let those obstacles stop him from owning his own business, from sending his youngest sister to college. If it weren't for his tomcatting reputation, he'd be too good to be true.

Ben frowned. "I'm sensing doubt, my lovely. What's wrong?"

She'd barely admitted it to herself, yet he sensed it. He was too intuitive for his own good. "I don't know, Ben. It's just that . . ."

"He's never made a move on you, and you've seen him out with other women. *Lots* of other women."

She gave him a sideways glare. "You're kind of creepy when you do that."

He shrugged. "I can't help it, Legs. It's a family gift. As far as Rousseau, well, he's a complicated man, I won't lie. But you have to trust me, all is not what it seems. It's you he wants. I've never seen him so out of sorts over a woman. He just needs the proper incentive." He took her hand in his, his thumb lightly caressing her knuckles until she shivered. "I can get him there tonight, keep the wolves at bay so to speak. But you have to let him know, without a doubt, that it's him you want."

"It's harder for women. If we push, we come off as too easy or aggressive. If we don't, you think we're prudes." Allegra leaned back in her chair with a sigh. "What if he says no?"

"Then he's a fool, and I'll be more than happy to personally relieve you of any and all of your pent-up frustration."

She tried to smile at his flattery, but she just wasn't sure if she still had the nerve she'd always been famous for. The stuff of legends, Michelle had once called her. No dare was too dangerous, no mountain too steep.

That's who she used to be. Before she'd taken one dare too many.

Being with Rousseau was the first thing in a long time she wanted enough to take that leap for. But he had so many beautiful women after him. She couldn't help but doubt that he'd be interested in a skinny girl with scars on her arms and legs. A girl who walked with a cane because, no matter how much physical therapy she'd had, or how many miles she walked, her left leg would never work right again.

Ben tsked, reading her thoughts again. "You are beautiful. All those luscious strawberry curls, the delicate freckles scattered across your creamy skin. He has a penchant for freckles. So do I. He'll want to lick every single one." He leaned in closer. "Your eyes alone would make any man fall in love with you. So big and blue. So lost. They turn a man inside out with the need to protect you. To make you smile."

Allegra glared. "I'm not broken. Not lost or fragile. I never have been. If that's what he wants . . ."

Ben laid his hand over hers. "He wants *you*, Legs. And I'm going to give you to him. But not without my price."

The price. When he'd first mentioned being a part of her plan, she'd thought he was joking. Allegra studied his intent expression and knew he wasn't. She knew he found her attractive. The parts of her he'd seen anyway. And she had to admit he was the exact type she used to fall for. The polar opposite of Rousseau in looks and demeanor.

Three wasn't the number Allegra usually thought of when she imagined herself and Rousseau together. Not that she'd never fantasized about it. What it would be like to have two men focused on her pleasure, touching her, taking her. It was just one of those adventures she'd never sought out. Surely Rousseau wouldn't take him up on it.

She bit her lip. What would she do if he did?

"You're not helping to calm me down at all."

His smile was devilish. "That's a good sign."

Allegra shook her head at his teasing. "I should go back to the apartment. If I'm going to be a femme fatale tonight I need a long soak in the tub. No man will find a woman who creaks when she walks irresistible."

Ben dug into the cheesecake in front of him. "He will if *you* do it, Legs. Trust me. And don't be late."

She dropped a tip on the table and limped away, mumbling under her breath. "Yeah, better not be late. Wouldn't want to miss my biggest crash and burn of all time."

CHAPTER 2

THE PLACE WAS PACKED. CROWDED AND LOUD, HOT WITH bodies and expectations.

Rousseau lifted a watered-down soda to his lips and grimaced. What had he expected? Even in September, the weekends still brought revelers to the Big Easy. He hated this. Why had he allowed Ben to talk him into leaving the loft? It was just asking for trouble. At home he'd be able to do the paperwork for the café. Finally get through that book he'd been reading.

You are nothing if not boring. You're also a liar. You merely want the chance to see her *through the window across the way. Maybe that Toussaint girl would be massaging her leg again. Mmmmm. Or maybe she'd be alone, walking around in nothing but those sweet pink panties with all that lace in the front. I'd love to tear those off with my teeth and stick my tongue—*

"Shut. Up."

"Talking to yourself again?" Ben's knowing grin set Rousseau's teeth on edge. Bastard. He knew better than most how much he disliked these crowded clubs in the Quarter. Full of drunken women and men, all looking for the same thing.

Sex.

It brought out something inside him he couldn't control. Something that kept him from having a normal life, from asking someone on a date where he didn't wake up with a stranger or two, surrounded by handcuffs, whips, and memories that would make even the lewdest of men blush. "Why are we here, Ben? You said you needed me. Needed to talk. We could have done that at the loft."

Ben took a long pull of his wet beer bottle, his throat working, eyes closed as he enjoyed the taste. Rousseau envied him, but he didn't trust himself with alcohol anymore. It made it too easy to lose control.

His friend set the bottle down and leaned back against the booth. "Relax, man. It's dark. We're hidden away in a corner booth. We can see the whole room from here, but no one is looking at us. And I do need to talk to you. About Allegra."

Here it came. He knew it would. How many days had he looked up from the line of ogling women to find her sitting at the table *he'd* put outside for her, laughing at something Ben was saying? Too many. "You want her. Be careful. She's Michelle's friend."

Ben laughed, shaking his head. "A man would have to be blind not to. And Michelle has no hold on me. Seems to think I'm a bad influence on Allegra. But I've told you before, it's not me she wants, though I do think she's attracted." Rousseau tensed and Ben sighed, leaning across the table. "Allegra Jarrod wants you, Rousseau. Not him. Not the experience. You. She doesn't even know he exists, but I sense she could handle it if she did."

That was the problem. If she knew, there would be no secrets, no possibility of disbelief or rejection. She would come to him. Or run away as fast as she could.

She liked the man she imagined him to be. But she didn't know what he was. Didn't know what his father's lust and arrogance had made him. And he didn't want her to know. "You *sensed* she could handle it? Your gift must be on the fritz. There is no woman who would want more than a night or two with me. No woman on this earth. And we both know it. I think it's better for everyone if we leave well enough alone. She doesn't need to know what I am. You can have her if you want. I'm going home."

"That's too bad. Because she's already here. She and Michelle just sat down at the table closest to the dance floor."

"Shit." He saw her as soon as he turned his head. Allegra. Ethereal and lovely in a long broom skirt and a sheer, long-sleeved blouse. She always tried to cover herself, but he'd seen her. All of her, enough to know she was perfection. Strawberries and cream with sprinkles of cinnamon. A delicious confection he hungered for far more than he was willing to admit.

He watched her tug on the thin, red, see-through material of her blouse. She was worried about her scars. He knew from Ben that she'd been a writer for an adventure travel magazine before an accident left her on an open-ended vacation. She'd been all over the world, climbing mountains and diving off exotic island cliffs. Beautiful *and* courageous. An irresistible combination.

Rousseau had never left the state of Louisiana. He'd stuck out the hurricanes and the breaking of the levees. His only escape came in books about travel, or stories the female tourists who ended up in his shop, in his bed, would share in the glow between rounds of hard fucking.

There is nowhere you could go that would rival the sights I've shown you. The heights, the sensations, the experiences you have had because of me.

He ignored the defensive voice in his head. He'd never leave New Orleans. He was tied here just as surely as if there were shackles on his legs.

Allegra may be here now, mending her body and soul. But she wouldn't stay for long. And no matter how much he wanted her, she wouldn't be able to accept his curse. He gripped the table and shook his head. "I'll see you tomorrow."

"Coward."

Ben's quiet words sent a gale of laughter echoing through his head, followed by a strong surge of power. "Damn it, *no*."

I do like that man. We only seek to give you what you want, Celestin. What you need. I find I am sick of your pathetic martyrdom. I thought we'd grown past that, you and I, until she came along. She has not asked for Bone Daddy by name, but before the night is over, I'll make sure she wants to. That way, we can all have what we truly desire. Everybody wins.

"QUIT FIDGETING, ALLEGRA. YOU'RE MAKING ME NERVOUS."

"You didn't have to come with me." She wasn't sure why Michelle had come along. Allegra had just wanted a few tips on seducing the opposite sex, or for her roommate to make her hair do something sexy despite the humidity. This was not part of the plan.

Michelle smiled as an attractive man tripped off the dance floor, too busy trying to look down her tight black halter to notice the step. Allegra sighed. She wished she had breasts like those.

"Are you kidding?" Michelle adjusted her strap as an excuse to check out the fit of the man's jeans while talking to Allegra. "I wouldn't let you come to a place like this without a chaperone. A chaperone who can protect you from yourself if you even *think* about chasing after Rousseau. Besides, after dealing with angry teenagers wielding finger paint and a subconscious need to destroy my classroom, I need a break. Maybe a new distraction."

Distraction was Michelle's code word for *man*. No relationship or boyfriend. Not for her. She was terminally single. Always had been. For some reason Michelle just didn't trust men. She'd told Allegra once that if she didn't enjoy the male body as much as she did, she would go after women instead.

Allegra shook her head. "How is it that you can have 'distractions' and I can't?"

Michelle kept her gaze on the clumsy hot guy, who noticed her studying him and nearly dropped his beer. "Because you don't have distractions, my friend. I can't count on half the fingers of one hand the amount of times you've been in a relationship. And I know for a fact you've never had a one-night stand. You take men far too seriously." She rose from her chair. "I'm gonna go grab some drinks for us. We can talk about all the reasons you should avoid one particular troublemaker when I get back."

Michelle walked away, and a knot formed in Allegra's stomach. What was Michelle not telling her? Was it more than fear that a Casanova would break her heart that kept Michelle protesting her choice? And where were Ben and Rousseau?

"Would you like to dance?"

She looked up at a twentysomething man with light brown hair and an open smile. He obviously hadn't seen her walk in, or he wouldn't be asking. Before she could shake her head and thank him for the offer, someone appeared at his side, towering over him.

"She is already taken, *mon petit*. Why don't you go ask your friend over there to dance? He doesn't look too happy to see you with us."

The young man's face turned beet red, his eyes widening and lips parting as he studied the magnetic man who'd spoken. She'd know that sexy voice blindfolded. Allegra didn't blame him for the once-over he gave Rousseau.

Sexuality rolled off him like heated steam. And he stood with a sensual confidence that she'd never seen in him before. Dangerously appealing. She imagined he was just as irresistible to the men in the room as he was to the women.

To her.

Rousseau arched one perfect brow. "The other friends you came with already know, little man. Why deny yourself the pleasure of his touch any longer? Dance with him."

Allegra felt her jaw drop when her would-be dance partner spun on his heel without hesitation, heading back to his table and holding out his hand to a shy, surprised-looking Latino. "How did you know?"

Rousseau shrugged, his gaze glued to the two males who walked to the dance floor, their steps slow, as though unsure whether they were headed to the guillotine or salvation. "He was easy to read. He just needed someone to give him permission to follow his passions. The same as every other human I know."

She wondered if he'd been drinking. Ben said he was different away from the café, but he seemed . . . transformed. His gaze clashed with hers and her heart skipped a beat.

"Your eyes."

"Can only see you, *cher*. Dance with me, I need to touch you."

Her thoughts were muddled, confused. His eyes—she'd thought they were hazel, but now they seemed more golden. Amber with flecks of green. He called her *cher*. Darling. And he wanted to . . . dance? Her hand searched for her cane where it rested against her chair. "I'm not sure you know what you're letting yourself in for. I can't really dance like I used to."

"We won't really be dancing. And you won't need that, *cher*. Not with me." He took her hand from the rounded top of the walking stick and lifted her easily from her seat.

She felt as though she were floating toward the middle of the dance floor, the toe-tapping jazz tune that had been playing giving way to a slow, sultry melody.

Her eyes closed at the first press of his body against hers. He was so hot. Blazing. One of his hands slid down her back and cupped her hip, dragging her closer. And hard. Oh God, he was so big and hard.

"Do you like what you feel, Allegra? So do I." He nuzzled her neck and growled softly. "I've wanted you this close from the moment I saw you. Only in a perfect world, you wouldn't have any clothes on at all, and I'd be inside you."

She shuddered at the image, her laughter huffing against his temple as he pressed a kiss to her chin. "I'd feel a little awkward if I was naked in the middle of a crowded club."

He pulled back and she opened her eyes to see his golden gaze, so like a cat's, focusing on her lips. "You'd never notice. Or if you did, you wouldn't care. I know you've fantasized about it, Allegra. Watching and being watched."

She shook her head. It was impossible to concentrate on much beyond the feel of his shoulders beneath her hands, his body swaying, chest brushing against her sensitive nipples. Who was this man and what had he done with her hesitant Rousseau? Not that she was complaining. She was just in shock. "I don't think I'd like an audience when I lose control. My fantasies aren't *that* wild."

I think they are. And I can prove it.

Had he spoken? She wasn't sure. The room seemed to tilt on its side, the sounds all around her suddenly muted echoes. Rousseau took a step back, tugging his black T-shirt over his head and dropping it to the floor, baring his smooth dusky chest to her gaze.

Damn, he was gorgeous.

She could see his tattoos clearly now, covering both his arms, lining his collarbone. She gasped in fascination when she saw the small metal rings piercing his nipples. His fingers reached up and tugged one of the loops, and he bit his lip in obvious pleasure, drawing her gaze to his beautiful mouth. "Do you like, *cher*?"

She glanced around nervously, wondering if anyone was watching his impromptu strip show. And they were. The dance floor was cleared and the crowd who'd been dancing beside them had formed a circle around them, watching as they touched each other, or themselves.

Rousseau cupped her cheek to turn her attention back to him. His fingers slid down her neck, inside the vee of her neckline and yanked, tearing the sheer shirt down the middle, along with the red tank top she was wearing beneath it.

"What the hell?" She tried to grab the edges of her shirt and pull them together, but she wasn't fast enough.

He gripped her arms and pulled her close, nibbling on her lower lip until she was trembling. "Not hell, *cher*. Heaven. *Your* fantasies. And theirs. All your deepest, hidden desires. Ah, Allegra, I knew you were a bad girl."

He lifted her breasts and plucked at her long nipples, moaning against her mouth. "Your nipples should be pierced. You're so sensitive here you might even come as they put them in. Not rings though. Maybe small bars that I could twist with my tongue."

He turned her around to face the crowd once more, bared to their avid gazes. Pierced? Her fantasies? His touch was swiftly turning her brain to pudding, and her inhibitions to dust.

A lusty groan drew her attention to the young man who'd had to work up the courage to ask his male friend to dance in public. What a difference a dance made. The Latino boy with the shy expression had his head thrown back in ecstasy, his body bent over the booth where all his friends were sitting as his lover fucked him from behind, slender hips pumping with the power of their need.

"Passion is sacred in all its forms, is it not, *cher*? Nothing that feels that good should be taboo." He cupped her breasts from behind, his breath hot against her shoulder as she watched the two men together, unaware of anything but each other. "Does it surprise you that I know? That the sight of them together only fuels the desire you've kindled?"

It should, but it didn't. She felt drunk, drugged, and thoroughly aroused at the scene playing out before her eyes. She hadn't thought about two men together being sensual, but seeing them, their two lean, masculine bodies straining together, their need for each other clear for all to see . . . it was beautiful. It made her want Rousseau's touch. Made her want more.

Allegra turned away from the climaxing couple to see a women facedown, her body lying across the laps of two men in business suits. Her pencil skirt had been tugged up over her hips, her white silk panties tugged down as the men took turns spanking the flushing cheeks of her ass. The woman was crying out her pleasure.

"You like that, don't you, Allegra? You like the idea of the forbidden. So do they. People's secret desires are often surprising, even to me, even after all these centuries. Yours most of all. And I find I'm having a hard time controlling *my* desire to see if you're wearing those pink lace panties that I love."

She felt the breeze on her hard nipples, between her thighs, before she became aware enough to pull her gaze away from the woman being smacked into orgasm and looked down at herself. Rousseau had lifted her loose skirt and tucked the hem into the waistband, leaving her body visible to the room. Everyone could see her scar-ravaged knee, her pale skin, her small breasts topped by long, pink nipples . . . and her peach lace panties. And she didn't care. She wanted them to look. Wanted to be seen.

"You are brave, aren't you? Lovely. This color suits you, *cher*. Perfect for such biteable curves. Now I have a sudden longing for peaches."

"I don't have any curves." Her voice cracked when his hot palm cupped her lace-covered sex. "Rousseau . . . that feels . . ."

"You have all the curves you need to drive a man wild with the need to touch you. I could make you come now, right here, in front of all these people. Make you scream with it. Have you begging for more." His voice was gravel-rough against her ear, his bare cock sliding against the lace. When had he taken off his jeans?

She was about to beg him to do it, to make her scream, anything he wanted, when she noticed someone had come closer to them on the dance floor. Ben Adair.

He licked his lower lip, his eyes on Rousseau's fingers as they slipped beneath the flimsy fabric to tangle in her strawberry curls. She couldn't contain her whimper when Ben undid the top button of his jeans, then the next, his own impressive erection straining against the denim.

"He's gotten to you, hasn't he? The idea of it. Of all of us together. We've shared women before, but never one so full of untapped passion. Never one so strong in her need."

They'd shared women before. The words penetrated the sensual fog surrounding her, but she couldn't make herself pull away. Was she a game to them? Just another notch? Did she even care?

"No. You are more, Allegra Jarrod. All you have to do is tell me what you want, and it's yours."

"I want . . ." Suddenly Michelle was there, blocking her view of Ben, kneeling at his feet as she took his cock into her mouth. Michelle? Ben moaned loud and long, his hands fisting in her curls, hips thrusting helplessly against her as she took him deep. Oh God, that shouldn't be turning her on, should it?

Rousseau pressed his finger against her clit, regaining her attention with a jolt of pleasure. "Who do you want, *cher*?"

"You. I want you, Rousseau." She was out of her mind with the need to come. The air around her filled with groans and cries of carnal delight. Rousseau's body felt like a furnace behind her, and she turned in his arms, rubbing her breasts against his chest, her nipples scraping the cool metal as she licked his neck. Salty. Delicious. Male. "Please, Rousseau. I want you."

He jerked in her arms, jarring her with the strength of his reaction to her touch. He pulled back, his jaw tight, eyes nearly glowing with golden lust and restrained power. "Call me by my other name. Tell me you want Bone Daddy. Say it out loud, and I can fulfill your every desire. Do it now."

"I see you, spirit. Back off."

Allegra heard Michelle's voice, but the words didn't make any sense. She said something else in Creole and a wave of dizziness washed over Allegra. A crash of the cymbals, the music and overloud buzz of the crowd resumed.

She looked around the room. The young male couple was still dancing awkwardly on the floor, smiling proudly at each other. The men and woman in business suits at the table were still deep in discussion, no sign of what they'd been up to only moments before. Had she just imagined the whole thing?

She looked up at Rousseau's pained expression. "What was that? What happened?"

He opened his eyes. Hazel. Full of regret. "I'm sorry, Allegra. I didn't mean to offe—"

Michelle was suddenly beside them on the dance floor. "We need to go now. I brought your purse and cane. Come on, Allegra. Trust me, it's time to go."

Where was Ben? Hadn't she just been with Ben? Allegra was still confused when Michelle took her hand, nearly dragging her away from a solemn Rousseau, standing silent in the mass of writhing bodies. Not doing anything to stop her from leaving.

It wasn't until they'd left the club that she stumbled, sharp needlelike stabs of pain shooting from her knee up to her left hip. She stopped on the corner, her knuckles turning white as she gripped her cane hard. "Chelle, my knee. It didn't hurt when I was dancing with Rousseau. I didn't even realize . . . How could that be?"

She'd lived with the pain for so long, it was hard to imagine she wouldn't have noticed it was gone, even for a moment.

Michelle looked over her shoulder, watching the door to the club, as though worried they would be followed. "I told you, Allegra. That man is trouble."

Allegra limped behind her, mind racing. She would suspect Rousseau of slipping something in her drink but she hadn't had one. Maybe he was a hypnotist. That might explain the illusory orgy she'd just witnessed. Participated in. Explain why his eyes had seemed to glow with an unearthly light.

Whatever the reason, she had to know. Her desire to have a mad affair with the café owner hadn't changed, but now her curiosity was as strong as her need. "Define *trouble*."

CHAPTER 3

"POSSESSED? LIKE *THE EXORCIST* POSSESSED?"

"More like Whoopi Goldberg in *Ghost* possessed. Sort of. Look, voodoo is my family's religion, not mine. It's hard to explain." Michelle had her feet propped on the desk by the window, blocking the view of Rousseau's apartment and twirling a letter opener in her hand.

Allegra sat on the fat, soft sofa bed in the living room, a book open in her lap, unable to keep her lips from twitching at her friend's announcement. "You *really* don't like him, do you? Only you could come up with something this creative. It's those paintings you've been doing lately. All those ghosts and graveyards and demons. Maybe the paint fumes have gone to your head."

Michelle made a face. "Laugh it up, but I'm serious. Mama gave me that book when I . . . a while back. She knows about Rousseau's case. He even came to her once, but she says she's not the one who can help him."

Michelle's mother was Mambo Toussaint, a voodoo priestess who ran a small shop on Royal Street, selling charms and special oils, giving the occasional reading. She was the genuine article, a fascinating and loving woman. She'd given Allegra an oil to put in her bath that worked better than all the strange liniments her therapists had tried on her knee.

But possessed? They thought Rousseau was hosting a spirit called a—she looked down at the book—a Loa? "Rousseau believes it, too? So the nickname Bone Daddy is actually . . . ?"

"The name of the Loa, yes."

"A *sex* Loa."

Michelle shifted, getting up from the chair and picking up her workout bag. "I know it sounds crazy. There isn't a day that goes by that I wish I didn't know any of this existed. But it does." She took a step toward the door. "I have a kickboxing lesson to get to. Just read the book. Mama put notes in the margins."

"Michelle?" Allegra tilted her head to study her roommate. "Are you okay? I mean other than being stressed at my recent crush."

"I'm fine, Allegra. Just busy. Thanks. Read that book, especially chapter eleven." She walked out the door, and Allegra fell back onto the pillows with a sigh.

Her friend was lying. Allegra wasn't so caught up in her own turmoil that she couldn't see Michelle had changed lately. Distracted, edgy, keeping herself so busy she never had time to breathe, let alone relax.

She understood Michelle's dedication to her job. Her work for New Schools for New Orleans, and her help rebuilding the charter program's art department, had been amazing.

When Allegra had first known Michelle, she'd just been getting a degree to escape from a town full of interfering family and bead-craving tourists while she worked on creating the perfect masterpiece. Now she was a leader in the education community. Allegra couldn't be prouder of all she'd accomplished. But it didn't seem to satisfy her. Chelle had to keep moving.

All those defense classes. Kickboxing. Karate. She'd even been learning capoeira, a Brazilian form of martial arts that looked like dancing. She envied Michelle's energy, but though they lived in the same two-room apartment, she barely saw her.

And what she did see concerned her. Allegra turned her head to the wall lined with Michelle's canvases. The nearest and most recent was disturbing. Three men, their features distorted and grotesque, their faces covered in blood. All three had ghostly figures behind them, figures whose arms thrust inside the men's bodies, as if guiding them toward the screaming woman curled up against the alley wall in front of them.

It was a dark piece. A scary piece. Especially since the woman looked an awful lot like Michelle herself.

Allegra picked the book up and rolled onto her right side, propping a pillow beneath her arm so she could read. It was a well-loved book, the cover lined with ragged threads. It was so old and worn smooth she could barely make out the title, but inside was everything she could ever want to know about voodoo.

An idea for a lifestyle article came into her mind, and she pushed it aside. She couldn't think about her old job now, her old life. She was too distracted by the present.

She flipped the yellowing pages until she found the right chapter, and read. The researcher in her was fascinated, lost in all the information.

Voodoo was an unusual mix of Catholicism and tribal ancestor worship. Loas were like saints or angels, intermediaries with the divine. But they all seemed to have their own unique personalities, and some less-than-angelic cravings and desires.

During rituals, the priests and priestesses of the religion, the houngans and mambos, were "ridden" by a Loa, possessed for a short time, giving body to the spirit and allowing them to revel in the joys of the flesh. Food. Drink. Sex. In return the Loa would heal, advise, and carry prayers with them when they returned to the other world.

Allegra sat up, wincing at the pain that ran like a current down her leg. How did this connect with Rousseau? She turned another page and saw writing in the margin beside a long list of Loa names and descriptions. "Bone Daddy. First arrived at peristyle, the ritual space, in the eighteen hundreds. Associated with sexual satisfaction, desire. Unknown origin, unknown family. Mischievous and magnetic."

Bone Daddy. There it was. That name. But no matter how interesting the topic, she knew she had just as hard a time believing in voodoo spirits as she did in vampires and aliens.

She'd been all over the planet, learned about so many different kinds of rituals and cultures, even different forms of voodoo in other parts of the world. She respected the beliefs of others, but that didn't mean she shared them. Allegra believed in what she could see. What she could prove.

She was back to square one. How did she explain Rousseau's behavior? Ben had convinced her she would have to be the aggressor. That she would have to tell Rousseau that she wanted him. But he'd turned the tables on her. He'd been the aggressor. More than that. He'd mastered her. Owned her. Surprised her with his overt sexuality.

Or had he? How much of that dance was real, and how much

had been in her mind? She'd be the first to admit she had an over-active imagination, but it wasn't *that* good.

Her nipples scraped against her tank top as she remembered what she'd seen. Last night had revealed an aspect of herself she hadn't been aware of. She loved to watch.

Real or not, that peek into the inner fantasies of others had been *her* fantasy. And he'd given it to her. Or . . . she imagined that he had.

Her fingers reached up to graze her sensitive breasts, the way his had. It had felt so real. His lips teasing hers, his hand be-tween her thighs. Unfortunately her hallucination, or whatever it was, had ended before she'd had the orgasm she'd been right on the edge of.

The air in the apartment grew warm and she pulled off her shirt, both hands reaching for her small breasts, desperate to ease the ache.

She closed her eyes, and an image of Rousseau immediately appeared behind her lids. He was smiling, watching her. She wanted him to watch. Wanted to show him what she needed. She tugged hard on her nipples, biting her lip at the sharp sensation.

One hand slid inside her shorts, beneath her panties. The pink ones. He'd mentioned loving them on her. Had he seen her through the window? Had he watched her, touching himself?

She let her fantasy Rousseau nod. Yes. Yes, he'd been looking. Yes, he'd stroked that thick, beautiful erection at the sight of her. "Oh God."

Was this magic—the way the mere thought of him made her feel? She wasn't this woman. This over-sexed, crazy stalker. She hadn't acted normally since she'd met Rousseau. Maybe he'd put her under some sort of a spell.

Her fingers slid through her arousal, her right leg bending so she could thrust deep, fucking herself, imagining it was him.

Two fingers, three, but she knew he was bigger. She'd felt him against her. She'd have a hard time taking him, it would be so tight, so full.

Four fingers. He'd stretch her wide, not stopping until every long, hard inch of him was inside.

She'd have to take it, take him. He'd torture her with slow, dragging glides, refusing her pleas to hurry.

Faster. Harder. Please.

Her body would cling to his, muscles tightening around him until he lost his control. He'd take her nipples between his teeth, tugging as he groaned against her flesh, his hips pumping her across the bed with the power of his need.

Yes. Yes. Rousseau. Harder. Fuck me harder. I'm coming!

His eyes lit with an eerie golden glow behind her closed lids as she came.

Call me Bone Daddy.

HE'D CLOSED HIS SHOP ON A SUNDAY. HE NEVER DID THAT. Monday was the only day Café Bwe was closed. It had been that way since his coffee shop had first opened.

She was hell on his schedule.

Rousseau walked down the dirty side streets that led to his mother's apartment complex, thinking about Allegra Jarrod's fantasies. She'd surprised him. He hadn't had any idea she was that passionate, that open-minded.

I knew.

"No, you didn't. Not until you touched her mind." If he had,

Rousseau wouldn't have been able to keep the Loa at bay for so long.

True. We should go back. She's thinking about us. About fucking us. I can smell it.

"We have to do this first." Bone Daddy grew quiet, understanding Rousseau's family obligations. He should. He was one of them.

Guilt swamped him. He was using his mother as a convenient excuse to get away from temptation. She'd asked him to stop by for weeks but he'd told her he was busy, even when it wasn't true.

He knew his reputation was as bad as his father's had been, that she'd heard the rumors about his sexual exploits. New Orleans, for all the tourists, was in many ways a tight-knit community. And he had no wish to bring his mother more shame, though she never asked him about what he did. Never acted as though she was anything but proud of her son.

Nothing had changed. The beautifully aging redhead who still spoke Portuguese when she was excited pulled him inside the large, rambling building that had long ago been converted to small apartment units. She shoved a giant plate of food in front of him, and showed him his sister's latest college grades.

He fixed the window unit, trying in vain once more to convince her to move to a new house. A house of her own. He would pay for it. He had the money. But she refused. She'd raised her children here, she knew all her neighbors, and this was where she would die. But she didn't argue as vehemently as she had in the past. Maybe he was finally wearing her down.

"Who is she?"

The change in topic startled him. "Who is who?"

His mother rolled her eyes. "You think I don't recognize that expression? I am too old to know love, passion, when I see it?"

Love? "I'm just full. I ate too much. I always do when I come here."

"Okay, don't tell me. I only hope she is good enough for you." Her smile faded as she studied his expression. "You *are* a good man, Celestin. I wish you would believe it."

He chuckled, hearing the bitterness in the laugh. "I'm glad you think so, Mom. But you don't know—"

"I know." She crossed herself, mumbling a prayer under her breath. "I know all I need to know. My son does what he has always done; he protects the people he loves. Now go, I have my book club coming over in a few hours. I love you, my angel."

She hustled him out the door, and he walked away in a daze. Did she really know? It had been seven years since his father died. Seven years since he'd discovered that along with a few gambling debts and a paternity suit or two to pay off, his father had left him one more token of his affection.

A blood debt to a Loa who didn't show any signs of moving on.

Where would I go, mon ami? Back through the Gate? There is still so much pleasure to give. To feel.

Mambo Toussaint, the voodoo priestess he'd gone to when he'd first accepted Bone Daddy's bargain to save one of his sisters from the fate, had told him she couldn't help him. "There's a way, but I'm not the one to discover it. Not for you."

So he'd lived with it. Lived with the lack of control. Lived with the knowledge that a woman or man could walk up to him at any time and, if they knew what to say, he would be bound to give them pleasure, without having any of his own.

You're lying to yourself again. We've known pleasures beyond what you knew before. It feeds us, fuels us. I've seen your fantasies, too. Seen and delivered. Made you face your passions head on, instead of avoiding them.

His piercings brushed against his shirt, a constant reminder, along with most of his tattoos, of the fantasies the Loa had indulged him in. Still, not being able to come for so long had an effect on a man.

He thought about Allegra again. What would she think if she knew all he'd done? How many ways he'd taken and had been taken? Her desires told him she might be up for all the things he wanted to do to her.

But what would she see in the morning's light?

She can be ours. Yours. Any way you want her.

And that was the problem. He wanted her to be his. Just his. He didn't want to share her with anyone. Not his friend, and certainly not Bone Daddy. He remembered what his mother had said and hoped it wasn't true.

Falling in love was the last thing he should do.

CHAPTER 4

THE HOMEMADE CHIME OVER THE DOOR JANGLED A JOYFUL note of welcome. Allegra limped in, her muscles aching from the afternoon walk.

She'd watched him through the window last night. Rousseau. Pacing back and forth like a caged animal. Naked and aroused. And thankfully alone.

She'd been glad Michelle was asleep in the other room. Her friend wouldn't let her hear the end of it if she knew Allegra was so greedy for a glimpse of the man that she'd taken to peeping.

He looked angry. Frustrated. Had someone turned him down? Left him, of all people, sexually frustrated? Somehow she didn't think so. Couldn't even imagine the possibility.

He was a glorious specimen, but it was her heart, not her body, that melted as she studied him. She wanted to soothe his hurt, his anger. Wanted to hold him, to make him smile like he had that first day when she'd gotten him to laugh. He didn't laugh enough.

Shit. She was falling for a man who, if Michelle could be believed, thought he was possessed by a voodoo spirit. Falling fast without any clue where she would land.

And that's why she'd had to come here, to Mambo Toussaint's voodoo shop. She had to know more about Bone Daddy. Psychosis or supernatural, she needed information.

She really loved the warm feel of the place. It was cozy, each shelf and nook filled with some herb or trinket. And books everywhere. Michelle had told her once that her mother believed that knowledge "took the hoodoo from the voodoo," allowed practitioners to find the true magic inside themselves, instead of being bogged down in superstition. Not that she didn't also carry items for the tourists, things people could take back with them when they went home that told others, without a doubt, they'd been to New Orleans.

"*Bonswa*, Allegra. How is that bath oil working for you?"

She smiled at the small woman in the bright head scarf behind the counter. "Very well, thank you so much. How are you today?"

The petite woman hopped down off her stool and rushed over to her, wrapping her in a warm embrace. "Better than you, I think. Come, sit and I'll introduce you to my friend Elise Adair."

Allegra allowed Michelle's mother to guide her to the small sofa in the corner of the shop, and looked over at the elegant blonde woman she'd assumed was a customer. "Are you related to Ben Adair?"

Elise gifted her with a wide smile and came to sit beside her, laying a hand on Allegra's arm. "Benjamin is my son. You must be the writer he's told us about."

Allegra blushed. "I wouldn't call myself a writer. Just a wannabe journalist currently on sabbatical. You don't look old enough to be Ben's mother."

"Oh, I like you. Please, call me Elise. Annemarie and I were just talking about our stubborn offspring, and bemoaning our lack of grandchildren. Thankfully you've come to take our minds off our maternal woes."

The women laughed together, and Allegra bit her lip, wondering how to broach the subject of Rousseau and his . . . issues.

"Look at her face, Elise. So beautiful to be so serious."

"Well, who can blame her? She's had to overcome too much. The skydiving accident, the rehabilitation, and now she's in love with Theresa's troubled boy Celestin. She's got a lot on her plate."

Allegra looked down to where Elise was touching her, recalling all the times Ben had done the same as he repeated the thoughts forming in her mind. Her memories.

She'd never told Ben. Never talked about it with her family. One night, when she'd first arrived in New Orleans, she lay in the dark telling Michelle about what had happened. She'd jumped from a plane hundreds of times, she loved the sensation of floating, falling—it was one of the perks of the job. She got to experience everything.

Even when the large gust of wind threw her off her landing course, she hadn't been concerned. Until she realized her chute had a tear in it. She aimed for the trees, believing it would be better than crashing directly onto the ground. She'd second-guessed her decision many times through the long night that had followed.

Elise cooed and patted her arm soothingly, as if she could see the image in her mind, feel the terror and loneliness that had washed over Allegra as she waited to be found. And Allegra knew, without a doubt, that she could. "Ben *did* say it ran in the family."

Elise threw back her head and laughed. "You're just as strong and smart as Benjamin said you were. Good. You'll need to be to get through what comes next."

Annemarie nodded, drawing Allegra's attention to her face. It was darker in tone, but so similar to Michelle's, even to the few scattered freckles over her nose and cheeks. She could only hope she looked as good as these two did when she was their age. "What comes next?" Allegra clenched her skirt with her fingers. "I have to be honest, I'm not sure that I believe that Rousseau is being ridden by a Loa. That he's possessed. From what the book said, long-term possessions just don't happen."

Elise nodded. "It *is* unusual, but then, Bone Daddy is an unusual spirit. Nothing like the rest of the Loa."

Annemarie leaned back. "True enough. Bone Daddy isn't like the others at all. He's a wild card to those of us who practice. Mischievous as all get-out, and so mysterious even The Mysteries, what we like to call the rest of the Loa, don't seem to know that much about him. Or maybe they just aren't talking." She shrugged, her vibrant, patterned caftan shifting with the movement. "Before he found Rousseau he'd pop up from time to time, always leaving sobbing women in his wake. He *is* a hard one to resist, but why would any normal red-blooded woman want to? He gives them pleasure beyond their wildest dreams, no strings, and they move on to find the pastures greener than they've ever seen, and good fortune shining on all their endeavors. It's a win-win deal with one sexy devil."

Allegra watched Michelle's mother fan herself and had to agree. How *could* anyone resist something like that? "Michelle isn't tempted."

"Oh, honey, my baby isn't normal; you should know that by now. No matter how much she wishes she was. That girl is running so hard from being special, she doesn't have time to see what's right in front of her. But that's another story. We're talking about you. Has he played with your mind yet? Showed you your fantasies?"

"Yes." How did they know? She'd almost convinced herself she'd imagined it.

Elise leaned closer. "His eyes change? Maybe his personality?"

"Yes. You two are scaring me. Are you saying that it's . . . real? That there actually is a Bone Daddy? That Rousseau isn't in control of his actions?" And what did it mean that his alter-ego was interested in her, but Rousseau had never asked her out?

"Bone Daddy would never take Rousseau down a road he wasn't willing to walk, if that's what you're thinking. He'll drag him kicking and screaming if it's one he wants, but *wishes* he didn't, but never anything he didn't desire. That's not his style."

Annemarie sounded so certain that Allegra found herself relaxing. A little. She still had to deal with the fact that she was beginning to believe what they were saying. That the man she wanted was, well, conflicted. "So what comes next? What do I do?"

Michelle's mother shared a look with Elise and shook her head. "That we can't tell you. But you're a smart girl, Allegra. I've always thought so. You'll figure it out."

"Words of wisdom, Mambo." The three women glanced up, startled by Ben's sudden appearance at their side. "My ears were ringing, so I thought I'd stop in and see what sort of mischief The Mamas were cooking up."

Elise blushed, standing and offering a cheek that her son dutifully kissed, his attention on Allegra. "Darling, we're talking about what we always talk about. Babies."

Annemarie Toussaint chortled as Ben helped her up off the couch and lifted her off her feet for an enthusiastic hug. "Put me down, scoundrel. Babies. As in, if you don't give us some soon we're gonna get desperate and stick a fertility bundle 'neath your bed."

"Don't blame me, Mambo. I'm trying to follow orders. I keep propositioning women, and they keep turning me down."

Elise sniffed, but her eyes twinkled delightedly at her son's antics. "That's your problem. You proposition when you should propose. At least you have impeccable timing. Can you walk Miss Allegra home so we can continue planning the end of your bachelor days?" She smiled apologetically down at Allegra. "Not that we haven't loved seeing you here, but I know you're anxious to get home and sort everything out."

She was. She had to be alone, to sort out fact from fiction in her head, to think about all she'd learned here today. Ben winked at Allegra, holding out his arm for her to take and bowing like an old-fashioned courtier. "I live to serve. Hey, you wouldn't want to get hitched so my mother can finally sleep at night, would you?"

Allegra stuck out her tongue. "Ha. I should say yes just to spite you. At least I'd know I'd have a great mother-in-law."

The older women's laughter followed them out the door and onto the busy sidewalk. Ben kept her close to the shops, his body protective beside hers as she limped at a slower pace than the rest of the crowd. "So what did they tell you?"

She huffed. "Something Michelle was trying to tell me. Something that, if it's true, a *friend* should have told me a lot sooner. Instead of trying to push me in the deep end without telling me there were piranhas in the pool."

Ben sighed. "I know you, Legs. You wouldn't have believed me."

"I'm still not sure I do. Although I am starting to wonder about that family trait of yours. You and your mother could go on the road with that telepathic parlor trick."

"It's not a trick, Legs. But I guess it *is* a kind of telepathy. I can sense what you're thinking, feeling, but only if I'm touching you. My mother's family has always had the touch." He grimaced. "It isn't always pleasant, but it gives me an upper hand in business, and it lets me know when people aren't telling me the truth."

"Sounds like a skill I could use right about now."

"No one's lying to you, Legs. We've just left a few blanks. I'll tell you everything I know. Rousseau sure as hell isn't going to do it. Stubborn ass."

Allegra looked up, frustration nearly making her growl. "That's my first question. Is it Rousseau that's actually interested in me? Or is it the spirit? The Loa?"

"Bone Daddy is interested in sex, period. But I wasn't lying when I told you Rousseau wanted you. You've shaken him up but good." He smiled. "Even before his, um, situation, Rousseau never had a problem attracting women, though he was so busy taking care of his family and saving to open Café Bwe that he rarely paid them any mind. I learned in high school that hanging out with him was the smartest thing a single guy could do. I don't know if you've noticed or not, but he's not a bad-looking man. Don't tell him I said that."

Allegra felt her lips quirk when he sent her a mock-threatening look. "How did it happen? When?"

"Bone Daddy? He's been around since a few days after Rousseau's dad was buried. I don't know all the details, but I do know it was something his father did that brought Rousseau to the Loa's attention. I know Mambo Toussaint told you, he's not one of the main Loa of the religion. But he is a strong spirit, stronger and more determined than most, I think. I wish I knew what his old man did to call down that kind of thunder, but the type of Loa that BD is gives me a clue. He affects people strangely. Even me."

They turned the corner of her building, and she reached into her purse for the key. As soon as she'd opened the door Ben swooped her up in his arms, making her shriek in surprise. "Service with a smile, Legs."

"Thanks." She was suddenly breathless with a sensual curiosity that surprised her. Ben's masculine scent surrounded her, his arm strong beneath her legs. This close she noticed the warm brown of his eyes, the small scar at his temple. She thought about the night at the club, what Rousseau, well, what Bone Daddy had said. "You've shared women with him before. With the Loa."

He'd closed the door and was taking his first step up the stairs when he paused to look at her. "He told you that?" His golden skin flushed while she looked on, fascinated. He continued walking. "The first time I thought it was Rousseau. Maybe a little drunk, but still just my best friend." His voice lowered. "It was incredible. The best sex of my life, and I knew part of it was watching the woman overwhelmed with ecstasy. Watching her face as we took her together."

Allegra clenched her fingers on his shoulders, her body heating at his words. "And after you knew?"

"When I put two and two together, Rousseau didn't deny it. He said he'd done things he wasn't proud of, but if he was going to share a woman, he'd rather it was with someone he trusted."

At the top of the stairs he put her on her feet, his brow lowering in concern when she flinched as she found her balance. Ben's hand came up to caress her hip gently in apology.

She opened her mouth, looking up at him with what she knew was confusion. Her mind was filled with images of Ben and Rousseau sharing a lover, surrounding her with their bodies, taking her higher than she'd ever been. She realized she'd replaced the faceless woman in her mind. She was the one the two men were touching, kissing.

Ben's chest rose on a harsh breath. "I'm touching you, Allegra. I can feel what you're feeling."

She licked her lips. "I know."

He groaned and lowered his head slowly, taking her lips in a gentle, almost hesitant kiss. Allegra felt warmth course through her limbs and she leaned closer. It was a lovely kiss, wonderful.

But not Rousseau.

Ben pulled back with a wry smile. "You're perfect for him, Legs. Exactly what he needs. Don't run away now that you know the truth."

He moved as though to leave but turned back, his hand reaching into his pocket. "Michelle's mother wanted you to have this. She said sleep with it beneath your pillow if you still need more answers."

"Thank you, Ben. For everything."

"My pleasure, darlin'. My pleasure."

Allegra waited for him to leave before turning to unlock the door to her apartment. The phone was ringing. "Damn it." She slammed the door shut, trying to race, but almost fell over before she got to the phone on the other side of the room. "Hello?"

"Did he fuck you?"

CHAPTER 5

"WHAT? WAIT—ROUSSEAU? IS THAT YOU?" ALLEGRA QUICKLY looked out the window and saw him, phone in hand, staring back at her. Her heart was pounding from the race to the phone and his blunt, vulgar question. If she had any self-respect she'd hang up the phone.

"I know I have no right, but I have to know. Is that where you went today? To him?"

Good-bye, self-respect. "You're right. It is none of your business. Unless I can ask you about all the people *you've* been with since I met you."

Silence. Her heart shouldn't ache at that, but it did. Just enough for her to want to tell him. "Ben and I are friends. He was nice enough to walk me home from Mambo Toussaint's. You know her, don't you?"

He didn't take the bait. "Nothing else?"

"He . . . We kissed." And I loved it. It was better than a chocolate caramel roll. All the things she could say to wound his pride ran through her mind, but her throat closed in protest. Ben's kiss made her warm, but Rousseau made her burn.

He lowered his head, swearing under his breath, and her hand flattened on the glass. She wanted to touch him. What was it about this man that made her long to comfort him and tear his clothes off all at the same time? "Did you want me to lie? Or avoid telling you altogether?"

She knew he heard the undercurrent in her voice. What she wasn't saying. That she knew the stories. That she was starting to believe them. She could feel his gaze heat her body, through the space and glass that separated them.

"No. No lies. Not from you."

Seeing him, hearing his voice, was washing all her anxieties and doubts away. Right, wrong, or insane, she wanted him. "No lies. That's good. Then I'll tell you that when he kissed me, I was wishing you were there, too."

"Too? I may kill my good buddy Ben. Too much honesty could be a dangerous thing, *bebe*."

"You don't like it? Then I won't share the fantasy I had about you the other morning. Or last night." She smiled at the heartfelt groan vibrating against her ear. She could get used to being brazen.

Her smile faded as he took off his shirt, bringing the phone back to his ear as soon as the cloth cleared his head. "Why don't you show me instead?"

Allegra hesitated. "Rousseau?"

"It's me. I need to see you. Just this once. I've been thinking

about you, too, *bebe*. Too much. I need you. Take your shirt off."
Allegra shuddered, her insecurity falling away with the excitement
of the moment, and yes, the safety of the distance between them.

She set the phone down beside her and put it on speaker, her
hand going to the top button of her blouse. "I can't believe I'm
doing this."

"I can. You're the sexiest woman I've ever known. Fearless."

Her fingers were shaking. She didn't feel that fearless, but she
was feeling sexy when he growled into the phone, coming closer
to his window, as if desperate to see more.

"Don't tease me, Allegra. I've been dreaming about your perfect breasts for days. Open your shirt for me . . . yes . . . yes, *bebe*.
Now caress them."

A warm breeze lifted her hair and her lashes fluttered in surprise. The window wasn't open, yet she felt it, curling around her
neck and down, moving beneath her hands to squeeze her nipples.
"What . . . ?"

Can't be left out, cher. *Let us show Rousseau how much you want
him. Want this.*

Allegra hesitated. That voice. Bone Daddy? But how, if he was
in Rousseau?

Just a little magic, cher. *Don't think. Feel.*

"Allegra? You still with me?" Rousseau's voice was rough,
tinged with need. A need she wanted to fulfill.

"Still here. Wondering why you haven't taken off your pants."

Two males laughed in relief, the "breeze" caressing her belly in
approval as Rousseau removed his last article of clothing.

Even from this distance in the daylight, she could see his erection. So beautiful. She wished she was closer. That's what she
needed. Him. Closer. Inside her *might* be close enough.

She lowered her hands to her skirt, loosening the drawstrings until the fabric fell whisper quiet to the floor.

"Fuck, *bebe*. You're killing me. I wish I could touch you."

"Why can't you?" She slid her hand beneath the lace of her panties, now simple ivory, and felt the wetness there. "I'm right here, and I want you to. I want—"

"*Don't*, Allegra. Don't tell me what you want. Just show me." *Tricky boy.*

Allegra bit her lip, feeling the magical caress of the air around her. It was trying to distract her, circling her nipples, riding between the cheeks of her ass, driving her crazy.

She recalled Ben's adamancy about telling Rousseau she wanted him, and her fantasy, where her golden-eyed lover wanted her to declare her desire for him, for Bone Daddy, out loud. Was that it then? In order to have him did she have to say those words?

And a clever girl. What a vexing combination. Whatever shall I do with you two?

"I won't say it, Rousseau. Not yet. I'll just show you." Where her audacity came from she'd never know. In broad daylight, with people walking below and Michelle capable of coming home at any moment, Allegra acted the part of a wanton.

One hand tugged hard on her tingling nipple, loving the sharp sensation, and the other pulled the lace aside to spread the lips of her sex to the delicate, licking breeze.

She watched Rousseau copy her movements, twisting his nipple ring and stroking his heavy cock in a slow, sensual rhythm. "What does it feel like? Your piercings?"

He didn't hesitate. "Love bites. Your teeth on my skin. Your mouth, your nails. I can feel the pull all the way down my spine, in my cock."

She gasped for breath. Ben had been right, Rousseau was irresistible without the Loa. But then, she'd already known that.

His husky voice came to her through the speaker. "Are you wet, Allegra? For me?"

"Yes. Oh God, yes." She rubbed her clit faster, her body on fire for this man. Allegra lost herself to sensation, climbing higher and higher, trying desperately to keep her heavy lids lifted, to watch her distant lover as his movements grew just as frenzied as her own.

"Come for me, *bebe*. Let me see you. Let me watch you come apart for me."

Her body obeyed his command. Her fingers slipped through her arousal, electricity shooting up her spine. She arched her back, feeling the air whip around her, intensifying every sensation, every shocking jolt of the powerful release.

She collapsed, grateful for the chair beside her as the strength in her legs gave out at her climax. "Rousseau! Oh God, *Rousseau*."

"*Yes.*"

The intense satisfaction in his voice made her focus, certain she would be able to watch his orgasm as he'd witnessed hers. But he was standing still at the window, focused on her, one hand holding the phone to his ear once more.

She wanted to ask why but he spoke before she could. "Thank you, beautiful Allegra. Since we're telling the truth, I'll let you in on a secret. You're the only woman *I've* had the honor of pleasuring in nearly seven years."

She heard the emphasis as he separated himself from Bone Daddy. "Seven years? But you didn't . . ."

She hated the resignation in his tone. "And I won't. I can't. But seeing you like that is worth every second I'll be spending under the cold shower in my future."

He couldn't? "I don't understand. Rousseau, I want—"

"Sleep well, Allegra." He hung up the phone and turned away from the window, disappearing from her view. Her special breeze had disappeared the moment he'd severed the connection, leaving Allegra completely alone with her heart still pounding, naked by the window.

He'd hung up on her. Given her the sexiest, and first, phone sex of her life, then hung up without an explanation. Talk about a cold shower.

Pain throbbed in her leg, interrupting her silent pique. She hung up her phone, walking slowly toward the bathroom. She needed a hot bath, and some of Mambo Toussaint's magical bath oils.

Thinking of the kindhearted priestess made her turn back toward the desk. Ben had given her something from the older woman, something she thought would give Allegra the answers she needed. And she definitely needed answers. Now more than ever.

SHE KNEW SHE WAS DREAMING BECAUSE SHE WAS SKYDIVING, falling fast through the air toward a far too familiar line of trees. She hadn't had this nightmare for months. Why now?

The wind surrounded her, slowing her descent, cushioning her body until she was floating safely to the ground. Definitely dreaming.

Darkness surrounded her, but she saw the flickering light of a fire through the trees and took off her gear, heading toward it. As she drew closer she heard the music, the chanting. It sounded like a party, but when she got to the clearing, the noise stopped, and one old man sat alone beside the fire.

Smooth ebony skin, white hair, and closely trimmed beard, the man didn't look up when she came to stand beside him, fascinated.

"You don't look like you're dressed for camping."

And he didn't. Suit pants, suspenders, and shiny shoes didn't fit with the rough landscape. He threw some moss into the fire, feeding it. "You're a journalist. You should know what things look like, and what they are, are rarely the same thing."

She sat down next to him. "I'm dreaming, but I don't know why I'm here. Why can't I dream about white sandy beaches filled with naked men and margaritas? Not that I'm complaining about the company." She patted his arm consolingly. "Just the setting."

He chuckled. "You have spirit, Allegra Jarrod." He lifted his hand and took a puff off his pipe. "As to the place, why *not* here? You are what life has made you, this place most of all. You learned to be strong here, not to take life for granted."

She looked around. She supposed he was right. Hadn't she promised herself a thousand things if only she lived long enough to be rescued?

She would be a better friend, a better daughter. She would stay in one place for a while, write a novel . . . fall in love. "I'd forgotten."

"And yet you still found yourself on the right road. Funny, isn't it, how that works?" The old man glanced over at her and winked, bumping shoulders with her as though they were old friends.

"So we know why I'm here. Why are you here?"

He used a cane to pull himself up, placing a straw hat that seemed to appear from nowhere at a rakish angle on his head. "Just helping out a friend. You have another question." He wasn't asking, and suddenly she realized what was going on.

"Mambo Toussaint's charm. That's why I'm having this dream. I have a million questions."

"Only have time for one."

"Is there a way to free Rousseau from Bone Daddy?"

He laughed, loud and long, making Allegra smile in spite of herself. "Not many women would ask that question. That alone would make you special." He shrugged, groaning and stretching, looking up to the sky. "As with most things, when you want something badly enough, you'll find a way to get it. Especially if you have something the other party wants in exchange."

The old man turned as if to go and Allegra stood up, confused. "Wait. What do you mean?"

He looked over his shoulder, his eyes sparkling with good humor. "That's two questions. But you're a smart girl. You'll figure it out."

"So they keep saying." She sighed. "Thank you . . . what did you say your name was?"

"I don't believe I did. But you know me, Allegra Jarrod. You always have. And we'll meet again." He disappeared between the trees, whistling. The wind picked up and Allegra glanced down at the fire just in time to see the flames shoot up toward her.

She gasped, nearly tumbling out of bed as she scrambled backward. Bed. She was in her bed in the living room. She concentrated on slowing her breathing, listening to the soft sounds of music coming from Michelle's bedroom, telling Allegra that she was home.

Allegra lay back against the back of the cushions with a sigh. She must have fallen asleep right after her bath, her muscles totally relaxed, her mind still in turmoil. She slid her hand beneath the pillow and pulled out the small sewn pouch. What did the dream mean? And who was that old man?

An exchange. Did he mean with Bone Daddy? And when had she stopped doubting he actually existed?

Today by the window. She'd felt him. Heard him in her mind.

According to Mambo Toussaint, Ben, and Michelle, the Loa only wanted one thing: sex.

She closed her fingers over the buttery fabric of the charm, a slow smile spreading across her face. A girl had to do what a girl had to do.

CHAPTER 6

"You sure about this, Legs?"

"You've spent weeks talking me into it, are you chickening out on me now that we're here?"

Ben leaned back in his chair at their private outdoor table at Rousseau's café, lifting his face to the sun for a moment before shaking his head, a wicked smile curving his lips. "No way. I just want to make sure you know what you're getting us into."

"I don't, but we're doing it anyway."

"Remind me to thank Mambo Toussaint for that gris-gris she gave you."

Allegra raised her eyebrow knowingly. "I don't think she meant it for you at all. In fact, I'm sure of it. I have a feeling she sees you as perfect son-in-law material."

Ben flinched. "Sadly, I'm afraid her matchmaker skills are off when it comes to her daughter. I'm the last person in the world Michelle wants. She's told me often enough."

Not "I don't want her" but "She doesn't want me." She'd been right. He had a thing for Michelle. Maybe she should have come alone this afternoon. "Are you sure *you* want to do this . . . with me?"

He reached for her hand, catching her gaze with his own. "Are you kidding? You are a fascinating woman, Allegra. More so by the day. Plus, I think you need a spotter."

She started to choke, pulling her hand from his to reach for her bottled water, and Ben's expression of innocent concern wasn't helping. "A *spotter*?"

"In gymnastics, a spotter is there in case someone takes a tumble." He shrugged at her disbelieving expression. "What? My mother loves the Olympics. The point is, I'm attracted to you, you're attracted to me, enough to turn BD on . . . and drive Rousseau crazy."

"How do you know it will drive him crazy?"

"Don't look now, but it already is."

Allegra turned her head to look through the café window. Rousseau was untying his apron, motioning the last of the female stragglers to the door, his angry gaze never leaving hers. "Uh-oh."

She watched, her heart in her throat, as he strode out the door, rounding the corner until he was standing beside them. "Café is closing early today. I'm going to need to take the table inside."

"I'll help." Ben started to stand up, but Rousseau's look froze him in his seat.

"What are you doing here?"

Ben shrugged lazily, his expression so relaxed Allegra had to admire his acting. "I believe we're here for a—" He glanced at

Allegra, who nodded adamantly. "Yes, I do believe we're here for a threesome. Is the café closed for that?"

"Jackass." Rousseau stepped closer to Ben, his fists clenching, and Allegra knew she had to do something.

"I want you, Bone Daddy."

Rousseau whipped around to face her, an expression of surprise and an excitement he couldn't quite conceal coming over his face. "Allegra. Damn it, Ben, take her upstairs."

She saw the golden glint in his eyes and her heart raced. Ben picked her up in his arms again and headed inside.

She leaned her head on his chest. "This is getting to be a habit."

"I'd carry you anywhere, Legs. And that's a fact."

"Why didn't he come with us?"

Ben shrugged, his expression tight, his eyes over-bright. "I think he wanted to give you a chance to prepare." He slid open the loft door with one hand, carrying her into the large room and setting her down on a narrow kitchen chair. "Or maybe this is where I'm supposed to tell you that Bone Daddy doesn't only want one thing. He craves it. It's like food to him, and each time he needs more."

Oh, God, it was only sex he wanted, right? She'd known this was coming, but the knowledge that she'd just invited a Loa to have sex with her suddenly made all the terrifying things she'd ever seen or heard about voodoo flash through her mind. What if he wanted more? A zombie army? The souls of innocent children? Blood?

That rich, sensual chuckle filled the air, and Ben took a step away from her to give her a clear view of the man leaning against the door frame. He'd certainly wasted no time, she thought, a little hysterically.

"What an imagination you have, *cher*. Morbid, but humorous. No zombies, no souls. And blood isn't what I want to taste on my tongue, to soak my fingers in when I touch you. I'm not *that* kind of animal."

He could hear her thoughts? Word for word? What was it with this city? Two psychic men prying into her mind and emotions was a little too much for her to take. But it didn't take a psychic to understand *his* graphic words. Sex. He fed off sex.

"Not just sex, *cher*. Satisfaction. And today, it is your satisfaction I crave. Rousseau and I may be in true accord for the first time since we met. Neither one of us can wait to make you come." He strode toward her, his motions confident, predatory. He was a jungle cat stalking his prey, eyes golden.

Allegra was still as a statue on the tiny wooden chair, feeling caught, helpless, as he reached behind him and pulled his white T-shirt over his head. The movement loosed his hair from its queue, and the locks fell over his shoulders, giving him the look of a warring conqueror. Damn, he was beautiful.

The muscles in his arms and abs rippled with leashed power as he reached for his belt. Every inch of skin revealed made her heart beat that much harder, that much faster. Made her mouth water in anticipation.

"Too late to back out now, *cher*. He tried to hold me back, give you a choice. But you made it months ago, didn't you?"

He was right. She had. But that was before she knew about his identity crisis. Bone Daddy threw back his head and laughed, letting his khaki pants fall to the floor. He wore nothing underneath. Oh dear Lord.

"Did my identity matter all those mornings you spent in the coffee shop, pretending not to follow Rousseau's every move? Or all those days you watched us from your window? Rousseau knew you were there. I told him. He watched you, too. Watched and felt an ache of longing at the sight of your sweet little body. The ache that you made that much worse when you came for us yesterday."

She caught movement from the corner of her eye, saw Ben's expression change to one of true surprise. See? He didn't know everything. He hadn't known she was a peeping pervert. But Bone Daddy did. *Rousseau* did. She felt her face heat, but in spite of her embarrassment, she couldn't stop her gaze from lowering to his erection. She'd felt it against her, seen it at a distance, but up close it seemed impossibly large. Her body felt hot, restless, and she shifted in her chair. A twinge in her leg brought her back to herself.

"We can't have that. Can't have anything distracting you from pleasure. I want all your attention on me. On us. At least until we are done." He knelt down beside her, his hand smoothing over her left leg, from hip to knee.

His touch was a fire on her skin. She was so lost in the feeling it took her a moment to notice the pain. Or the lack of it.

Allegra gasped. The pain. It was gone again. Her leg hadn't stopped hurting once in over a year, until the other night at the club, and then yesterday . . . Bone Daddy, with a single touch, had made it disappear. How had he done that? And did he say it was only temporary?

Her shock must have shown in her expression, and he gentled his eternally wicked smile. Repeating the words that had echoed through her mind the day before, he said, "Don't think, Allegra Jarrod. Just feel."

He kissed her. Bone Daddy. Rousseau. It didn't seem to matter to her body which one it was. His lips were just as soft as she'd imagined, just as warm.

Her body trembled with adrenaline. Free from pain, drowning in arousal, she wrapped her arms around his neck and opened her mouth to his, welcoming him in.

He pulled back enough to look into her eyes, his own flickering like a golden flame. "Benjamin, since you've taken it upon yourself to be our third, I'll ask you to make yourself useful."

"I'm on it, BD." She heard Ben's footsteps taking him farther away, wondering at her confidant, masculine friend's instant obedience, but she quickly forgot him again as Rousseau's mouth pressed against hers once more. It was him. Bone Daddy. He had a way about him. It clouded your mind. He was a walking aphrodisiac.

He ate at her mouth, biting at her lips, then soothing the pain with tender licks. She felt him tug her dress down once more, willingly lifting her bottom off the chair long enough for him to sweep it away completely, along with her brand-new pair of pink lace underwear.

Her inhibitions seemed to shed along with her clothes. His taste, the feel of his smooth skin burning beneath her hands was addictive. She needed more.

Allegra wrapped both her legs around his waist and pulled him closer. Her blood raced through her veins at the contact. *This.* This was what she needed, what she had laid awake dreaming of night after night. She pressed closer, kissing his delicious lips with all the pent-up passion stored inside her.

He growled, pulling back as he stood with her in his arms. "Knew you'd be like this. Knew you had a fire to match ours. You couldn't hide it from me."

He walked across the spacious living room toward the large platform bed against the wall. Allegra held on tight. "Rousseau thought you a hothouse flower, delicate and fragile. He didn't think you'd be able to take what we wanted to give you. All the depraved and wicked things we wanted to do to you. We showed him your fantasies, your willingness to . . . experiment."

He stopped, looking down at her with a surprisingly uncertain expression. "But was he right after all, *cher*? Should I turn Benjamin away, and cover you with rose petals? Should I grope you carefully in the dark beneath the covers? Is that what you want? Tell me now."

She didn't hesitate. "No. That's not what I want."

"Then what?" He moved forward again until his knees hit the side of the bed, his gaze alert as he studied her. She could see the Loa, but she was starting to see Rousseau in there as well. Two distinct entities, both waiting to hear her answer.

She meant to sound confident, sure, but her voice came out in a whisper. "All the depraved and wicked things you want to do."

She heard Ben groan behind them. "Good girl, Legs." He dropped a handful of condoms, a small bottle of lubricant, and what looked like a wooden bowl of dark liquid on the bedside table. Her eyebrows rose.

Rousseau's golden eyes sparkled. "No, Benjamin. *Bad girl.* Just the kind we like." Without warning, he tossed her on the bed.

Allegra laughed, a carefree, joyous sound that she'd almost forgotten. This was what she wanted. No pity, no careful touches. *This*. Fun and fire and passion.

Ben and Rousseau stood over her, neither man hiding the hungry gleam in his eyes. If their arousal was even half of what the sight of them side by side was doing to her, she didn't know how they were still standing.

Darkness and light, the two were opposite sides of the same heart-stopping coin. Ben with his blond, all-American good looks, and Rousseau, exotic, erotic, and irresistible. The only thing they had in common was the approval in their eyes as they studied her naked body on the bed.

She slid her legs against the cool sheets like a contented feline, loving the freedom of motion, loving how their attention followed her every move. Her hands caressed her thighs, uncaring of the small ridges scattered over her skin. The ones she'd been so insecure about earlier.

It was impossible to ignore their admiration, their desire. Her scars didn't bother them at all. And suddenly, they didn't bother her either. Instead, they were proof of life. Of survival.

"That's right, *cher*. You are a warrior woman." The harsh voice growled in Rousseau's throat. "In my world, you could be queen." He motioned to Ben, who'd unbuttoned his linen shirt, revealing broad shoulders and a well-defined chest. "We will not share her this first time. You may watch."

Ben held up his hands and stepped back. "With pleasure, BD. You know how I love to watch. As long as there *is* a next time." He winked at Allegra, disappearing from her line of sight as Rousseau leaned over her body, his hands landing on either side of her head, his hair hiding them behind a sweet-smelling curtain.

Allegra licked her lips, loving the weight of him against her, his cock hard against her thigh. He bit her chin. "I don't think any of the others we've had have ever felt as right as you do, *cher*. There is something special about you."

She narrowed her eyes, surprising herself by lifting her head and biting his jaw in return. "Note to Bone Daddy, mentioning other women is not high up on my list of exciting foreplay options."

He purred, his eyes flashing. "Oh, I like you, little one. We've never told anyone what we are, other than Ben. It's very liberating, this honesty. I don't know why we've never tried it before. Shall I tell you what Rousseau thought of the very first time he saw you?" He smiled. "No. Perhaps I should just show you instead."

He slid down her body, his breath hot against her nipples, the soft curve of her belly. "Freckles. You have freckles everywhere, *cher*. They are distracting." He stopped to lick a small patch of them clustered on her hip, making deep sounds of pleasure.

"You, ah, you really do like freckles then? Oh, that feels . . . *mmm*."

"Like cinnamon sprinkled over your body. They taste just as sweet to me. Rousseau never understood my fascination. But he does now."

His lips glided along her hip to her thigh, his fingers coming up to tangle in the wet red curls of her sex. Her body curved toward him, already attuned to his touch. Burning for more.

He smiled against her skin. "Good. You aren't shaved. So many women are these days. Strange fashion trend."

He tugged and Allegra felt her clit pulse in response. "This is what Rousseau thought about. He wanted to fall to his knees and press his face between your thighs. Wanted to lift your legs over his shoulders and drink you down until he was drowning in your honeyed juices. He was hungry for you, *cher*. I've never felt that kind of hunger inside him."

He lifted her legs over his shoulders, kneeling on the floor beside the bed, and sighed. "She's so wet. So pretty and pink and wet."

"She's beautiful."

Allegra's body jerked as she looked over Rousseau's shoulder to catch Ben's avid gaze. His blond hair fell over his glittering eyes as he watched them together. She'd almost forgotten he was there, that he could see everything.

It didn't make her as nervous as she thought it would. Instead, a rush of excitement shivered through her body at the thought of Rousseau taking her, claiming her in front of him. And another part of her, apparently more debauched than she'd realized, was hoping that *he'd* get another chance to touch her as well.

Bone Daddy tugged on her pubic curls again, a little harder this time. "I must be boring you if that pale empath can take your attention away from me. I think I'll have to do something about that."

His fingers spread the lips of her sex open, his tongue exploring her newly exposed flesh.

"Oh! *Yes.*" Allegra's back arched off the bed, her eyes closing in ecstasy at the sensations flooding her system. It had been so long. And it had never felt like this. She'd always believed she wasn't an oral sex kind of girl. But she'd been wrong. Totally. Completely. Wrong.

He sucked her clit in his mouth, his tongue swirling to gather every drop of her arousal. He groaned aloud at her taste, gripping her hips to pull her closer, burying his face deeper between her thighs.

Her hands curled into fists around the fabric beneath her, and the heels of her feet dug into his back as his coarse hair scraped her thighs. His tongue thrust deep inside her core, and feral sounds of approval rumbled in his chest as her hips pumped against him, fucking his mouth.

More. She didn't know whose thought it was, but it repeated in her head like a mantra played to the beat of her pounding heart. Her skin was on fire, spine tingling with the power of her rising arousal.

His hands slid from her hips to the cheeks of her ass, squeezing, caressing, spreading. She was drenched with need, her sex and thighs soaked with it. Rousseau's fingers, too, were slick and coated with her heat.

Allegra's eyes opened wide when she felt the firm pressure of his thumbs against her ass. Without lifting his mouth from her he met her gaze, his own glowing with determination and untamed passion. He wasn't asking for permission, he was demanding she submit.

She breathed out on a trembling sigh, and the pressure increased. She'd experimented with toys in the past, curious, but she was sure she would never allow anyone to take her there. She'd been sure of a lot of things this morning. Sure she wasn't into threesomes, voyeurism, or pain mixed with her pleasure.

She must be under some kind of spell. Bone Daddy's doing no doubt. How else could she explain her wicked behavior? Her sudden impatience to feel him filling her from behind?

His growl grew louder, and his thumbs pushed inside her in small, short thrusts. Fiery bursts of pleasure exploded through her body. Oh God, it was overwhelming. His mouth, his hands . . . it was too much.

Her cry was loud in the stillness of the loft. Her neck arched at an impossible angle, eyes sightless with the strength of her orgasm. She was shaking, her flesh nearly sizzling with electricity.

An irresistible urge to lift her head overtook her. She wanted to see him, to look into those golden eyes and know she'd pleased him as much as he'd pleased her.

Her vision cleared in time to witness the battle. He hadn't stopped drinking her down, if anything he was more voracious, greedier for her taste. But his eyes were changing, flashing hazel and gold and back again. She knew instantly what was happening. Rousseau wanted out. Wanted to experience her firsthand.

Yes. She shivered, and her hips jerked against his mouth as the waves of her climax continued to break over her. She pushed against his thumbs, loving the sharp, stinging stretch—already wanting more.

He lifted his head, his full lips shining with the evidence of her pleasure. His upper lip curled, snarled as he pushed away from her, standing to step back from the bed. Every muscle in his body tensed. His hands tightened into fists at his sides.

Allegra knew Rousseau was still struggling for control. He paced as she fought to recover from the most intense climax of her life. Her breathing slowed, body cooling as she thought about what it must be like for Rousseau, to have his choice taken away, his body used by another. What had happened? And what did his father have to do with it?

Golden eyes turned her way. "The only trouble with honesty is how inconvenient it can be. No lies, isn't that what you said, *cher*? Benjamin, take off your clothes and get on the bed. I will tell you both a bedtime story."

He stroked his thick cock as he watched Ben obey, coming to sit behind a nervous Allegra. She wanted to turn around, to study Ben's bare body, wanted to lean into the heat she felt coming off of him, but she couldn't tear her gaze away from Rousseau.

He tightened his fist around his erection, knowing he had a captive audience. "Once upon a time, there was a man who wanted to fuck. He didn't want to fuck his adoring wife, the mother of his three children. He didn't want to fuck the lovely little piece he had on the side. No. He wanted to fuck a woman who didn't want him or trust him. A woman who was not swayed by his charm or beautiful features, who saw him for exactly what he was."

He stepped closer to the bed, and Allegra couldn't help but lower her eyes to his erection. The way he was touching himself ensnared her. She wanted to touch him that way. She heard him speak again and fought to focus on his words.

"He was a practitioner of the voodoo religion. More faithful to it than he'd ever been to any woman. He should have known better, but he asked the spirits for help. He wanted to force the object of his desire to love him. He wanted her to want him more than she wanted to live."

Ben's hand had been gently stroking her lower back, but it stilled at those words. "I thought that was taboo. A Loa can't make someone do what they don't want to do."

Rousseau's lush lips quirked. "Can and should, Benjamin. Two very different words. We *can* do anything. But most Loa wouldn't poke a request like that with a stick."

Allegra was beginning to understand. "Except for you."

He shrugged. "I am too soft-hearted. He was a desperate man. And what he was offering in return was . . . impossible to resist." His fist tightened around his cock, and he thrust into his own hand with a groan.

"He offered you his son." Ben sounded disgusted at Rousseau's father. She'd like a few minutes alone with him herself. "And he died before he could fix it."

The laugh was distinctly Bone Daddy's. It gave Allegra a sensual shiver. "As if he would. He laid his family out on a platter for my sampling pleasure, so I gave him what he asked for. The woman loved him well that night. Loved him as though she would die without him inside her. The next morning they found them both dead in the hotel room, she with a gun in her hand. Seems after all he went through to get his true love, the damn fool refused to leave his wife for her."

He lifted a hand to Allegra's forehead, pushing a strawberry curl out of her eyes. It was gentle, totally at odds with the ugly story he'd just dropped in their laps. "Don't be sad, *cher*. Sadness doesn't feed me. It isn't the way to get rid of me either."

Something in his tone narrowed Allegra's gaze. If sadness wasn't the way, that meant there had to be another. A way to get Rousseau out of his father's debt to the Loa. A way to satisfy Bone Daddy. Just like the old man had said.

He sent a look of surprise her way, then his smile widened. "No more stories. You've had enough time to recover, *cher*. Are you ready for round two?"

CHAPTER 7

THE TWO MEN SHARED A SPEAKING GLANCE, AND BEN GOT to his knees. "Turn around, Allegra. Look at me."

His blue eyes held a strange mixture of melancholy and desire, mirroring what she was feeling. She couldn't stop her body's reaction to what she'd just experienced, what she was about to experience. But a part of her regretted her need, and the fact that Rousseau might hate her for giving in to it.

Ben smiled, his hands cupping her jaw. "He wants you, Legs. They both do." His expression heated. "Hell, I do, too. But this is all I'll get, sweet Allegra. All I'll ever ask for. And all of a sudden I'm wondering why I didn't snatch you up for myself."

Her brow furrowed. What was it he was asking of her? What did they want her to do? She felt the hot, sweet breath on the nape of her neck, heard foil tearing behind her as she got her answer.

Bone Daddy's harsh growl sent a powerful shudder down her

spine. "Every dirty and depraved thing I want. That's what you said. Well, now I want you to bend over and suck Ben right down your sweet little throat. Suck him dry while I fill your ass with my cock."

Was she really going to do this? This was Ben in front of her, her confidant. Her friend. It was Rousseau she wanted. Right? Then why was she so aroused by the sight of Ben Adair's naked flesh? One man at a time was more than enough for her. Had always been. Was she any different than Rousseau's loose father?

"I can hear you thinking, *cher*. If you left one man's bed to go to another you could worry. We know who and what you want. And all *we* want is to please you. Taste him, Allegra. Let me watch."

Allegra whimpered, her skin flushing with revealing heat. Ben's smile grew knowing, and he reached for the bowl. "Honey rum. Your research must have taught you how much the spirits love rum."

Rousseau reached over his shoulder to dip his fingers in the liquid. "The others haven't tasted Allegra. She's far more intoxicating." She felt him trace damp lines on her lower back, the cheeks of her ass.

Ben drenched his own fingers with the liqueur, drizzling it on his hard shaft. It smelled delicious. Her mouth watered and she grabbed his wrist, pulling his fingers to her open mouth and licking them clean.

Bone Daddy growled against her shoulder, and Ben's fingers tensed in her mouth.

"Shit, Legs." He gathered her hair gently in one fist, holding it back from her face. Ever the gentleman. She released his fingers and bent over his lap, the rum making her lips tingle.

Allegra trembled between them, her body wound tight with

excitement, with desire. She slowly, teasingly licked the sweet, sticky liquid off the head of Ben's cock, bending lower to reach the base of his shaft with her tongue. Salty and sweet. Potent. "What I saw in the club . . . were those just my fantasies?"

Bone Daddy chuckled behind her. "No, *cher*. Your fantasy was to watch. And to be with me. You saw what the others wanted, but were too afraid to take."

She thought so. She looked up at Ben, her lips coated with cum, her heart pounding. "You're wrong about her, Ben. She does want you. That night? I was watching her doing this to you." She opened her mouth wide over his cock, her cheeks hollowing as she sucked him deep inside.

She heard the surprise in Ben's inhalation, felt his erection grow in her mouth. His fingers pressed against her temple, and she knew he was sensing the truth of what she'd said about Michelle, even as he reveled in the feel of her mouth.

The last of the rum had just disappeared beneath her tongue when she felt it. Rousseau was licking *her* skin, tasting the rum he'd drawn on her flesh. She arched against his mouth.

He reached for something beside her, and then a different, cooler liquid poured between the cheeks of her ass. Strong, callused fingers rubbed it in, and then his thumb pressed against her once more. But gently. Hesitantly.

Allegra raised her head to look over her shoulder at Rousseau struggling against the Loa once more. He'd bitten his lip so hard it was bleeding. His struggle for restraint was clear for her to see as he watched her with Ben. But if they wanted to please her, he had to stop holding back his own passions. And she knew just what to do.

"I want you to fuck me, Rousseau. Any way you want. Any way Bone Daddy wants."

His voice was guttural. "You've never been taken this way. We have to go slow. You need to be prepared."

She smiled into eyes that were momentarily hazel. "If you go slow I may kill you. You'd never hurt me. Either of you." She repeated the words she'd heard earlier. "Don't think, Celestin 'Bone Daddy' Rousseau. Just feel."

The golden glow returned and his eyes narrowed. "No more outs, *cher*. I won't hold back. It's not in my nature."

She knew. God help her, she knew.

Ben's fist tightened on her hair and she turned back toward his approving expression, bending down to take him in her mouth once more, breathing deeply to calm her racing heart.

Allegra closed her eyes, her senses on overload. The taste of honey rum and Ben filled her mouth. The feeling of Rousseau behind her, his massive erection sliding between the cheeks of her ass, the lube he'd applied coating him as well.

He spread her cheeks apart with his hot hands, the tip of his cock pushing slowly inside, stretching her. Despite his warning, he took his time.

"Ahh." The pressure was intense, but so was her arousal.

The intimacy of the moment was startling. She hadn't expected it. Hadn't expected her emotions to be in such turmoil. She wanted to pull away, or push closer. She wanted to cry, to beg him to speed up, to take her hard and fast.

"Sweet Allegra. Warrior queen. *Yes*. Open for me. Take everything." One hand gripped her hip, while the other slid up her spine to hold her shoulder, pulling her back toward him. Allegra cried out around Ben's shaft, feeling impaled as Rousseau filled her completely. She wasn't the warrior he thought she was. She wasn't sure she could take much more.

"You are, *cher*. And it will never be enough." His rough rasp scraped over her flesh, the need in his voice twisting her heart. And then she couldn't think, could only feel as he began to pump his hips against her.

Her body felt stretched out, hyper-aware, her nerves strung tight. Light burst behind her eyes at the painful pleasure. Shallow thrusts grew to deep, powering drives inside her, his tightening grip the only thing keeping her grounded.

She sucked Ben's cock deeper into her mouth, feeling him hit the back of her throat, his moan mingling with hers. With Bone Daddy's.

Ben's free hand reached down to pluck at her nipples, squeezing the sensitive tips hard, the way she loved it. She slipped her fingers between her thighs, thrusting two inside her sex, feeling Rousseau's cock on the other side of the thin barrier. She pressed against it.

"No, *cher*. Mercy, *please*, you mustn't—"

"Yeah, baby. Fuck, I'm gonna come."

Ben's cry of passion mixed with Rousseau's agonized plea, both sounding like white noise to Allegra as the lightning struck her body again. She sensed the energy arc between the three of them, as though she were the conduit of pure, unadulterated bliss.

Rousseau's hands burned into her flesh. He began to pull out of her just as Ben pulled her head away from his cock, his own fist pumping once, then twice before he came in his hand.

Allegra only had time for a moment's regret for not getting to taste him. In the blink of an eye Ben disappeared with a shocked shout. She spun around, her body still shaken from her earth-shattering climax, to see Bone Daddy holding Ben by the throat, his feet dangling in the air. She shook her head, trying to focus. No human man was that strong.

"What? Jesus, Rousseau!" Ben choked out his surprise, but nothing swayed the angry Loa.

"She does not belong to you. She will never belong to you. Not her mouth, not her body. You will *never* have her. Your price has been paid."

It didn't even sound human, that voice. A moment's fear shimmered up Allegra's spine, but she pushed it away. Ben was turning purple. "Stop this right now." She crawled off the bed and put her hand on one of Rousseau's bulging arms.

"He was thinking—"

"Private thoughts during an orgasm. Thoughts people don't usually share. Unless you have a piggybacking spirit along for the ride."

He growled, but lowered the wheezing Ben to the ground, releasing him. Allegra's shoulders slumped in relief, and then tensed again when his golden glare turned her way. "I'll kill him if he touches you again."

"I don't think Rousseau would like that very much." She watched his expression turn to one of confusion. "And I know I wouldn't."

He stepped away from her, looking down at Ben, who was still clutching his neck protectively. He shook his head. "This isn't what I wanted." His eyes rolled back, and Rousseau/Bone Daddy collapsed on the floor like a sack of potatoes.

"Rousseau!" Allegra fell to her knees beside him, her fingers searching his neck for a pulse. It was faint, but there.

"That was incredibly promising."

Ben's hoarse voice brought Allegra's head whipping over her shoulder in shock. "He almost killed you, Ben. How is that promising?"

He came to kneel beside her, his gaze dropping to the still body on the wood floor. "I told you, this isn't the first time we've shared a woman. I've seen BD in action enough to know that this"—he pointed toward Rousseau—"is *not* the norm. Bone Daddy's MO is kinky, but fixed. He fulfills the deepest, darkest secret desires of whatever woman he's with, gaining energy from every climax, and then he sends them off with a smile on their face and a little something extra. Some change in their lives. Like your leg."

Allegra's hand instinctively moved to her left thigh. It was a powerful talent, being able to give a person anything, everything they wanted. The allure was almost irresistible. Almost. "He said it was temporary."

"Unless he decides it isn't." Ben sighed. "He always gives a gift to his lovers. That part of the rumor is true. He'll never come, but the next day you may win the lottery."

Awareness throbbed painfully in her temples. He hadn't come. In fact, when it looked like he might a few minutes ago, he'd seemed concerned. Scared.

No. It couldn't be true. Rousseau's cryptic words on the phone came back to her in a rush. "He's *never* come? Wait a second, are you telling me that in *seven years* you've never seen him have an orgasm?"

Ben shook his head. "Rousseau told me on a rare night when he allowed me to get him drunk. He'd started railing at his father for sticking him with a Loa who needed other people's orgasms to survive, but never let *him* come."

And those times she'd watched him through her window. He *always* had an erection. It wasn't because he got aroused at the drop of a hat. He was just never allowed relief. She rose up on her knees, gripping Ben's shoulders excitedly. "Is there anything that can hold a Loa? Silver? Candle wax? Anything?"

Ben's expression was wary. "Well, he isn't a werewolf, Allegra.

He's a spirit. A strong spirit, and his powers . . ." He shrugged. "I don't know, Legs. I'm not sure anyone's ever tried to hold one. Not anyone I've ever heard of."

"Not that you've—haven't you ever *tried* to help Rousseau get rid of his spirit?"

He jerked as though she'd slapped him. "You have no idea what I've done for him. What I would do. Do you think I want him to be controlled by the Loa's passions forever? I am not immune to BD's talents. He allows me in at his leisure, but as you can see, he rarely lets down his guard."

Allegra ran a hand through her hair. "I'm sorry, Ben. I have no right. And I'm not one to talk."

She didn't have time for this. He could wake up at any moment. "Does Rousseau have ropes or chains? Maybe we can use belts . . ." She stood up, looking around the room.

"No. Nothing like that." He paused. "Of course, there are those handcuffs."

"Handcuffs?"

Ben blushed. "They're under the bed, connected to the posts. There was this blonde who liked—"

Allegra held up her hand. "Stop. Talking. Now. Handcuffs, huh? Why didn't you say so in the first place? Help me get him to the bed before he wakes up."

"What is going on in that brain of yours, Legs?"

She took Rousseau's legs and grunted. Man, he was heavy. "Ever seen *The Exorcist*?"

Ben huffed, his muscles straining as he half carried, half dragged his friend toward the bed. "Yeah. So?"

"This will be nothing like that."

CHAPTER 8

"Am I crazy?"

"No more than anyone in love, Legs. Are *you* sure you want me to leave?" Ben looked worried.

Allegra shrugged, climbing up onto the bed and straddling Rousseau's thighs. He was still hard. Even when he was sleeping. "No. But I think he'd like it. It might help him drop his guard."

"I'm handcuffed to a bed without a stitch of clothing on. How much further down can a man's guard be?"

Allegra jumped, nearly kneeing Rousseau in the groin. "Careful now." He shifted on the bed, rattling the cuffs. "I have a feeling you're going to want use of that particular part of my anatomy. At least, I'm hopeful."

Hazel eyes. For the moment. "Rousseau?"

His gaze was fixed, unblinking, on her breasts. "Mmm-hmm?"

"I think that's my cue. Try not to screw this up, buddy." Ben leaned over and kissed Allegra on the forehead. "Good luck, Legs. And thank you, for everything." From the look in his eyes she had a feeling he was talking about more than what they'd done together. He was talking about Michelle.

Rousseau snorted. "I'd call you a traitor if you hadn't left a beautiful naked woman on my lap."

"You're welcome, lucky bastard."

"I'm sorry about earlier."

"Keep it to yourself. My story is I knocked you out and got you handcuffed to a bed. Who do you think people will believe?"

A surprise chuckle escaped Allegra's throat. Their easy banter reminded her of the way she was with Michelle. This was the Rousseau Ben had talked about. This was the man she wanted.

Ben's footsteps faded and she heard the door open, then slowly close behind him. She stared at Rousseau without blinking until he lifted his gaze.

"So why am I tied up again?"

Allegra swallowed at Rousseau's question. She wasn't sure herself. She didn't know if it would work. Bone Daddy was strong, but she was getting to know him. He might be intrigued enough to give her the time she needed. All she was sure of was that if he touched her, she might not be able to go through with her plan. And she needed to. Everything depended on it.

"My chute failed."

His perfectly arched eyebrows rose. "Excuse me?"

"My accident? It was my own fault. I wasn't careful, never was. Always jumped first, asked questions later. That particular day, my luck ran out. I got tangled in the ropes, hanging by my arms and legs for eleven hours waiting for the searchers to find me. After I lost all feeling in my limbs, all I had was time to think. I realized I'd been on the move for years, never stopping long enough to find love or make any friends. Michelle doesn't count; she adopted me. I had no choice in the matter, thank God."

She rubbed the scars on her arms. "I took chances. Thought I was being brave. But after tonight, I know I was fooling myself."

Rousseau was listening intently, compassion in his eyes. "Why tonight?"

"Something made me realize that brave isn't always the mad woman jumping from the plane without double-checking her chute. It's the person on the ground, watching and ready to catch you. It's the person who sticks around, even when it's hard. People like Ben. And you."

He looked away. "I'm not brave, Allegra. It's not like I had a lot of choice in the matter."

She knew better. "Bone Daddy said, 'He laid his family out like a platter.' His whole family, not just his son. You offered yourself, didn't you? To save your family from your father's mistakes."

His expression told her everything she wanted to know. She'd been right. Rousseau had taken the Loa into himself willingly. "That's what courage is, Rousseau."

His laugh was haggard, bitter. "What an imagination you have. Would you be so quick to canonize me if you knew how many women I've had sex with? How many men? The Loa isn't particular, love. He just wants to fuck. And I've never said no. Never tried to fight it. I'm no hero, I'm a dirty bastard."

She slid her hands up his chest, making him shudder. She tugged lightly on his nipple rings, and he gasped. "And how many of those others ever stopped to wonder if you were satisfied? How many wanted nothing but to make *you* come? To make you happy?"

A flash of gold kindled in his hazel eyes, and Allegra watched as he was taken over by the Loa once more. She sat up straighter. Game time.

Bone Daddy smiled. "Why would you worry about that, *cher*? I am satisfied when you scream out in ecstasy. When your body quakes at the touch of my tongue, my fingers. That is all it takes to make me happy."

"But none of your lovers have ever given you an orgasm, have they?"

He shrugged lazily. "When you are given a sumptuous buffet after a lifetime of famine, do you wonder if the person in the line behind you is hungry? Or do you feast?"

Allegra felt the truth like a punch in the gut. She'd been no better. She'd reveled in her climax, not realizing until it was pointed out to her that Rousseau hadn't had the same release. How many women left his side the morning after, thinking they had had the best sex of their life, and never wondering about him again?

She sighed. "I'm sorry, Bone Daddy. But I'm on to you now." She lowered her chest, scraping her hard nipples across the cool metal on his. His smile wavered. "You want to satisfy me?"

His gaze heated to molten gold. "More than I imagined possible, *cher*."

Her hips pressed against his, her mind already fighting the haze of arousal and remembered pleasure at the feel of his smooth, muscular body against hers. "Good. Then this shouldn't be too hard." She smiled. "No pun intended. I won't be satisfied until I make you come."

Allegra kissed him, loving his taste, his full, succulent lips. Rousseau's lips. Everything about the man called to her, always had. She only hoped she had the strength to outlast him. And that he wanted her enough to give her the chance.

Her lips lifted and she shifted on his body, lowering her head to place hot, open-mouthed kisses on his neck, his chest, the tense muscles of his stomach. "*Cher*, come back up here. I want to taste you again. Give me your sweet pussy."

She chuckled against his hip. "Not now. I'm busy."

He rattled the handcuffs, his arms bulging as he struggled against the bonds. Allegra ignored him, spreading his powerful thighs with her body. Her mouth watered at the sight of his thick cock. She hadn't wondered with Ben, but with the revolving door of partners Rousseau had just admitted to, she had to ask. "Have you ever had sex without a condom?"

He snorted. "I'm older than you know, *cher*, and I'm not stupid. Of course I haven't. If this body got a disease, it would put an end to my fun. Why?"

Allegra didn't answer his question. Not with words. His surprised moan as she took him in her mouth was gratifying. He didn't need a coating of honey rum, he tasted sweeter than any liqueur all on his own. Her own personal addiction.

Her lips stretched wide to take more of his thick cock in her mouth, her fist trying to close around the base of his shaft. So big. God, she wanted him inside her.

"Unlock my chains, *cher*. Set me free, and I will give you what you need."

She licked her finger, slipping it between his thighs until she reached what she was aiming for. Allegra lifted her mouth and licked her lips devilishly. "If I did that, how could I give you what *you* need?" Her finger pushed through the tight muscles of his ass, and she watched as shocked desire widened his eyes.

Her tongue traced the veins on his flushed cock while she studied his reaction to her invasion. He liked it. She knew he would. She pressed deeper, finding the spot that she'd read about, the spot she knew would drive the sexual Loa, and Rousseau, insane.

"*Fuck*. Allegra, please."

"Please what? Please stop sucking your cock? Please *don't* make you come?"

He clenched his jaw. "Please don't make me come like *this*. Ride me, *cher*. If you are going to do this, do it right. Ride the Loa. Let me feel your sweet pussy around my cock."

There lies the danger, she thought to herself. Her body heated, thighs tingling at the thought of taking him inside her. It was a big temptation. To please him without giving in to her own need. A lot was at stake. And he knew it, clever man.

She rose, reaching for the condoms beside the bed, her body trembling with excitement. Allegra's hands shook as she rolled the condom down his long shaft, a spark of feminine fire lighting in her belly at the proof of his desire. She straddled him again, aligning her knees with his hips.

"That's right, *cher*. I can feel your heat from here. Think of how I'm going to fill you, fuck you. Think of how hard I'm going to make you come."

She lifted her chin, looking him straight in the eye. "*You* think, Bone Daddy. Think about how tightly I'll grip you, how good you'll feel when *I* make *you* come."

Long lashes shuttered his golden eyes from view. "You talked to the old man. I can see him in your mind. What if he was wrong? What if giving me what I want changes nothing?"

"That's a chance I'm willing to take." For love. Allegra laid her hands on his chest, slowly lowering herself onto the tip of his shaft.

Her thigh muscles tightened, making her aware once again of what he'd done to her leg, how he'd taken the pain away.

"You're so wet, *cher*. So ready for me." He glanced down at her leg. "You know what I can give to you. What I want to give to you. Shall I show you more?"

Her arms and legs began to burn and tingle. She looked down and gasped. The scars on her arms and legs were gone. Not a trace remained. It was as if the accident had never happened. She met his gaze, unable to stop the instinctive tears welling in her eyes.

"Let me go, Allegra Jarrod. Let me go, and I will give you more pleasure than you ever imagined. I want to take my time with you. Days and nights of nothing but paradise. And when you finally leave my bed, you will never have to hurt again. Never have to hear the whispers of pity from your family, from strangers. You'll be free."

She hovered over the head of his cock, her body frozen, her mind in chaos. He'd just offered her everything she'd wanted every day since the accident. A second chance with a whole body. Freedom from pain.

But the cost was too high.

"I'll be free. But Rousseau won't."

His expression grew dark. "What do you care? You barely know the boy. You lust for him. Is that enough to refuse what I'm offering?"

"It's more than lust, and if you can read my mind then you know it." She didn't look over her body again, not even when she felt the tingling, knowing he'd returned her scars. She wanted Rousseau, scars or no scars. She lowered herself onto his cock, moaning at the impossible fullness, her body struggling to accept all of him despite her arousal.

She set a slow, teasing rhythm, while her internal muscles massaged him. She loved his sensual growls, the helpless jerk of his hips as he tried to quicken her pace. His cheeks flushed a deep bronze, his full lips tight with need. He was irresistible. She bit the inside of her cheek, determined to fight the desire to give in, the desire to release him and let him take her.

Allegra lifted her hand and cupped her breasts, teasing her nipples while he watched.

"You're playing with fire, *cher*." Her sex tightened around him once more, and he moaned. "Do that again."

She did, her own sound of pleasure mingling with his. She quickened her pace, watching as he closed his eyes, his head tossing on the pillow, lost to the moment. "Yes, that's it, *cher*. Fuck me. Make me come. Take what you want."

Allegra couldn't hold back. She arched her spine, dropping her hands to grip his thighs as she took them both closer to the edge. She wasn't sure how much longer she could last. It felt too good. But she needed him to come. Everything depended on it.

She twisted her hips, rocking against him, faster and faster, his groans guiding her movements. "*Yes*. Oh, *cher*. Allegra. I feel . . . it's been . . . *yes*." His eyes flashed, joy and wonder overtaking his expression as his cock pulsed inside her.

They came together as thunder crashed overhead, shaking the small loft and covering their shouts of pleasure. Allegra collapsed against him, shuddering and crying with the power of her climax.

"Are you okay, *bebe*?"

Bebe? She sniffled, lifting her head to look into his eyes. Would he still be there? Bone Daddy? Glowing behind Rousseau's eyes?

His smile was gentle, happy. And his eyes were a sparkling hazel. Not a trace of gold. "You did it, Allegra. He's gone."

Was it true? She studied his face, looking for any trace that he might be deceiving her. His grin grew. "I swear to you, love. He's gone for good. You gave him something no one has since I met him. I think he decided you'd more than paid what was left of my father's debt."

Allegra dove on him, covering his face with joyful kisses. "Thank heavens. I wasn't sure I could do it, or if it would even work."

"Well, it did. And I'd be happy to pay you back if you let me out of these handcuffs."

She pulled away from him with a frown. "You don't owe me anything, Rousseau." She hopped off the bed, grabbing the keys and unlocking his hands without looking at him. She didn't want gratitude. Not from him. Not for this. "Anyone would have done the same. I don't expect any kind of payback."

He sat up and grabbed her waist, pulling her onto his lap. "Allegra, I didn't mean it like that. Don't you know how much I wanted you? From the first moment I saw you, I knew you were mine. But I couldn't approach you, I didn't want what I was going through to scare you away."

He pressed his forehead against hers. "He knew you were someone I could . . . care for. More than care for. He let me feel what you were feeling. More than sex and desire. Love, Allegra. Your love, not for him, but for *me*. I think the real reason he decided to let you win was because of that. I do believe that libidinous Loa was actually matchmaking."

She grinned. "With a little assist from Ben. And Mambo Toussaint. And—"

"They'll hold *that* over my head forever." His expression sobered. "And I'll let them."

He kissed her, and she felt his cock stir against her hip. She tore her lips from his, surprise in her eyes. "Already?"

Rousseau laughed. "I've had seven years of lessons from the master of kink. I'm impatient to show you all I've learned."

He tossed her beneath him and she giggled, gasping when she looked down at her legs. "He healed my leg but he didn't take away my scars? Why?"

Rousseau shrugged. "He liked you. More than I was comfortable with." Rousseau traced one particularly jagged scar on her arm. "And he loved these. They make you even more beautiful, you know." His lips brushed over each scar he came across, and Allegra shivered. Through his eyes she *felt* more beautiful, and stronger than she had in a long time. A warrior.

Yes. My warrior queen.

Bone Daddy?

Thank you, cher. *I'd forgotten how good it feels to come, it's been so long. That boy is stubborn, you know that, right? But then again, you were worth the wait. Knew you were a smart one.*

Where will you go from here?

Don't worry about me. Just take care of Rousseau. He loves you, cher. *And you may see me again, sooner than you think. Ben needs a good woman. Or man. We'll see.*

Think Michelle.

Bon Dieu, that woman hates me.

Rousseau ducked his head to get her attention. "Where'd you go?"

"I think Ben's in trouble."

"Huh?"

Allegra beamed, grabbing his long locks and pulling him toward her for another kiss. "Nothing. Nothing at all."

He came over her, taking her mouth with all the desire she'd imagined when she first planned this crazy seduction. She'd had no idea what she was in for, but she didn't regret a thing.

Thank you, God. Oh, and Bone Daddy.

A far-off devilish chuckle echoed through her mind before Rousseau took charge, distracting her so thoroughly that she had no time to think about Loas or voodoo spells. No time for anything but pleasure.

And love.

❧ RECLAIM ME ❧

CHAPTER 1

She needed to move.

When Michelle had agreed to come back to New Orleans, her mother had found her an apartment with a ready-made roommate. She'd known Stacy from high school, and she'd desperately needed a roommate to help with the rent.

But a few important rental features had been left out of her mother's description. The most important being that Michelle had thought she'd be living across the street from a coffee shop, not her very own voodoo sex show.

And if her mother hadn't known *exactly* what she was subjecting her only daughter to by setting her up in this location, Michelle would eat her shiny green hat.

She vaguely recalled Celestin from high school. Two years ahead of her, he was the attractive but distracted friend of the bane of her existence—Benjamin Beauregard Adair.

She'd had no idea that it was Celestin Rousseau who owned Café Bwe, or that he and Ben were still thick as thieves.

Even more surprising, Rousseau had found a new friend while she'd been away.

Bone Daddy.

The Loa possessing him made the handsome café owner practically irresistible. His body glowed with extra life, the spirit clinging to his skin like a glove. And Michelle could see him. Them.

She'd asked her mother, a priestess in the voodoo religion, how a man could be held so long in the thrall of a Loa. Annemarie Toussaint had just given her a stack of books and told her to study.

If Michelle was going to take over the shop, she said, she had to learn the ways of her ancestors, had to learn about and respect their family's traditions. But Michelle had no intention of becoming a healer or priestess, no intention of becoming involved in the voodoo religion.

She only wished her mother would believe her.

The priestess might be more willing if Michelle hadn't allowed herself to be talked into coming back home.

Why had she? Nearly losing her mother and the family home to the hurricane had been a damn good reason, but Michelle knew it wasn't the only one.

The abilities she'd had as a child, the ones she'd pushed down with medication and therapy, had returned with a vengeance a few years ago, ruining her perfect life.

She'd been in New York, working in an art gallery. Handsome, sophisticated lovers vied for her attention, and her friends were the elite of the art world. Sure, she wasn't painting, but there were no dangling chicken feet, no family expectations, and not a single irritating Southern man to be found.

The mugging changed everything. People got mugged all the time in New York City. In fact, a few of her friends said you couldn't really claim native status until you were.

But this had been no ordinary mugging.

The man who'd attacked her hadn't been alone. Someone, or some*thing*, had been directing him, controlling him. When it realized Michelle could see it, it stopped trying to steal her purse and jewelry, and attacked. If a coworker hadn't come along . . . she didn't want to think about what might have happened.

After that the medicine her therapist had given her hadn't worked. She could see everything. The veil had been lifted once more, and the world that had seemed so magical to her when she was young took a frightening turn.

That was when she knew she had to come home. Had to understand. Why her? Why had she been given the ability to see all the things that went bump in the night? Was there a reason—beyond driving her insane? And if not, how could she get it to stop for good?

Maybe it had been the wrong decision. Being back home had felt good, but after four years, she found she still couldn't bring herself to talk to her mother about her renewed abilities. And now, well, if she hadn't returned, Allegra would never have moved here to recuperate, Bone Daddy would never have met her . . . and Michelle wouldn't be watching through her window as the possessed Rousseau and Benjamin Adair fucked her friend into an orgasmic stupor in the loft above the coffee shop.

It wasn't Allegra's fault she'd given in. Despite all her warnings, Michelle knew how hard it was to resist the pull of a Loa, especially one as magnetic as Bone Daddy. The voodoo spirit wasn't entirely to blame either. He never hid his agenda from anyone. He wanted sex, and he was willing to do whatever he had to do to get it.

If anything it was Ben she was angry with. *He'd* been the devil whispering in Allegra's ear, encouraging her crush on Rousseau. Flirting for his own wicked purposes. And he didn't have the excuse of being under the influence of a spell or spirit. He was just born trouble.

Too bad he was so damn fine. It made it harder to hate him, wanting him as badly as she did. And it made it impossible to tear herself away from the window when he shed his clothes, his body perfectly profiled as he stood beside the bed. He was watching Allegra writhe on the sheets, Rousseau's face buried between her thighs.

Michelle was watching Ben.

He was a golden god. Sandy blond hair with a tendency to curl at the ends when he left it too long. Strong, square jaw that constantly seemed to have a day's worth of stubble. He always looked as though he'd be more at home on a surfboard in California than the steamy streets of New Orleans.

And his body. It was the stuff of wet dreams. Lean and muscular, his chest was sprinkled with light brown hair that she wanted to tug, wanted to run her fingers through.

Her gaze honed in on his erection. He was stroking it lightly, grazing it with his short fingernails while he studied the couple on the bed. Michelle wanted to touch him, wanted to take him into her mouth and taste every thick, delicious inch.

Rousseau stepped back from the bed, Bone Daddy's aura bright around him, and Ben turned to crawl onto the bed. The lamplight fell on the paler skin of his perfectly bitable ass, and she saw it. The small tattoo on his right cheek.

Mimi.

His nickname for her inked on his behind for all to see. A sudden memory of when and why he'd gotten it flooded her mind.

The exact details of her eighteenth birthday were foggy. She'd let her friends get her drunk in celebration, and gone to a strip club when she probably shouldn't have.

She'd been spouting off again, about how beautiful women were, better than men in every way, and her friends had called her on it. They'd dared her to share a dance with a stripper, to kiss a girl. After downing yet another sazerac, it sounded like a good plan. So they'd gone to the club.

And run into Ben.

He'd been twenty back then, home from college, and even more full of himself, if that were possible. Her friends had drooled after him, inviting him to join the party, which he had, despite her glares.

When they shared her belief that women would be better lovers than men, he'd challenged her. More than challenged.

He'd double-dog dared her.

The dare was simple. Ben would pay for her private lap dance . . . for a price. He would get to be in the room with them, and if she actually had the nerve to kiss and touch the other woman, he'd have her name tattooed on his ass.

To the drunken Michelle, this challenge had seemed perfectly reasonable. He'd dared her, after all. She had no choice but to comply.

She remembered thinking the blonde woman he'd chosen was beautiful, as slender as Michelle was hopelessly curvy. The same type of girls who'd always hung around him in high school.

They'd gone into the VIP room and the woman had started to dance for Michelle with Ben sitting on the other side of the room, his face hidden in the shadows.

The music had flowed through her, and she'd gotten up to join the dancer, unable to merely sit and watch. Her movements were hesitant at first; she was too aware of Ben, and of the fact that something in her wanted to arouse him, despite their antagonistic relationship.

The blonde had slid her hand up to cup one of Michelle's heavy breasts, turning slightly so the male in the room could easily see what she was doing.

They were rocking back and forth together to the rhythm, inching closer, by accident or design, to where Ben sat, unmoving, in the corner.

She'd been more aroused by the dance, by the stripper's touch, than she thought she would be. But she knew, without a doubt, it was Ben's presence that was adding the extra heat.

"Let's get rid of this."

Michelle's eyes, closed as she lost herself in the sensual beat of the drums, popped open when the woman untied her halter top, the top of the shirt dropping to reveal Michelle's bare breasts.

"*Damn*, Mimi."

Ben's voice had her raising her hands to cover herself, but the stripper grabbed them, distracting her with a knowing grin. "Relax, darlin'. It's just you and me in here. Just a dance."

The blonde pulled the straps off her minuscule shimmery dress and it pooled at her feet, leaving her clad in only a sheer thong and high heels.

Her breasts were small but sexy, and Michelle envied her slender, boyish body—her creamy skin. Not to mention the glorious ivy tattoo that wound around her waist. The blonde came closer, tossing her hair back over her shoulder before touching the tips of Michelle's hard nipples with her own. "Men love this," she'd whispered into Michelle's ear, leaving a gentle kiss on her lobe.

The pained masculine groan from the shadows told her the woman had to be on to something. Michelle thought about all the girls she'd seen him with throughout high school, all the times she'd caught him making out in the spot that had been *their* special place when they were children, and felt the desire to pay him back in kind.

She licked her lips, her hips following the knowingly seductive sway of the stripper's as they pressed against each other. Michelle spun around so that she was facing Ben's direction, her own hands lifting her breasts, presenting them for his inspection. She bent forward, pressing her curved backside against the blonde's slender hips, and the stripper laughed breathlessly.

"You're a fast learner."

"She is, isn't she?" Ben had leaned forward then, his hands clenched into fists on his thighs, his cheeks flushed. Their eyes met, and Michelle had had a sudden, sinking feeling she was in way over her head. "Touch her, Mimi. Kiss her. Otherwise you forfeit the bet."

Lose a bet? To him? "Never have, never will." Michelle straightened, turning back toward the stripper with wobbly legs, determined to show him up. "May I?"

"Why not?"

Michelle traced the twining ivy image, so stark against the pale skin, and slid her arms around the lovely blonde, leaning in to kiss her.

When the soft, feminine lips touched hers, she'd closed her eyes to enjoy the sensation. But all she'd seen was Ben. Ben cupping the curves of her hips and pulling her closer. Ben's tongue flicking her lips teasingly. Ben moaning in delight when her mouth opened, inviting him in.

Michelle felt her world turn sideways as large, male hands gripped her shoulders, pulling her away from the woman and into his arms. He took her mouth with a low growl and she made a sound of approval, thinking this was so much better than she'd imagined—the dark taste of him, his rough fingers cupping her breasts, his erection pressed against the curve of her belly.

More than the physical embrace, she felt that familiar mental connection. The connection she hadn't felt since they were young, when he had touched her and known what she was thinking, feeling. He'd known what she wanted then, and he knew what she wanted now.

His other hand slid down to the hem of her short, snug skirt, yanking so hard it rolled up around her waist, revealing her plain cotton briefs to his searching fingers.

Yes, touch me.

He slipped them beneath the fabric and lower, between her thighs, groaning into her mouth when he'd found the wetness there. "Mimi. Baby, I want—"

"Your tip was big, but not big enough for this. Not that I'm not enjoying watching for a change, but you two might want to take this somewhere a little more private before the boss decides to poke his head in."

Michelle pulled away from Ben's embrace, noticing the stripper smirking as she leaned against the wall, watching them.

"Oh, shit."

As though someone had pushed her under an ice-cold shower, Michelle had instantly sobered. Ben. She'd been kissing Ben. Topless, no less. He'd never let her hear the end of it. Oh, God, her friends—they were right outside. She'd backed away from him, retying her halter and lowering her skirt with shaking hands.

"Mimi, damn it, wait."

Ben reached out as if to grab her and she stumbled, bumping against the stripper with a mumbled apology. She couldn't look at either of them. "Don't touch me. Ever again. I'm drunk. This never happened."

That was the first and last time she'd kissed Benjamin Adair.

A few days later he'd passed by the patio restaurant where she'd been working for the summer, and, right in front of the amused and slightly horrified tourists, he turned his back and showed her his new strategically placed tattoo. She'd left for school a month later, vowing to never forgive him, and to do her best never to see him again.

The fogged window obscuring her vision drew her back to the present. She ran her forearm down the glass, wiping off the moisture, and felt a small pang of disappointment. And a relief she didn't want to think about.

He was dressing again. How long had she been lost in her daydream? Long enough to miss his part in their strange ménage, apparently. He was leaving Rousseau cuffed to the bed with Allegra beside him, her expression determined. What was that girl up to now?

Ben kissed Allegra on the forehead and looked toward the window. Michelle slid closer to the wall, knowing he couldn't possibly see her. It was dark outside, and the lights were all out, but she could swear he was looking straight at her.

Ben turned to leave and Michelle knew she should look away, give her friend privacy, but something kept her frozen in place.

Allegra was pleasuring Rousseau, kissing and caressing him, and Michelle could see the Loa inside him struggling against his own pleasure. The energy ebbed and flowed, Bone Daddy's form superimposing over Rousseau's as Allegra rode him.

Michelle didn't question her arousal at the scene playing out before her eyes. She would worry if she *wasn't* turned on by the sensual attack her friend was launching on the helpless Loa and the man he currently inhabited.

Allegra was beautiful, in spite of her scars. *Because* of them. And Rousseau obviously felt the same, if the intense ecstasy on his face was anything to go by.

She really should have taken that man she'd flirted with the other night up on his offer. She'd told Allegra she needed a new distraction. After tonight it would jump to number one on her priority list.

"Holy shit."

Michelle pressed closer to the window, amazed at what she was seeing. As Allegra and Rousseau climaxed, their bodies arching off the bed with the power of it, the Loa slipped to the edge of the bed . . . then disappeared. Bone Daddy had left Rousseau? How? Why?

She studied the two lovers carefully, looking for any sign, any remnant of the spirit who'd been a continuous presence in Rousseau since Michelle had moved back. But she couldn't see a thing.

"Well, I'll be damned." She watched them embrace, and recalled something she'd read from one of the books her mother had foisted on her.

There is no hex, nor dark spell of any kind, that can't be overcome by a selfless act of love.

Had she been so focused on keeping herself busy, on keeping Allegra away from Bone Daddy, that she hadn't noticed her friend had fallen in love with Rousseau? That perhaps he'd fallen in love with her right back?

A strange tingle shot down her spine, pulling her gaze away from the couple's first private moment together and down to the street below.

Ben.

He stood beneath the street lamp on the corner, heedless of the scattered groups walking by as he stared up at her window, watching her.

She didn't move, didn't blink. Some part of her was terrified he would come closer, knock on the door. Some part of her wanted to let him in. To ease the ache created by what she'd seen tonight, by him.

He smiled. A wide, wicked grin that was pure temptation. Pure Ben. She didn't breathe again until he turned and walked slowly down the street, hands in his pockets.

Good. The last thing she needed was another run-in with Ben Adair. She turned away with a sigh, feeling the need for a cold shower, or maybe she'd practice her capoeira moves first so she could impress her teacher at tomorrow's class. She had a feeling she would need to exhaust herself to get any sleep tonight.

When she dragged her sweaty body to the shower an hour later, the showerhead sputtered, spitting out boiling hot water despite how much she fiddled with the faucet. She had to laugh.

She *really* needed to move.

CHAPTER 2

"*Bonjou,* BEN! WE NEVER SEE YOU UP AND ABOUT SO EARLY. And certainly not on a Saturday. What's the special occasion, little one?"

Ben chuckled at Mambo Toussaint's bright welcome when she answered his knock at her door. He would always be the *little one* to her. Other than his mother and another woman who was currently driving him bonkers, she was his favorite female. But unlike the other two, *she* spoiled him rotten. "I haven't been to your house in a while, and since when does a man need a reason to visit the most beautiful woman in the Crescent City?"

"I thought *I* was the most beautiful woman in New Orleans, Benjamin."

Elise Adair appeared over Mambo Toussaint's shoulder, a dog-eared book in hand. *Love Spells.* Ben bit the inside of his cheek. His mother had never been subtle.

"I should have known. Where one Mama is . . ."

"The other's nearby," the older women said in unison, all of them laughing together at the familiar saying. The two had been best friends long before Ben was born.

The lives they led when apart couldn't have been more different. His mother was a pampered housewife to a wealthy businessman, with a house in Europe and a Louisiana mansion.

Annemarie Toussaint was a mambo, a voodoo priestess, who'd never missed a day of work. A woman who'd raised a child on her own, not to mention any stray that needed her help.

To any onlooker, their friendship would be unusual, but he knew The Mamas were opposite sides of the same coin, the gifts they shared, their secrets and their heartaches, kept them bound tightly to each other.

"You're both too lovely to choose from. I'm an innocent victim of circumstance."

Mambo Toussaint threw back her head, hair wrapped as it always was in one of her brightly patterned scarves, and guffawed. She stepped inside and pulled him close behind her, past the homey, crowded kitchen and into the living room.

He'd loved this house when he was a child. The statues of saints and images of colorful icons that hung on the walls, the smells of Cajun spices and rose oil permeating the air. It was a warm house, full of magic and music and laughter. He hadn't had to keep his clothes clean or his shoes on, and he could talk as loud as he liked.

His mother squeezed his arm before going to fold herself elegantly onto the quilt-covered couch, and he noticed her bare feet. He had a feeling his mother liked it for the same reasons. Pristine mansions with furniture that hadn't been created to sit on got old after a while.

She tilted her head in his direction, her straight, silvery blonde bob sliding forward with the movement. "Something's wrong. I'm sure half the female population of Louisiana is bound for disappointment, but I would think you'd be relieved that Celestin is free of his father's debt with the Loa. Not to mention that sweet Allegra's injury being healed."

"Do you know how disconcerting it is to have your mother know things before you tell her?"

She wrinkled her nose at Ben. "Don't change the subject, Benjamin. I wasn't looking. Michelle told Annemarie a few days ago. Though how she found out when we all know Café Bwe's been closed for several days now, and no one's heard one peep from the lovebirds . . ." Elise shrugged casually, though she was watching her son with an interested glimmer in her eyes.

Ben knew how Michelle had found out. He'd felt her watching, knew she'd seen him with Allegra and Rousseau, that she'd seen him on the street below. The little voyeur.

It had taken all of his willpower to turn and walk away without banging her door down and finding a way to touch her. If he could just get his hands on her, he'd know if what Allegra had said was true. Was *he* Michelle's secret fantasy?

He had to find out. He'd spent the last few days climbing the walls, his happiness for Rousseau and Allegra muted by his own frustration.

Michelle Toussaint.

He couldn't remember a time when he wasn't in love with her. At the age of five, he'd looked at the giggling three-year-old talking to herself in the garden and lost his heart.

Everything about her drew him in; her cocoa curls, her large, strikingly green eyes, her feistiness. And when she took his hand, he could see that he wasn't alone in the world, that someone other than his mother had gifts similar to his own.

Ben had always been able to sense what people were thinking and feeling, but with Michelle, he could also see what she saw. With one touch he knew she hadn't been talking to herself at all, but to a young man in strange clothing, the rosebush still visible through his head. A ghost.

They'd been inseparable after that. Ben, Michelle, and Gabriel, her twin brother. Though Gabe had no abilities, he'd still joined them on their adventures, sticking close to his sister's side. Ben had been sure they would always be friends.

Things had changed after Michelle's father decided to return to Italy, taking his son, but *not* his daughter, with him—Michelle had been devastated. Nothing he did could console her. At ten years old he couldn't understand why she pushed him away. At thirty-six he was still chasing after her.

He looked down at the two women sitting patiently on the sofa. The Mamas had always known how he felt about Michelle.

When she left for college in Texas, then moved to New York, deciding not to come back home, he'd gone a little crazy. Not that he'd ever been a saint, but for a while there, he knew his mother was worried he might have lost his way.

Four years ago she'd come back home, and he'd held out the hope that they could renew their friendship. But she avoided him, and when she couldn't, when their families got together for annual crawfish boils or birthdays, she made sure he never got the chance to touch her. And Ben had been forced to accept that.

But not anymore.

He sat on the small footstool at Mambo Toussaint's feet, and took her hand. "I need a reading. And a little help from the both of you."

The priestess shared a look with his mother. "It's about damn time."

* * *

MICHELLE WAS TIRED. GOOD TIRED, BUT STILL, SHE NEEDED to find a new obsession. What had started as a way to make herself stronger, to feel safer after the mugging, had become a manic compulsion she didn't know how to stop.

By now she knew so many ways to kick ass, she could probably give Jet Li a run for his money. As if any amount of physical training could protect her from the strength of a Loa, let alone a demonic entity in possession of a body. But it made her feel better, and it had made her leaner than she'd ever been in her life.

She'd never be as thin as Allegra—she had too much on the bottom and top for that—but she could definitely hold her own.

Right now, though, all she wanted was an actual shower, and the only place she was going to find that was at her mother's house. Hopefully the landlord would send someone out about her own recently departed shower in the next day or two, but she wasn't holding her breath.

"Mama? Where you at?" She rolled her eyes. How many years had she worked to get rid of her accent? And when had it come back so completely?

She walked through the kitchen, grabbing one of the candied pralines on the table and popping it into her mouth as she headed down the hall. The red door was closed; that meant her mother was granting someone a reading and she wasn't to be disturbed.

She'd just hop in the shower, and maybe she could avoid running into whoever it was. She entered the bathroom, dropping her gym bag and stripping out of the sweat shorts and black sports bra.

Turning the water to the perfect temperature, she started the shower, glancing at herself in the mirror before she stepped in.

"Not bad at all." If she did say so herself. She needed someone else to say it, and soon. She was so restless she'd even flirted with her cute Brazilian instructor today. He'd ended the class early, chattering nervously about his boyfriend making special plans for dinner.

She shrugged. Maybe she'd go out tonight. Without Allegra to look after, she'd be free to find the perfect distraction for the night.

Michelle stepped under the shower and moaned. This wasn't exactly what she needed, but it helped. She reached for her favorite lavender soap, the soap her mother made herself, and lathered her body.

Her hands lingered over her breasts, her belly, as she let her thoughts drift to the evening ahead. The blues club she usually went to might not do the job tonight. She was too needy. She wasn't in the mood to flirt coyly, hoping her intended target could work up the nerve to flirt back.

She slipped her fingers between her legs, shivering as she washed the sensitive lips of her sex. Yeah. She needed a sure thing tonight.

Ben would be a sure thing.

Her inner voice had a strange sense of humor. Even if it was right, Ben Adair was and had always been off limits. She just hadn't been able to get the other night, and his part in it, out of her head.

She groaned, turning to let the water pound against her skin like a heated massage, relaxing the tight muscles of her back until she was leaning against the colorfully tiled wall, boneless.

"I wasn't sure what he saw in you. But I know now. I have never seen such a sweet ass, *cher*."

"Son of a bitch!" Michelle screeched and grabbed for the towel rack beside her head as soon as she heard the casual male voice behind her.

She ripped it from its moorings, whirling around with her weapon outstretched to meet . . . air. The porcelain bar hit the wall of the shower with a loud crash, breaking off several chunks of tile in the process.

"I don't think the mambo will be too happy with what you've done to her shower. I know we got off to a rocky start, *cher*, but surely we don't need to resort to violence."

Michelle felt her jaw drop and her fingers loosened in shock, the towel bar clanging against the tub at her feet. "No way. It can't be."

"Mimi, honey, are you in there? Damn it, I'm coming in." Ben's concerned voice was quickly followed by a large bang as he broke through the locked bathroom door.

She closed her eyes. Of course. She was naked in the shower with a beautiful, if noncorporeal male, and Ben. He always had a fantastic sense of timing. "Go away, Adair."

"I heard you scream and heard something break. Are you bleeding, baby? Just tell me if you're hurt, or I'm coming in there after you."

The man standing beside her started laughing, his white linen shirt and pants unaffected by the water pouring through him and onto her.

Michelle wasn't finding the situation nearly as humorous. "I'm glad someone's enjoying themselves."

"Enjoying— Mimi, what are you talking about?"

His voice was closer and Michelle panicked. "No blood, Ben. I'm fine. Go away before I tell my mother to hex you."

She heard the relief in his voice. "Your mama loves me far too much to harm a hair on my pretty head. Now turn off the water, and I'll toss a towel over for you. I'm not leaving until I can see for myself that nothing is broken or out of place."

"You know he means it, *cher*. Ben is just as stubborn as you are. Not that I mind. The longer you resist, the longer I can ogle all that . . . *flesh*."

His voice was seductive. The way he openly surveyed her body. He had no shame. But she'd never imagined he did. No one could ever accuse him of being a gentleman. "Okay, Ben, turning off the water. Let's get this over with."

"Good girl," Ben praised, all good humor once more. "For some reason I'm reminded of all those baths we were forced to take together after The Mamas would pull us out of whatever mud puddle we'd been rolling in. Maybe I should just come in there, relive the good old days."

"Try to pretend you aren't a total pervert for five minutes, can you? Hand me the damn towel."

Ben tsked, throwing a plush green towel over the shower curtain and through the smirking Loa beside her. "Listen to that language. In your mother's house no less. Good thing I closed the door."

Michelle wrapped the towel around her, tucking the corner into her cleavage securely before ripping open the slender curtain. "I'm fine. See? *Fine*. Now you can go and let me get dressed and out of here before I lose my mind."

"You are fine, Michelle. You make me wish I had a body at my disposal. Think I could convince Ben to loan me his for the night?"

"No!"

Ben frowned at her sudden outburst, looking around the room

suspiciously. Before she had a chance to back away, he pounced, pulling her out of the shower and into his arms. Touching her.

Ben swore. "Sweet holy heaven."

Michelle sighed. No avoiding it now. "Yep. That about sums it up. Say hello to Bone Daddy. I believe you two know each other."

CHAPTER 3

"THAT *IS* A NEAT TRICK, *CHER*. CAN HE HEAR ME, TOO?"
Bone Daddy stepped out of the bathtub as though he were exiting
a limousine, just adding to the dreamlike feel of the moment. Michelle wished she was dreaming, but her luck hadn't been that
good lately.

"I can. Fuck me runnin', I really can. But I thought you'd gone.
How can you still be here . . . a Loa without a host?" Ben sounded
fascinated, but not enough to loosen his grip on Michelle. She bit
her lip as his thumbs caressed her wet shoulders. If he didn't stop
soon, she wouldn't be responsible for her actions.

He pulled her closer and she felt that tingle along her temple,
recalling why she'd avoided his touch all these years. Bone Daddy's
sensual voice was just the distraction she needed.

"I find I'm not ready to go back just yet, *mon ami*. Even without
a horse to ride, I still enjoy the pleasures of this world more than

the other." He glanced meaningfully at Michelle's towel-clad body. "Can you really blame me?"

Horse to ride was a voodoo euphemism for possession. She'd seen her mother embrace the Loa spirits time and time again during the rituals she'd been allowed to go to when she was young. It had never scared her. It was just a part of their life. A part of their beliefs. Now she couldn't imagine giving up that kind of control to anyone.

She leaned against Ben's hard body and studied the Loa in front of them. He was almost too beautiful. Short dark curls framed a sinner's face. His lashes were long, his lips full and pouty, and his eyes were the color of whiskey in the sun. He was lighter than her brother—"high yellow" was the term her grandmother would have used. It made her wonder, not for the first time . . . who was this Loa? Where did he come from? Most of the spirits that watched over and guided the believers and practitioners of voodoo had a story, a beginning. Bone Daddy had appeared out of nowhere.

"*Cher*, I can see the wheels turning in your head. You are a stubborn one. How can you think when you are practically naked, surrounded by men who find you irresistible? Weren't you just caressing your body in the shower, wishing someone would release all that passion inside you? Relieve your need?"

Oh God. Ben's body stilled against hers, his fingers stopping their unconscious caress as he leaned back to meet her gaze. "Mimi, is he right?" He closed his eyes, the feel of him inside her mind more arousing then invasive. "Fuck, he is. I can sense it. I'm right here, Mimi. I can give you everything you need."

It was tempting. Being this close to him, the scent of him, was doing things to her. She looked at the base of his throat, the rapid beat of his pulse. She wanted to place her lips against that spot. Her tongue. She leaned closer.

"Ben? Michelle Francesca Toussaint, you tell your mother that you're okay."

Her forehead fell momentarily on Ben's shoulder, her mother's voice reminding her of where she was, *and* what she shouldn't be doing. "I'm okay, Mama. I slipped in the shower and broke the towel rod."

She stepped back slowly, away from Ben's touch, bending to grab her fresh clothes from the open duffel bag. She ignored the men watching her as she slid on her thong and jiggled into her jeans, using her towel to shield herself from their view. She turned her back on them and dropped her towel, slipping a tank top over her head to the tune of their groans.

"You're an evil temptress, *cher*, to tease him this way when you know how he wants you."

Michelle whirled around to face the Loa. "You—stay away from me. And Ben"—she grabbed her bag and held it protectively against her chest—"thank you for your concern, but I don't need you to help me with anything."

She flew past her mother with an apology and a promise to call tomorrow. She had to get out of there. And she knew exactly where she was going tonight. Somewhere she could forget about spirits. Forget about Ben Adair. Somewhere she could only feel.

Ben knew Bone Daddy was nearby. He hadn't been able to see him since those few shocking moments with Michelle earlier, but he could sense him. And if there was one thing he'd learned to trust over the years, it was his senses.

That's why he was here instead of waiting outside of Michelle's apartment. He'd had her skin beneath his hands long enough to receive some very interesting images. Including her decision to come to this place, a bar he'd been in once before a few years ago, before Michelle had come home.

She wasn't here for the music.

He hesitated outside the nightclub, thinking about the reading Mambo Toussaint had given him before the crash in the bathroom had sent him running to the rescue.

The priestess had pulled out a handful of chicken bones and tossed them on the table while Ben and his mother sat in respectful silence. "You're a watcher. A listener. Gifted in more ways than one man has a right to be, and for sure you know it."

Ben blushed, ducking his head when she looked up at him with one raised brow. She lowered her gaze to the bones once more. "You have to do more than watch this time. You have to act. You have to fight." Her forehead wrinkled with concern, and Ben felt the hairs rise on the back of his neck. "There is an obstacle in front of you and what you want. I see darkness."

She shook her head and stood up, gathering the bones in a patterned pouch and putting them away. "I'm sorry little one, I think I need to consult more than the bones." She took his hand and Ben sensed her worry, worry about Michelle. He also heard a phrase that echoed loudly in his ears.

Bon ange.

In voodoo they believed the soul of a person was split into two parts. The *ti bon ange* and the *gros bon ange*. The little and big guardian angels. His mother had told him that it was the *ti bon ange*, the flyer that left the body in sleep, that also made way when the Loa rode a body during a ritual.

"*Bon ange*? Are you worried for her soul, Mambo?"

Mambo Toussaint sighed. "When twins are born, the Loas known as the Marassa twins watch out for them. Occasionally, the Marassa gift one or both of the newborn twins with special abilities."

Ben nodded, he'd heard all this before. "Like Michelle."

The petite priestess nodded. "Like Michelle. They're called *bon ange* by some. Guardian angels on earth, who use their abilities to help others. But like any gift, if it's used for negative ends, or in my daughter's case, rejected out of hand, the good of it can be twisted, can call the darkness instead of helping to protect the light."

He leaned back in his chair. Michelle had rejected her gifts for most of her life. Running from who and what she was. And he'd always understood why.

"She thinks her father and brother left because of her," he said softly.

His mother glared at him and went to stand beside Annemarie, wrapping her arm around her friend. He stood as well. "I'm sorry, Mambo. I didn't mean to imply—"

"Her father was a decent man. At least, he seemed to be at first. He just had one too many old-fashioned ideas and too closed of a mind. I should have told her long ago, I just didn't want to hurt her anymore."

Elise shushed the priestess, holding the smaller woman protectively close. "He was a jackass, Annie, and that's the God's honest truth." She glanced at Ben. "When she caught him forcing Michelle to stand in a corner while Gabriel played in the same room, she confronted him. He said Michelle had to stay there until she promised to tell her brother that there were no such thing as ghosts. That she was a liar. She'd been there for four hours, not even allowed to have a drink or go to the bathroom. She was brave even then, poor child."

The bastard. Ben's jaw tightened with disbelief and anger at the redheaded man he barely remembered. The man who'd made his own daughter ashamed of her abilities.

The priestess took a shuddering breath, and for the first time Ben thought about how hard it must have been on her, not only finding out she'd cared for a man who disregarded her beliefs, but also losing her son, and watching her daughter grow up believing—no matter how hard she tried to change her mind—that her gift was a curse.

"A Toussaint has lived in New Orleans since the city was built. My ancestor was blessed by Marie Laveau herself." Mambo Toussaint lifted her chin, her stare fixed on Ben. "But not in love. None of the Toussaints have chosen wisely in love. And no man has loved them enough to fight for them."

The Mamas looked at him with a hope in their eyes that was plain to see. Hope that he would be the one to break the family's run of romantic bad luck. But it wasn't his choice that was the problem, he'd made it a long time ago. It was Michelle, as usual, being the stubborn one.

Ben was pushed out of his memories when a drunken straggler bumped into him before rejoining his group on the sidewalk. He shook his head. Luckily most tourists didn't know about this place. From the outside, it looked exactly like what it was, an abandoned building that had seen better days. The owners had kept up the plywood they'd nailed to the windows after the last storm. There wasn't even a sign over the entrance. But then, this wasn't the kind of place that advertised.

He opened the door and was instantly overwhelmed by the sound of hypnotic techno music and the scent of sex. Two large men appeared beside him and looked him over, taking his money before nodding and melting back into the shadows.

He'd known the people who owned this place for years. During the day, they ran a T-shirt shop a few streets down. What had started as a safe haven for their monthly swinger and BDSM education party had turned into this weekly gathering of pleasure seekers. He hadn't been aware that Michelle knew about it.

A raised platform in the middle of the room where an exhibitionist couple was performing was surrounded by several booth-like daybeds where the audience could watch, or participate in their own chosen love play.

Small wicker bowls full of protection and different types of lubrication were placed on every table, and bottled water was stocked in coolers in each corner. No liquor was served here, no food. Just fantasy. Just escape.

Upstairs, he knew, were the rooms for the more intense players. Domination and bondage. It was there he and Bone Daddy, while he'd still been "attached" to Rousseau, had taken a woman with some intriguing fetishes. He got hard just thinking about it, instinctively imagining Michelle in the nameless woman's place.

How many nights had he woken from *that* dream? Michelle bound and open for his pleasure, her ass dark and flushed from the palm of his hand. If anyone needed a good spanking, it was her.

But his Mimi would never go upstairs. At least, not without him. And not without an audience. He knew what she truly craved.

The music changed to a sensual tribal rhythm with an irresistible beat the moment he found her. She was talking absently to a man who had his arm around her, staring at the couple on the stage.

The man gave her a squeeze and a small push, and she was walking up through the groping couples and to the edge of the platform.

The man and woman who had been kissing and caressing each other looked down when she started talking and nodded, smiling as they helped her up onto the makeshift stage to join them.

Ben shoved his fists into the pockets of his jeans and leaned back against the wall, attention riveted to Michelle. She was in a flouncy indigo skirt that fell to her lower thighs, and a snug, golden half-shirt with buttons down the front that showed her tight stomach muscles off to perfection.

The spotlight overhead began to pulse in time to the beat, and he watched as she closed her eyes and started to move.

Her hips flew back and forth too fast for his eyes to follow, her hands gliding up her body like a lover's, touching her breasts, her neck, lifting her shoulder-length curls up over her head.

Ben knew all eyes were on her, how could they not be? She was stunning. When the nearly naked couple beside her came closer, touching her body as she bent back in an arch that made his dick jerk against the confines of his jeans, he had to hold himself back.

The muscular male lifted her skirt slowly, showing the crowd the smooth skin of her thighs, the muscles controlling her flexing movements. Ben wanted to feel those thighs wrapped around his waist, wanted to hold them wide and taste her, finally, on his tongue.

The flat-chested female beside Michelle was fascinated by her large, luscious breasts. She slid open the buttons of her half-shirt, spreading it wide to reveal a bra made of violet lace.

This was how he'd felt all those years ago when he'd dared her to dance with the stripper. He'd wanted her then so much it physically hurt. No woman, no matter how practiced or lovely, had ever been able to bring out this kind of hunger, this level of need in him from that day to this.

Michelle covered the woman's hands with her own and her

eyes opened, gazing in his direction. She saw him. She knew he was here.

She turned toward the woman, leaning back against the man so that she was sandwiched between the two, still gyrating her hips and moving to the quickening rhythm.

Seeing the man's large hands against the skin of her hips, pumping lightly against her through the fabric of her skirt, made him growl. Michelle lifted her chin, and Ben knew the game she was playing.

It was a dare. Neither of them had ever been able to resist a dare.

He caught a flash of movement beneath the dizzying lights, noticed the man who'd sent her toward the stage was walking closer, headed directly for her.

Not fucking likely.

Ben pushed off from his position against the wall, his legs eating up the distance between them, reaching the stage at the same time as the other man, his gaze focused on Michelle.

The music changed, and the lights stopped their rapid pulse. The couple thanked Michelle with a friendly embrace and went back into each other's arms, leaving her standing alone, her body shimmering with unsatisfied desire.

Ben didn't blink, refused to look away. He held out his hand to her, his heart thumping hard against his chest. He knew the other man was looking at him in confusion, but he didn't care. He could only hope a bit of Bone Daddy's mojo had rubbed off on him, that she would, just this once, find him as irresistible as he found her.

She hesitated for a painful moment, glancing toward her intended partner and biting her lip. Ben almost hollered in relief when she shook her head, slipping her hand into his.

He'd never let her go again.

CHAPTER 4

MICHELLE HAD LOST HER MIND. THAT WAS THE ONLY EX-plantion she could come up with. Mindless, faceless sex. That was all she'd wanted.

Hadn't she just renewed her promise to herself to stay away from Ben Adair? And yet, a part of her had known he would find her tonight. Had known when she got up on that small stage that she was performing for him. Again.

Her body was on fire, her mind hazy as he dragged her through the crowd and through the old kitchen. He seemed to know exactly where he was going.

He opened the back door and stepped outside, reaching behind her to close it before pushing her against the outside wall.

The alley was dark and narrow, the building across from them full of light and life. Anyone could walk out onto the balconies and see them. Or pass by on the street and see the man with his hips pressed between her thighs, his hands holding her wrists above her head.

God he was sexy. Especially now. The easy smile that always drove her mad was gone, replaced with an intensity that took her breath away. Desire. For her.

But she wasn't going to give in easily. "Slumming, Ben? I was sure you'd be back at Rousseau's place for another threesome. Or is it not as fun without Bone Daddy around?"

His brown eyes narrowed. "We're even now. You've watched me, and I've watched you. It ends tonight, Mimi. Let other people watch as I fuck you, as I make you come. From this moment on, if anyone's going to touch you, it will be me. Meet your new distraction."

The last time he'd kissed her, she'd been eighteen and overwhelmed by the power of it. After all these years, the touch of his lips against hers still hit her like a punch in the stomach. He opened her mouth with his own, his tongue tangling with hers as though he couldn't get close enough, couldn't taste her enough, kiss her enough.

Her distraction? He could never be that. She'd always known it. She was too drawn to him, too affected by his touch. The touch that could read her so well.

She struggled against his hold, wanting to wrap her arms around him, run her fingers through his hair, but he wouldn't let her go.

One leg came up to wrap around his waist, pulling him closer as she arched her hips against his denim-clad erection. So good. He felt so good.

He gathered her wrists in one hand and pulled his mouth away from hers. "I'll buy you a new one." The words came out rough and garbled. He curled his fingers around the small bow design

that held her bra together and yanked, ripping it open and expos-
ing her breasts to the night air.

She'd forgotten her shirt was open. She was completely bared
to his burning gaze and his words suddenly made sense. Her thighs
clenched, and she arched her back as he stared at the hard peaks
of her nipples. Did he like them? She'd only seen him with smaller
women. Maybe he thought they were too big.

He groaned. "Fuck, Mimi. Don't you know how perfect your
breasts are? How much I want to suck them, slide my cock through
them, squeeze them as I make you scream my name?" His hips
jerked against hers, and he shuddered. "You never need to doubt
it, babe."

"You talk an awful lot for a distraction. I think I'd rather you
show me."

She slapped down the part of her mind that was shocked at
what she said, at the fact that she wasn't turning tail to run as fast
as her heels would take her. But she was tired of fighting it. For
tonight, anyway, she desperately wanted to give in.

He lifted one full breast, his exhalation rough against her skin.
"Anything you say, Mimi."

She watched his head lower, felt him press an open-mouthed
kiss against her neck. She shivered, surprised at the flood of desire
that simple touch evoked.

When his tongue traced a path from her collarbone to her
nipple, she couldn't stop the moan that escaped her. His grip
on her wrists loosened, and she pulled out of his grasp to clench
his head in her hands.

"Come on, Ben. Don't be a tease."

She pulled him closer, and her eyes nearly rolled in the back of
her head when he sucked her nipple hard against the roof of his
mouth. The scrape of his teeth against her skin heated her blood,

her sex. He knew just how to touch her, to bite her, to drive her crazy. God, his mouth was dangerous, but she wanted more. She wanted to taste him, too.

"You're the dangerous one." He lifted his head to whisper against her nipple. "All those wicked thoughts. You're tempting me to take you right here. Just bend you over and make you mine." He pressed her breasts together, taking turns licking and sucking each nipple in turn.

Michelle let her hands glide down his broad shoulders, over the cloth heated by his skin until she reached his ass. She squeezed. "Tempting you to take me? No. I'm not tempting you, Benjamin . . . I'm *daring* you."

He raised his head to look at her. His cheeks were flushed, and a hank of his sandy blond hair had fallen over one eye.

She couldn't resist. "Double-dog dare ya."

He closed his eyes for a moment, taking a deep breath. "Oh, Mimi." His lashes lifted, pinning her with a gaze that sent a jolt of excitement, and a purely feminine thrill through her body. And then he grinned. "You are in so much trouble."

She cried out in surprise when he spun her around to face the wall. She could have sworn she saw . . . But Ben wasn't giving her time to look around or get her bearings.

He threw up her skirt, growling at the sight that awaited him. "I can see I'll be spending a lot of money at the lingerie shop." Her underwear fell apart like cobwebs in his hands and her knees wobbled at the wildness, the passion in him.

Ben cupped the curves of her ass with his palms and he groaned. "Just as lush as I remembered. I've been dreaming of this ass, Mimi."

Her fingers curled into the stucco wall and she arched her back, spreading her legs, knowing he could see everything. Wanting him to. He lifted his hands and she heard the click of his buttons as he ripped open his jeans.

"I hope to hell you brought a party favor."

Ben froze and swore beneath his breath. When she heard the sound of foil tearing, Michelle lowered her head in relief.

He pressed his lips against her shoulder. "I can't believe I almost forgot. You drive me crazy, woman."

She felt his erection slide between her legs, his hand glide across her belly and down to touch her heated sex. She held her breath when he found it—the small bar that pierced her clitoris. He fingered it curiously, twirling the tiny ball already soaked with her arousal until she cried out in pleasure. "You're full of surprises. Did you get this on another dare, Mimi? How does it feel?"

She couldn't concentrate. "*Please.*"

"I love the sound of that. I wanted to explore every inch of your body. Wanted to make sure you were so *distracted* you couldn't think of anything but me." He scraped his teeth lightly over her chin. "But I can't wait, Mimi. After all these years, I can't wait one more second."

He gripped her hips, and she felt the head of his cock push inside her. She was so wet, desperate for him, but the fit was still snug. "Ben."

"*Yes.*" His knees bent and he slung his hips forward, filling her with a powerful thrust that made them both shout out loud, uncaring who heard. "Yes, Mimi. So tight, Michelle. So ready for me."

He was in her. Deep. In her body. And her mind. She pushed her hips back, demanding more, taking him even as he took her. He growled, and she heard him clearly in her head.

"I don't need a spanking," she panted, her nails struggling for purchase on the wall. "You do."

I didn't say that out loud, Mimi.

She could sense his hesitation. His disbelief that she'd heard him. She couldn't think about why that was important. All she knew was she was too close to something amazing, too close to the strongest climax of her life to let him hesitate now.

"I know. Oh, God. Ben, don't stop."

One hand left the wall and she reached down, her fingers circling his shaft as it slid out of her, her thumb pressing against her piercing with every thrust.

"*Fuck*, Mimi."

There was no more thinking, no more talking, just two bodies clinging to each other, racing for the end they both could feel waiting just out of reach.

His hand covered hers between her thighs, increasing the pressure of her grip. "Come, Mimi. I want to hear you. Feel you fall apart around me."

Michelle couldn't hold back. A wave of pleasure so intense it was blinding crashed over her body. Her pleasure. And his. She could feel him, feel the lightning lash his spine, the blood pound in his cock as he came hard against her.

It's never been like this. Never.

Was that his thought or hers? She couldn't tell. She leaned her forehead on the rough wall and tried to catch her breath as ripples of her orgasm made her legs quiver.

He caressed her hips, still inside her, still in her mind. It was overwhelming. She'd never felt so vulnerable. So exposed.

"I don't mean to interrupt. But that was beautiful." The soft, female voice coming from the doorway of the club took them both by surprise.

Ben pulled out of Michelle and turned, his body protecting her, a little too late, from the watchful eyes of the younger female.

Michelle looked over his shoulder. She'd thought she'd seen a flash of someone before Ben distracted her. The woman was all in black with black hair. She even had black lipstick. But underneath the makeup Michelle knew she had to be in her early twenties. "Um, thank you?"

Ben huffed out a laugh, his breath ruffling the curls on her temple. He tucked himself back in, and then buttoned her shirt over her broken bra, his gaze tender.

She had to get out of here. Michelle turned and started to walk down the alley toward the street without a word.

"What the hell?"

Michelle heard Ben's rapid footsteps behind her, and walked faster, ignoring him as he matched his stride to hers.

"So that's what a distraction gets? A quick fuck against the wall, forget the pillow talk, and you're gone?"

"There are no pillows in seedy alleys, Adair." She crossed the street, tugging on her skirt, uncomfortably aware of her lack of underwear as a breeze picked up around her. She muttered under her breath. "That Goth girl probably kept them as a keepsake."

"You mean these?"

Michelle saw the shredded thong dangling from his finger and rolled her eyes. "Don't suppose you're going to give those back."

"Don't suppose so." But Ben wasn't laughing. He looked . . . mad. Michelle felt her stomach knot at the grim look on his face and turned away, picking up her pace.

He followed her home in silence. She unzipped the hidden pocket in her skirt, pulling out her keys, and he jerked them out of her hand. He opened her door and followed her up the stairs.

"Ben, I—"

"Don't worry, Mimi. I know you're not inviting me in." He reached around her and opened her door, his lips a breath away from hers. "But you and I both know what happened between us, and what it means." He stepped back and let her see his determined expression. "This is the last time I let you run away."

She watched him jog down the stairs and when the door closed behind him she leaned against the doorframe, closing her eyes. This wasn't good. What had she been thinking? She'd stayed away from him all these years for a reason. She knew this would happen. Knew her feelings for him would be too strong to shrug off.

"What are you so afraid of, *cher*?"

She walked inside her apartment and slammed the door. "I refuse to talk about my love life with you."

Bone Daddy walked through her door, following her as she stepped out of her heels and headed to the bedroom. "So you love him."

"Not listening." She turned off the light, falling on her bed and pulling her pillow over her head. She just needed to sleep. Maybe in the morning she'd find out she hadn't just let her hormones make the biggest mistake of her life.

"Well, you may not want to listen, *cher*. But I'm not going anywhere until you do."

She squealed into the pillow in frustration. "Why? Why do you care?"

He paused for so long she thought he'd gone. She was just starting to relax when he spoke into the darkness. "Damned if I know."

CHAPTER 5

"I CAN'T BELIEVE YOU NEVER TOLD ME YOU HAD THIS ABILITY. I tell you everything. Is he here right now?"

Michelle handed one of her student's change from the money box and nodded at Allegra. "Yep."

She and the other teachers in the art department had decided to raise money for New Schools for New Orleans by having the kids sell their artwork in Jackson Square. It was a chance for them to learn responsibility and show off their talents, as well as give back to the foundation that was trying to improve the districts.

She'd invited Allegra a few weeks ago, but she'd been surprised to see her this morning. Even more surprised that she'd found herself admitting that she could see Bone Daddy. But after what Allegra had gone through with Rousseau, she'd already known things like Loa existed. And it was nice to have a girlfriend to talk to. "Did you finally tire Rousseau out? Or did he realize the café had to be open in order for him to make money?"

Allegra blushed, her pale, freckled skin flushing at the question. She lowered her voice. "You know I've been looking forward to spending some time with you. Besides, I'm the one tired out. That man is a *machine*."

Michelle choked on her raspberry ice, laughing as her friend turned the same shade of crimson. "Oh, poor Allegra. But what a way to go."

"That's what I always say." Bone Daddy sat beside one of the teenager's canvases, studying the subject. "Michelle, I do believe this child is a prodigy. He's perfectly captured the pain-filled plight of the adolescent male. The bikini-clad woman on the hood of that sports car just screams, 'No one understands me.'"

She sighed, closing her eyes. "Do you remember if that book I loaned you mentioned how to shut him up?"

Allegra's blue eyes widened. "No. What's he saying?"

Bone Daddy crawled closer to Allegra, through the bodies of the people walking around the teenagers' art show. "Tell her I'm saying how much I wish I'd had another taste of her sweet honey. That I almost regret the climax that took me from her, because I didn't have the chance to lick every delicious freckle on her body."

"He says hi."

Allegra snorted. "I bet." Her expression turned serious. "I wanted to ask you . . . about Ben."

Michelle's jaw tightened. She'd been doing her damnedest not to think about him all day. But between Bone Daddy's continuous lectures and her own body's traitorous desires, it wasn't working. "What about him?"

"It's just that we—that I—the other night—"

"I know, Allegra. And for the single ladies everywhere, I salute you." Michelle clapped her hands with a humorous smirk.

"You aren't upset?"

Allegra really looked worried. Why? As far as she knew, Michelle hated Ben. She couldn't know what they'd done last night, what she wanted to do again. Could she?

"I showed her your fantasy that night at the club, my beauty. Don't be upset with me. She knows you wanted him."

"Great."

"What? Is he talking again?"

Michelle leaned forward in her chair and grabbed Allegra's hand. "Hon, I love you. I'm so relieved that you're happy. You followed your heart and it worked out. Rousseau is a lucky man. As for Ben"—she shrugged and tried to smile—"it's complicated. But not because of you."

Allegra's shoulders slumped in relief. "Thank God. Because I desperately need you to come to dinner with us tonight."

"You desperately need me to go out to dinner with you?"

"Yes. And Rousseau's family. And mine. And Ben."

Michelle was glad she was sitting down. "Your family is in town? What aren't you telling me?"

Allegra pushed her strawberry locks behind her ears and bit her lip. She was practically beaming, and Michelle had a sneaking suspicion as to why.

"True love, *cher*. This is what happens when a boy meets a girl, and the boy's Loa tempts her into his bed. A fairy tale. It's what could happen for you if you stopped avoiding poor Adair like the plague."

Bone Daddy was getting on her last nerve. She focused on Allegra. "Did he ask you to marry him?"

"You know, I think he did." Allegra was nearly jumping out of her seat. "I told him we had all the time in the world. That his life had been stolen for seven years." She paused and looked into the space between their chairs. "No offense, Bone Daddy. I said I wasn't going anywhere. But he wouldn't . . . Well, let's just say he convinced me he wouldn't take no for an answer."

Michelle was surprised when she glanced toward the Loa and saw him flinch. Had he never thought about what it might have been like for Rousseau? He wasn't a devil, but every human deserved to control his own fate. His own body.

Why was she feeling sorry for him? He was a Loa. Immortal, powerful. Though outside of a body he seemed lost and kind of sad. Did he miss Rousseau? Miss being a part of his life and circle of friends?

Allegra squeezed her hand. "Please say you'll come. You know how my parents are. So . . . so . . ."

"White-bread and stuffy?" Michelle broke in, making Allegra laugh.

She nodded, still giggling. "Exactly. I need you."

Michelle noticed Bone Daddy pretending he wasn't listening. He wasn't very subtle. Beautiful, yes. Subtle? No. Damn. She hadn't wanted to run into Ben again so soon. "For you? Anything." She sighed. "And tell Adair he should invite his mother along. She's really good at smoothing rough edges."

Allegra got out of her chair and knelt at Michelle's feet, giving her a grateful hug. "You're a genius, Chelle."

Bone Daddy leaned back on the ground, heedless of the people walking through him and watched the two of them embrace. "Am I the only one turned on right now?"

"NOT THAT I DON'T LOVE TO BE MY SON'S ARM CANDY, BUT why am I here again?"

Ben smiled down at his mother, watching her nod and wave regally at some of the familiar faces in the restaurant. He was thankful she'd been available to come to Allegra and Rousseau's engagement dinner on such short notice.

"You're here as a buffer. You already know Rousseau's mom and sisters, and apparently Allegra's parents are easily intimidated."

"Oh, lovely. I'm glad I wore your grandmother's pearls. They always remind me to be on my best behavior." She patted his arm affectionately. "I'm just grateful you aren't here to rub my nose in the happiness of other people's parents. At the rate Celestin is going, Theresa should have grandchildren by next spring."

"Rousseau thinks he's wasted enough time. He loves Allegra, and she's proven she loves him. He deserves some happiness." And so did he. Ben wouldn't have missed this celebration for the world, but he had another reason for coming.

Michelle.

Twenty-four hours had never gone by so slowly. After he'd left her last night he'd gone for a ride on his bike around the ports, to clear his head.

Should he have stayed, made her admit her feelings for him? Maybe he was too afraid to find out what those feelings were. He'd wanted her for so long. Loved her. If she couldn't, or wouldn't return his feelings, what would he do then?

"Benjamin, I don't mean to pry, I truly don't. But the feelings you're giving off are so strong." The always cool Elise Adair stopped in the middle of the elegant dining room and looked up at him worriedly. "Annemarie and I have known you and Michelle were soul mates from the moment you met. But I never meant to push you. I love Michelle as if she were my own, and after all she's gone through, she deserves some happiness. But if she can't appreciate what an amazing man you are . . ."

He'd never seen his mother flustered. He knew she was worried about him, so worried that her maternal instinct to matchmake was overridden by her need to protect him. He sent her a wave of love. "Sheathe those claws, Mama Adair. She knows. Now let's go. You need to wow the Jarrods. And I need to woo Michelle."

The hostess led them to the private room reserved for celebrations, and he saw her. His mother went immediately to work, hugging Theresa Rousseau and the girls, dazzling Mr. and Mrs. Jarrod, who seemed to be in a perpetual state of shock.

Ben walked down toward the end of the table where Rousseau, Allegra, and Michelle were laughing. "Legs, are you sure you aren't a changeling? You don't look a thing like your parents."

And she didn't. The Jarrods were both brown-haired, brown-eyed wrens to her flaming phoenix. Even their clothes were varying shades of beige.

Allegra stood up to embrace him, smiling. "I'm so glad you're here, Ben. No, they're mine all right. Luckily, Michelle was right. Bringing your mother was the right idea. I think I actually just saw one of them smile."

"Your parents are lovely, *bebe*. Although I think your mother nearly fainted when you introduced me as your fiancé. Hey, Ben." Rousseau stood to shake Ben's hand with a carefree grin.

"Congratulations, you lucky bastard."

Rousseau looked happier, more relaxed, than Ben had ever seen him, even when they were in high school. His long hair was severely constrained in thick braids, and he was dressed in a colorful linen shirt and black pants, tantamount to a tuxedo for Rousseau. Yep. He was definitely in love.

Ben glanced down at Michelle. "My mother was your idea, then?"

She shifted in her chair, refusing to look him in the eye. "I'm a good bridesmaid."

"And I'm a lucky best man." He sat down in the empty chair beside her, silently thanking Allegra for the seating arrangement, and gave his order to the hovering waiter before turning his attention back to Michelle. "You look beautiful tonight, Mimi."

And she did. She wore a knee-length dress that looked like a long white poet shirt. It fell off her shoulders, leaving them beautifully bare, with flared sleeves and crisscrossing ties up the front that Ben wanted to undo with his teeth.

His gaze dropped to her breasts, and he imagined he could see her dark nipples through the fabric. Unfortunately the fabric wasn't sheer enough.

He slid his hand beneath the table and cupped her knee, needing to touch her, and knowing she wouldn't make a scene in public. At least, not in front of his mother.

"Copping a feel under the table, are we, Benjamin?" Bone Daddy's voice was smug. "A man after my own heart. I remember a few years ago, a charming young culinary student who had a food fetish and a magnificent streak of exhibitionism—"

Michelle went into a fake coughing fit, glaring at the wall to her right where Ben could see Bone Daddy leaning against the decorative wine rack. Ben leaned close to whisper in her ear. "How long has he been here, Mimi?"

"He hasn't left my side since I got home the other night."

Rousseau wrapped his arm around Allegra, glancing down the table to make sure the others were occupied, before turning back to Ben and Michelle. "Allegra told me about that. He hasn't tried to take you over, has he?"

"I resent that, boy. I really do. I don't invite myself to places

I'm not wanted." Bone Daddy crossed his arms over his chest, obviously annoyed.

"I think it's nice that he's here. He did help me discover the way to set you free from your father's debt. He wanted us to be together." Allegra leaned her head on Rousseau's shoulder, and Ben watched his friend relax.

"She's such a clever girl. She's writing a book about me, you know. Said I inspired her."

Ben continued caressing Michelle's knee, shaking his head at the Loa's words. "I can't believe you're still hanging around, BD."

Michelle's eyes dilated a little at his touch. He loved how she reacted to him; it gave him hope. She quirked her lips. "I think he likes us."

"*I* think it's so amazing that you can see him. Talk to him. Both of you. I had no idea when I decided to move to New Orleans I'd be surrounded by people with such amazing gifts." Allegra chuckled. "I feel pretty average by comparison."

Rousseau cupped her cheek in his hand, lifting her chin to catch her gaze. "There is nothing average about you, *bebe*. You have a magic no being, Loa or other, can resist."

Ben heard Michelle sigh as the couple kissed and slid his hand higher up her leg, to her thigh. Her expression had softened, lips parting, and all he could think about was kissing her, taking her.

"To the happy couple." Rousseau's sister, Angelique, home from college for the occasion, raised her glass in a toast, bringing their attention back to their families. "My brother is the best man I've ever known. And I know he'll love Allegra, be true to her, and never leave her side. Love is a gift, precious and rare. May you trust in it, and each other, and may you give my mother plenty of grandchildren so she doesn't have time to harass me about my love life."

The full table lifted their glasses, laughing, but as soon as he set his glass down, Ben felt Michelle pull away from him, mentally and physically. She scooted back her chair and excused herself to visit the ladies' room.

Allegra bit her lip, following her friend with her gaze, obviously worried.

Ben rose. "Stay here, bride-to-be. I'll take care of Mimi."

"Will you?" Her blue eyes were solemn.

He reached out to touch her hand, allowing the knowledge of her concern, her hope for Michelle to find happiness, to soak into his senses.

"You're a true friend, Legs. And yes, I will. I promise."

As soon as he could convince Michelle Toussaint to let him.

CHAPTER 6

"WHAT IF I HAD TO PEE?" MICHELLE GLARED AT BONE Daddy in the mirror "Do you have some perverted story about another woman to fit that occasion as well?"

"Actually I—"

"Don't even think it." She held up her hand to shut the Loa up. "Why me? Seriously, I know I can see you, but surely someone is performing a ritual requesting help for their less-than-stellar love life. Why not go to them?"

Bone Daddy stepped up to stand beside her at the sink, watching her try to get herself together. "You need me more, *cher*. And I find I've grown rather fond of you and the others. I . . . care about you." He shifted his feet, seemingly uncomfortable with the emotion. "About your pleasure, of course. The kind of pleasure you've only found with Benjamin."

She sighed. "You're not as bad as I thought you were. You have a one-track mind, but you're sweet to worry about my sexual happiness. I'm sorry you're between jobs right now, but I'm not interested. In spirits or in Ben."

"You're a bad liar, *cher*. You care about Benjamin, more than you want to admit. And the things you see as well. The first time I noticed you could see me, you were scared. Not surprised. Scared. That always puzzled me. You know enough about your family's religion to know I would never hurt you."

"Not you, no. But it's not like it's never happened. The priests who work with both hands, the dark sorcerers—*bokors*, right? They call spirits to possess people in order to accomplish horrible acts."

Bone Daddy's gaze narrowed, and he seemed to tower over her. "What do you know of dark magic? Of the *bokor*? Remember I've seen your paintings now. Have you seen things like this? You are *bon ange*, a shining light to lost spirits. Has someone hurt you?"

She looked down. "I was just using an example. No need to get all macho."

"You need looking after, my beauty. Whether you know it or not."

A jiggle of the knob and a firm knock at the door had her rolling her eyes. "Occupied."

"I know, Mimi. But if you don't let me in right now, I'm going to make a scene and embarrass my poor, fragile mother. And Allegra's parents. Do *you* want to be the reason her mother passes out in shock?"

"Son of a bitch." She unlocked the door and pulled him inside before anyone could see him. "They have a little boys' room, too, you know."

Ben looked around the elegant washroom and whistled. "No

wonder you women love to come here. This place is nicer than your apartment."

"Ha ha." She'd never admit he was right. Even though the red velvet chaise and marble floors were lovely. Not to mention all the plumbing worked. "You're going to get us thrown out of the restaurant. What was so important that it couldn't wait until I got back to the table?"

"This."

At the first touch of his lips, Michelle moaned, her body instantly melting into his. She'd had no idea how much she'd craved this, craved Ben, until this moment.

"Beautiful."

She pulled back to catch her breath. "Go away, Bone Daddy. We're busy."

"Not this time, *cher*. No. This time I want to see your beautiful face at your climax. To hear your sounds of passion. Surely my good friend Benjamin will not begrudge me that."

Heat pooled low in her belly when Ben just smiled, lifting her with arms around her waist until the backs of her knees hit the velvet chaise. "Of course not, BD. She likes it when people watch, don't you, Mimi? Loves knowing people are right on the other side of that wall, that they could find us at any moment."

He was touching her so it was pointless to pretend. There *was* something exciting about the potential of being caught. Something forbidden about being here with Ben. And yes, with Bone Daddy.

Michelle was on the chaise, Ben caressing her bare shoulders. Her eyes were level with the unmistakable bulge behind his expensive gray pants, and she couldn't resist.

She reached up and undid his belt, feeling his grip tighten on her shoulders as he realized what she was doing. "Mimi, baby, what are you up to?"

The sound of the zipper lowering echoed off the marble, and she looked up at Ben through her lashes. "Fulfilling a fantasy." She spread the fabric, and her mouth opened on a gasp. He had nothing on beneath his pants. She gripped his hot, silken shaft in her hands and licked her lips. "Or trying to."

Her mouth closed over the flushed head of his cock, tongue exploring, savoring his taste. Salty, delicious. She'd been craving it for so long. Ever since that day she'd caught him with one of his many high school girlfriends at the isolated spot he and Michelle used to play in as children.

The girl had been taking off her shirt, her cheeks red as she watched Ben lying on the blanket at her feet, stroking his erection.

Michelle hadn't been able to look away. Everything about his bare body had been fascinating, but the sight of his hand stroking his cock, the perfect pearl of pre-come that had appeared right at the tip, had sent her running back home cursing him. She'd touched herself for the first time in her bed that night.

"Oh, Mimi. I never knew you were there. That feels so good, babe. I can't tell you how many times I woke up coming, dreaming of your mouth on my cock. Only you. Always. Yes. *Merde*. Shit, yes."

He filled her mouth and her lips stretched to take more, to take everything. She relaxed her throat, inhaling the clean, male scent of him while her nails traced the muscles of his thighs.

"*Mimi*." Ben's hands slid into her curls, clenching in her hair, and she hummed in pleasure, causing his hips to jerk.

"There's enough room on the chaise for two, Benjamin. Lift

her dress and show her how good she makes you feel. Drench your mouth with her taste."

Michelle heard Bone Daddy's rough growl, and then Ben was pulling back, lifting her up and taking her place on the red, backless sofa.

He caught her hips and dragged her down, until her thighs were straddling his face, her dress around her waist and her mouth once more a breath away from his erection.

She released a shuddering breath when he pulled her panties to the side, revealing her to his gaze. And the Loa's. Michelle turned her head to see Bone Daddy, now naked, stroking his less-than-solid shaft as he studied her soaking sex.

"I may have to change my mind, Michelle. Your smooth pussy is so pretty. And pierced? Mmmm. I bet Benjamin's tongue pressed against that lovely silver ball would make you want to scream. But you can't scream. If you do, someone will come to the door. You have to be quiet, Michelle. So very quiet as he fucks your pretty pussy with his tongue."

Michelle bit her lip until she tasted blood, pressing her forehead against Ben's hip. He growled against her thigh, just as aroused by the sight of her, by the Loa's words, as she was.

He pressed the flat of his tongue against her sex, the tip curling over her clit before flicking out again to taste her arousal. His grip tightened and he moaned, pulling her closer. As though he were starving for more of her, demanding to be fed.

Michelle lifted her head and saw that white pearl forming on his cock. Her tongue lapped out to taste it, and her eyes closed. So good. Pure Ben.

Her mouth opened over him once more, and she became lost in sensations. Hers and his. His tongue stiffened to thrust inside her and she muffled her shout around his flesh, sucking him deep until her cheeks hollowed and his hips lifted off the chaise.

"That's right, sweet. You should see his face. He is so hungry for you. Take him to heaven, *cher*. Give him what he needs."

Michelle felt a warm breeze wrap around them, and knew it was Bone Daddy, knew he was touching them the only way he could. It whipped around the base of Ben's shaft, slid between the cheeks of her ass, increasing their pleasure.

The wind whipped over the ties of her dress, unlacing the top and sliding beneath her heavy breasts suggestively.

Michelle took the Loa's cue, lifting her breasts out and rounding her back to press Ben's shaft between them while she sucked hard on the head of his cock.

Fuck. Fuck. Fuck.

He was there. In her mind. And she knew she'd thrown him over the edge. His thumb rubbed her clit as his tongue thrust deep inside her once more, and Michelle joined him in his climax. Her body shuddered against him, throat working as she swallowed him down. He was moaning, caressing her with his tongue, drinking her in until her heart rate returned to normal.

God, she loved him.

Both of them froze at her thought. Shit. She needed to get out of there. She looked up at Bone Daddy in panic. He was smiling in satisfaction, like he was solely responsible for their orgasms. He was dressed once more in that same white linen outfit. When he saw her expression his brow furrowed.

Michelle almost sobbed in relief when someone knocked on the door.

"Be out in a minute!"

She scrambled off Ben's body, grateful for the spotless condition of the bathroom as she practically fell on the floor beside the chaise. She jumped up and adjusted her dress, looking in the mirror and retying her laces. "Hurry up, Ben. I don't know how we're going to sneak you out of here without causing a scene."

He stood behind her, buttoning his pants and tucking his shirt in as he watched her. The knock was more forceful, and Ben smiled. "We better let that poor woman in. Come on, Mimi. We've had our appetizer. I think I can keep my hands off you long enough to eat dinner."

She tilted her head, suspicious. "You being agreeable makes me nervous."

Ben chuckled. "What? I just fulfilled several fantasies in one go. I'm always agreeable when I'm satisfied." He put his hands on her shoulders and nuzzled her wild curls with his chin. "Are you always so paranoid? I should know now since I plan on having dessert as soon as possible."

He winked at her and she made a face, heading toward the door and almost guaranteed embarrassment.

She turned the lock, pulling open the door to come face-to-face with . . . "Mama Elise."

The older blonde lifted her gaze to the ceiling, avoiding Michelle's deep blush. "I see nothing. I know nothing."

Ben smiled as he pushed Michelle out the door. "I love you, Mama."

"Well, of course you do. I didn't raise a fool."

CHAPTER 7

"Spend the next twenty minutes working on your individual projects."

"Yes, Ms. Toussaint."

Michelle smiled at the obedient-sounding chorus. She loved her students. They drove her crazy, but she remembered what it was like to be a teenager in New Orleans. Most of them started out in the class, thinking art would be an easy grade. But, if she did her job right, they'd all leave with a better understanding of the historical, social, and personal importance of art in their lives.

At the very least they'd have a safe outlet to express themselves.

What had started out as an easy degree in education had become a godsend. Who would have thought that she'd ever be happy out of the whirl of the New York art scene, teaching students with minimal supplies and constantly fighting for the art department's right to exist?

Yet here she was, in jeans and a paint-spattered T-shirt instead of stiletto heels and the latest runway fashion, and she didn't miss a thing.

The greatest perk was that she was painting again. She looked down at her half-finished canvas and wrinkled her nose. Sort of.

When had her artwork gotten so dark? For the last year everything she'd started painting turned into demonic spirits and dark figures attacking helpless victims. Sometimes those victims looked a bit too familiar for comfort.

In quiet moments she admitted to herself that she was still afraid. Still afraid of the darkness she'd seen, and that the fact that she could see it at all meant there was something wrong with her.

She stepped back and studied her current work in progress. She was using lighter colors again, and the scene, while still violent, held signs of passion as well.

Two lovers embraced. The woman had two faces, and one of them was being attacked by a ghostly entity. And there, watching from a nearby building, was another familiar form.

All in white, tall and almost angelically beautiful, was Bone Daddy. She looked around, making sure he wasn't hovering over her shoulder. He'd gotten bored with her class schedule and slipped away a few hours before. She hated to admit it, but she was starting to get used to his presence.

The bell rang, and her students made a mad, loud dash to the door. She waved at them as they called out to her, then picked up a wet sponge, pressing it against the top of her canvas and watching as the water made the color run together—rivers of red, yellow, and gray. Maybe next time she would try a landscape.

"Why ruin a work of art?"

Michelle attempted to tear her attention away from the hypnotic patterns to answer the female voice. "One man's art . . ." She glanced up and froze. "You."

"Me?" A pale girl with black hair, black clothes, even black lipstick stepped into her classroom, and shut the door. "Me, the girl who watched that handsome blond have his wicked way with you the other night? *That* me?"

"No." Michelle swallowed past the dryness in her mouth, her hands slowly sliding across her supply table, searching for one of the palette knives she used for texture. "Not that you."

The girl tilted her head curiously, a thoroughly creepy smile curling her caked lips. But it wasn't really her Michelle was looking at. It was him. It. No matter how many years had gone by, she'd never forget it. The entity from the mugging. The one who'd wanted her dead.

Damn. She couldn't find the knife. It didn't matter. She couldn't hurt this girl. She mumbled a phrase her mother had taught her, a demand for the spirit to depart from her sight.

The girl laughed. It was a grating, high-pitched sound. "Nice try. But you are no houngan or mambo, no voodoo shaman to send me packing so easily. I've been watching you for a long time now, Michelle Toussaint. I know all about you. All about your mother. Your friends. Ben." She walked by one of the student's stations and gagged. "That is *not* art. You've gone down in the world since we last met. A simple teacher in a poor neighborhood. That crook wouldn't want to rob you now."

Michelle's body was vibrating with fear. And that fear made her angry. "So, you've just been stalking me for four years? That sounds pathetic. Don't you have anything better to do?"

"I wouldn't say stalking as much as admiring from afar. Not all the time, mind you. I do have a life of my own. Such as it is. I just like to check in on you from time to time. It soothes me, knowing that if I wanted to be seen, I could be." The petite, possessed twenty-something skipped closer to Michelle's desk, her eyes bloodshot, her face slightly bruised beneath the pancake makeup.

"I appreciate the attention." She had to get out of here. Michelle could feel the walls closing in on her, snapshots of that evil face leering over her body as the thug attacked flashing in her mind.

The Goth shrugged. "Just protecting my property. He doesn't want you, you know. Doesn't know you the way I do. I think you'd be wise to break it off. For his own good, you understand."

Ben? It was threatening Ben? "Leave him alone."

"I will if you will." She came closer to Michelle, circling the desk so she could see the ruined painting. "You really shouldn't do that. You have talent. More than you know. I've waited a long time for someone like you, Michelle. And I realize I was wrong to have lashed out at you that last time. You need to be cherished. Kept safe. Touched."

The black nails on the small white hand held her riveted for a moment, and then instinct took over. Michelle ducked beneath the outstretched arm, sweeping the girl's legs with one of her own, sending the entity and the body it held tumbling to the floor.

She reached the door, her hand just closing over the doorknob when she was stopped by hands clawing at her hair, flinging her against a nearby easel.

"I'm not. Done. Talking." The girl reached back and touched her head, drawing back fingertips covered in blood. "Look what you did. You don't know what a rough night I've already put this body through."

The being brought the girl's fingers to her mouth, tasting the blood. "She was the one who wondered what was going on upstairs. How far she could take her interest in pain. But she's weak. Much weaker than I originally thought. I'll have to find a new one now. Just another disappointment."

Michelle rolled to a standing position, fighter's stance, knowing she didn't have the strength to fight this kind of entity. "How inconvenient for you. You obviously don't enjoy being disappointed. Why do you bother?"

"To feel, of course. I could feel your hair in her hands. I can feel her terror right now. Her pain. And yours. And it makes me want to feel more."

"*Cher*, I've been waiting for hours. Aren't you done yet?" Bone Daddy walked through the door, and the irritation on his face quickly turned to rage as he noticed the carnage, and the spirit holding fast to the girl's body.

Michelle felt cold shock weigh down her limbs as the Goth girl fell backward onto her hands and feet, crossing the floor like a monstrous, deformed spider at rapid speed until she reached the window. How had she done that?

"I hadn't expected company. I would have worn a better outfit." With that the girl threw herself out of the open first-floor window, losing herself in the crowd of children ambling toward the parking lot.

Michelle collapsed to the floor. It was him. He knew her, where she lived. About her mother. A sob of panic choked her throat.

"Oh, *cher*. Don't cry. I wish I could hold you. I can't do a damn thing like this. Outside of a body, I don't have the same power."

She shook her head, not really hearing him. "It didn't work. I tried to cast him out, but it didn't work. I couldn't save her." She grabbed a handful of paintbrushes and bits of easel and tossed them across the room. "Why the hell do I have the ability to see something I can't fight?"

"Michelle, you shouldn't stay here. You need to go to your mother's house. The priestess will know what to do."

She looked up at the worried Loa, tears blurring her vision. "I haven't told her about that." She pointed toward the window. "I haven't told her anything."

"I have never understood it. This belief you humans have that standing alone makes you brave. You have family and friends who love you. It's love that makes you strong, *cher*. That takes the power out of the darkness."

"Who do you have?" Michelle wasn't sure what possessed her to ask him, and she immediately regretted it when she saw the yearning that rolled in like rain clouds over his beautiful face.

"No one, *cher*. I have no one."

THE DOOR TO HER MOTHER'S COTTAGE WAS OPEN, PUTTING Michelle's already frayed nerves into overdrive. "Mama? Mama, are you okay?"

Elise Adair came rushing through the kitchen, her finger to her mouth, more frazzled then Michelle could remember seeing her. She lowered her voice. "Where is she? Has something happened?"

Elise looked her over and gasped. "Michelle, honey, you're bleeding."

She glanced down. Her shirt was torn, a long bloody gash from her fall across her stomach. "It's nothing. I need to see my mother."

"I just need to tell you—"

"Your call sounded urgent. What's going on?" Ben threw the screen door back with a bang, his gaze instantly honing in on Michelle. A pulse began to pound at his temple when he saw the blood. "Who did this to you?"

"I didn't call about her, Ben. I was going to ask you to pick up Michelle, break the news gently." She took a deep breath, looking over her shoulder before turning back and leaning closer. "Gabriel's in the living room with your mama."

Michelle stumbled, and Ben half dragged, half carried her to the nearest chair. He rushed to the sink to wet a washcloth, coming back to kneel beside the chair and clean up her wound. "You're okay, Mimi. Move your hands, that's right, let me see the damage."

He focused on her injury while talking to his mother. "He just showed up, out of the blue? How long has he been here?"

Elise paced beside them. "Long enough. Annemarie is trying so hard to hold herself together. He isn't exactly affectionate. I've never seen a more awkward reunion. I'm sorry, Michelle, but that father of yours better be glad he didn't show his face, or I would have had to break it. Taking a woman's own child away from her like that."

Elise's vehemence shocked Michelle out of her own shock. Her twin brother. Here. After all these years. "I don't know how many more surprises I can take today."

"Mimi, I need to know who did this to you. The wound is shallow, but ragged. You may need stitches, baby."

She pushed Ben's hand away absently. "I don't need stitches, I need answers." She stood up. "And I need to see my mother. Now."

Michelle pushed past the concerned Adairs, heading into the living room. She stood in the doorway, watching her mother fiddle with her hands, a nervous gesture that was so uncharacteristic it almost seemed false.

A man, with his hair trimmed so close to his head there was no hint of curl, sipped iced tea slowly, warily, as though it might be poisoned.

He was handsome. His jaw was clean-shaven, his casual outfit perfectly pressed, even his nails were neat and trimmed, obviously manicured. And he had green eyes, just like hers.

Gabriel. Her twin brother. He set his glass down and glanced up, a friendly, if distant smile curving his lips. "I can't believe it. Michelle? You look like you've been in a bar brawl, but I'd know those eyes, those curls, anywhere."

He stood up and walked over to her, wrapping his arms around her in an awkward hug. "I've waited years for this."

Michelle didn't respond. Didn't return his embrace. She wasn't sure how she felt, but it wasn't what she'd imagined she would feel. There was no instant connection, no affection for the brother she had adored. There was only confusion and doubt. "Hello, Gabriel."

She walked over to her mother and put her hand on the trembling shoulder, trying to infuse her with all the love she felt.

Her mother looked up in gratitude and gasped. "What happened, Boo? Sit down, right now, and let me have a look."

"I'm fine, Mama. Don't worry about it right now. Gabe is here. How is your father?"

Your father. Her brother raised one eyebrow, showing he noticed her emphasis. "Fat and happy. He's vacationing in Venice with wife number five at the moment. He sends his regards."

She doubted it. She remembered her father well. The way he used to look at her. The punishments. "What brings you stateside?"

"I come now and again for business. California. New York." He laughed. "I actually thought I saw you once a few years ago at a gallery opening. Are you sure we weren't triplets?"

"That was her. Michelle worked in one of the most prestigious galleries in New York. She came home to help her mother after the hurricane." Ben came into the room, filling it with his energy, his strength. Michelle was grateful, since she felt she might shatter at any moment.

"Ben Adair, you old dog. Still following our Mimi around on her adventures, I see."

"Michelle. No one calls me Mimi anymore." *Except Ben.*

Gabriel held up his hands. "My apologies. I can see this may not be the time for a long reunion. I'm staying at the Royal Crescent Hotel for the next few days, and I'd really like to catch up with my sister." He walked over and kissed her mother lightly on the cheek. "You, this place, it's all exactly as I remembered it. Thank you for being so welcoming, Mom."

"Of course, Gabriel. I'm . . . so glad you came to see me. You'll always be welcome here."

"I appreciate it. I know this is all a little surprising to say the least. But better late then never, yes?" His smile didn't reach his eyes, and he walked passed Michelle and Ben without another word.

Michelle watched Elise appear beside her mother, helping her out of the chair and walking into the back room without another word.

Her mother looked as lost as she felt. A stranger. Gabriel was a total stranger. Two demons from her past had reared their heads in less than two hours.

She needed a drink.

Ben slipped his hand in hers. As he had every time she'd fallen and scraped her knee, every time one of the kids on the corner made her cry. Always there. Until she'd pushed him away.

He tugged her into his arms. "You tried, Mimi. Lucky for you, I'm stubborn." He drew her back through the kitchen and down the cottage steps, where his Harley sat glimmering in the fading light.

"Wait, where are we going?"

Ben looked at her with an expression she didn't want to define, as much as she craved it. "The Mamas are going to be fine, Mimi. They have each other. I'm taking you home. My home."

She didn't have the energy to deny him. She didn't want to. She needed to be with Ben. Needed to feel safe. Loved. She lifted her leg over the vibrating machine and wrapped her arms around his waist.

"Take me home, Ben."

"Oh, I like the way you say that, babe. I really do."

CHAPTER 8

BEN TURNED ONTO ST. CHARLES AVENUE, TOWARD UP-
town, and he was stunned to realize he was nervous. She knew
where he lived. He'd moved her mother into his house for the
duration of Katrina, where she would be safe from any potential
flooding. The mambo's cottage house had been fine, of course,
she'd told him it would be. She'd only come to put his mind at
ease, leaving to help those in her community as soon as he'd let
her out the door.

The Mamas had been tireless in their efforts to get food and
water to those trapped by the flooding and all that had come after.
He and Rousseau had helped out wherever they could. It was during the aftermath, when he'd been helping to replace a shattered
window in a nearby complex, that he'd realized Michelle had come
back. That she was moving into the apartment across the street
from Café Bwe. She was home.

Almost.

He pulled up the drive slowly, feeling her hands tighten in surprise on his waist as she looked up. Whenever she was confronted with symbols of his wealth, she backed away. He knew it made her think of her father's family and their irresponsibility.

But this house wasn't about his family's wealth, since he'd split with *his* father's company and had begun making his own investments years ago. The family gift had helped him know who to trust, when to go all in and when to pull back. Everything he had now was his.

Except the house. He'd bought it for Michelle.

Had he realized that was what he was doing at the time? Had he known, even then, even when she had a life so far away from home, a life that didn't include him? Probably.

He'd gotten it nearly eight years ago, after a business trip to New York, business that could have easily been done by phone or computer.

He'd wanted to see her.

She'd been working the room at a gallery showing, looking so different from the wild girl he'd known. Her hair slicked back in an intricate knot, her black sheath dress sleek and backless. She'd had that smile. The smile his mother had long ago perfected for these types of social functions.

Ben had kept to the outskirts of the room, watching her flutter like an exotic butterfly through the crowd. When a man appeared beside her, his hand caressing the skin of her lower back, he'd left, sure the girl he'd known was lost to him forever.

Not two weeks later he'd bought the old place. To remind him of her.

"I knew you lived up here but . . . this white elephant? Ben, isn't this . . . ?"

He helped her off the bike and came to stand beside her as she gazed up at the aging mansion. "Yeah. It is. I told you I'd buy it one day so we could find the treasure little Emmanuel knew was inside."

"Isabel's treasure," she whispered, the remembered wonder in her voice making him smile.

Ben led her up the stairs and unlocked the door. "When the old man's son decided to bring him to Florida to live with his family, they sold it to me. I haven't found the hidden panel yet."

Emmanuel had been a ten-year-old ghost, who, judging by his period clothing, must have lived in the early eighteen hundreds. He'd play with Ben and Michelle from time to time, and tell them about a secret panel that held a special woman's most treasured possessions.

He showed them the old mansion where he'd lived with his sister. Isabel had been her name. And the treasure was hers.

Ben remembered how Michelle had loved hearing about Isabel. How she'd made the ghost go on and on about his beautiful older sister, her gowns, the dances he'd watched from the rafters . . . everything.

Ben walked Michelle through the cavernous foyer and pointed her in the direction of the music room. "I'm going to get you a new shirt and something to put on that wound."

He raced to the second floor, making sure nothing was out of place in case she wanted to come upstairs. Gathering a white T-shirt, some Neosporin, and a bandage, he loped downstairs in time to hear her laugh. She walked slowly, noticing all the detail on the fireplace he'd restored. He paused at the piano just as she stopped, tilting her head up to notice the framed drawing on the wall.

"Oh, you're kidding me."

He set his supplies on the grand piano and followed her gaze. "What? I'm a collector of fine art. That thing's gonna be worth a fortune someday."

She shook her head. "I cannot believe you still have that. You should have burned it."

"It belonged here." And it did. A seven-year-old's rendering of what she had imagined Isabel looked like fit perfectly in the warm room. Sometimes he'd look at it and just know he was about to hear a stampede of children's feet and laughter.

He wanted those children with her.

She cringed, her hand coming up to touch her side, and he turned her toward him. "Let me take a look at that."

"It's fine, really."

He ignored her and lifted her by her hips onto the top of the piano. "Don't be a baby. Take off your shirt."

Michelle glared at him. "I'm not a baby." She wrenched off her shirt and winced at the movement. "Damn it."

He focused on slowing his breathing as he tended to her wounds. There were other scratches, and a wood sliver or two, but the worst one had cut a jagged line down her stomach. "How did this happen, Mimi?"

"I fell."

"You were thrown, *cher*. Why are you lying to him? He deserves to know."

Ben, who was touching her skin as he smoothed on the bandage, froze beside her at Bone Daddy's words. The Loa was pacing beside them, glancing out the windows with a telling agitation.

"What do I deserve to know?"

Michelle growled, struggling to get away from him, but Ben pulled her closer and opened his mind. The angry being possessing the girl from the club, a being Michelle recognized—one who'd attacked her before in New York—Ben sensed it all. Felt Michelle's fear and her feeling of helplessness.

Why hadn't she told anyone? Him? Was this why she'd been pushing herself so hard? Taking all those defense classes?

Pain knotted his chest, making it hard for him to breathe. He wanted to kill the bastard for tormenting her. Wanted to shake her for keeping something this important from him. He'd almost lost her before she'd even come home. And she'd never said a word.

"I don't like this house, Benjamin." Bone Daddy looked around uneasily. "It's making me edgy. I'm going to look around, make sure that *djab* isn't about."

Michelle looked up. *"Djab?"*

He saw Bone Daddy grimace as though he'd tasted something sour. "A wild, rogue spirit. Not unlike myself. But this one seems to feed off pain and fear as opposed to pleasure. I didn't recognize him."

Ben narrowed his gaze on the frustrated spirit. "You didn't recognize him? And you can't ask, can you? You're ignoring the other Loa, staying under the radar so you don't have to go back yet."

"You're judging *me* for hesitating? Get your own house in order, Benjamin Adair." Bone Daddy disappeared through the fireplace, rocking the picture frame above with the force of his anger.

"That wasn't really fair, Ben." Michelle's voice was soft with reproach. "I'm starting to like that sinning specter. And I think he knows lonely better than—"

"Than I know you?" He finished her sentence, pressing his forehead against hers. *"You're* the one I'm worried about, Mimi. The Loa may be sad, but he's immortal. You're not. Instead, you're alone, facing God knows what that thing was. And you can't lie to me and say that your mother never told you how to deal with this kind of thing, because I know better."

MICHELLE GAVE A WATERY CHUCKLE. SHE NEEDED TO BEAT something up, to do something. Vulnerable wasn't her style. She didn't like feeling weak. Didn't want to need him. Yet, ever since she'd seen that *djab* thing, seen her brother, all she could think about was being alone with Ben. That she'd be safe with him.

It was a dangerous train of thought, thinking she could rely so completely on someone other than herself.

Coming here had only made it worse. He'd bought their dream house, Isabel's house. He'd hung up the drawing she'd worked on night and day, hoping to have it ready in time for his ninth birthday.

Had she always been such a blind fool?

"Ben, please. Not right now. I don't want to—I *can't* think about this right now."

She watched him hesitate, could practically see the wheels turning in his mind. He wanted answers. But she didn't have any. And she didn't want to think about the questions. She wanted him.

She reached behind her to unsnap her bra, letting the straps tumble down her arms. "You said you'd be my new distraction, Adair. I could surely use one right about now."

His jaw locked, but his attention slipped to her breasts. He started to reach for them, but his palm passed over her bandage and he pulled back. "I don't want to hurt you."

"Then don't leave me wanting."

Her legs wrapped around his and her fists curled in his shirt, pulling him in for a kiss filled with all her pent-up frustration, her passion.

He matched her aggression with his own, his mouth ravenous as it fought for supremacy with hers. He dragged her by her legs, her butt sliding across the smooth black surface until her sneak-ered feet landed on the piano bench, and then he tore his mouth away from hers. "Stand up, Mimi, and turn around."

She smiled down into his hungry expression, obeying without a word. This was what she wanted. What she had to have.

Her shoes and socks, jeans and lavender butterfly thong were all methodically removed as she stared in the direction of Isabel's picture above the mantel. But she couldn't see it. All of her energy was focused on Ben.

He wasn't talking, wasn't caressing, wasn't kissing—yet she found her arousal growing with every moment that passed.

When she was completely naked he stepped back. She heard the sound of his clothes being removed and she started to turn around, but his rumbling growl stopped her in her tracks. "I'll spank you if you do, Mimi. And I'll enjoy every minute of it. Kneel on the bench."

She stopped turning and knelt, but she couldn't hold in the laugh that bubbled out of her mouth. "If that's your deterrent, big man, you'll have to work on a new angle. I'd love to be spanked by you." The palm of her hand made a cracking sound as it landed on her right cheek. "Here." She slid the same hand around her hips to cover her bare sex. "Or here."

He was silent for so long she was worried she'd shocked him. She was about to disobey and turn around when he swore under his breath.

"You've had too many distractions for my peace of mind, babe. I think there's only one thing I can do."

She groaned. "If you're about to say get dressed and catch a matinee, you should know I'm a black belt."

His sensual laugh sent shock waves down her nerve endings. How much longer was he going to wait to touch her? She bent forward, lifting her ass in the air and placing her arms on top of the piano, feeling the cool ivory keys brush against her heavy breasts. The sensation felt surprisingly arousing. "Oh. Um, so . . . what is the only thing that you can do?"

Ben leaned down to whisper in her ear, his breath hot and delicious. "Make you forget them all."

She heard the scrape of a chair against the floor and then he was there, hands on her hips, placing openmouthed kisses on her ass where she'd smacked herself.

"I love your ass, babe. I have to admit there were times I'd get you riled up on purpose, just so I could watch you walk away. Watch the sway of your hips, the curve of your round bottom bounce. It made me want to kneel at your feet and beg for a bite."

He scraped his teeth across her skin, biting down with just enough force to make her whimper. One hand dropped from her hips to seek out her wet sex, groaning when he discovered the wetness there. "You want me. For more than just a distraction. I felt it all those years ago. I sense it now. Why, Mimi? Why did you keep me at arm's length for so long?"

He didn't give her a chance to answer. And then she had a hard time thinking at all. Two thick fingers filled her, slipping in and out of her while another caressed her piercing.

His other hand gripped one cheek of her ass, spreading her wider for his inspection. "Damn, Mimi."

Michelle's body jerked, her breasts mashing against the loud piano keys when she felt his tongue trace a line up her ass. "Oh my God."

Her body was taut, a fine vibration running through her as he devastated her with his fingers, his mouth. When his tongue probed her ass, she cried out.

His fingers gathered her arousal, his mouth lifting long enough to coat her with her own juices. His thumb applied pressure, pushing through the tight ring of resistant muscles.

I'm going to fuck you here, baby.

"Yes!"

He stood up abruptly behind her, the chair crashing to the floor as he bent down to grab a condom from the pocket of his jeans. She felt a pang of disappointment that anything would come between them.

He laid the flat of his palm against her back, catching the thought and releasing a shaky breath. "Mimi, baby, don't tempt me."

His cock filled her sex, thrusting deep, and they were both lost for a moment in the intensity of the pleasure, the connection. He pulled out, and she moaned. But he had other plans.

Michelle's temples started tingling and she felt his need, his desire to go slowly, not to hurt her. But she didn't want slow. "Fuck me, Adair." Her demand was breathless. "Do I have to dare you?"

"You are amazing, baby." *I love . . .*

She sensed the unfinished thought as he spread both cheeks wide, the head of his now soaked cock seeking entry. She took a few slow breaths, trying to relax her muscles, to open for him.

Her arms were shaking, barely able to hold her up. Two hearts pounded as one as he filled her. Inch by agonizing inch. Stretching her. Claiming her.

There were no words after that. No sounds beyond the straining breaths and moans of pained pleasure at the profound feeling of fullness.

Michelle sensed the moment he lost control, and screamed in

approval as he quickened his pace. He thrust deep, dragging his cock back through her clinging flesh.

He reached around to rub her clit with rough fingers, and she arched her spine, unable to hold back the flood that crashed around her with her climax.

"Yes, Mimi. Fuck, I can feel—" He came with a shout of male triumph, hips pumping against her, teeth closing over her shoulder in a passionate love bite.

You're mine, Mimi. You've always been mine.

Tell her something she didn't know.

CHAPTER 9

A SHARP PAIN IN HIS NECK WOKE HIM UP. HE SAT UP ON the small antique sofa and rubbed it, groaning a little at the aches and pains making themselves known all over his body.

"That's the last time I sleep on this thing."

He had a perfectly decadent bed in the master bedroom. He'd had plans for that bed, kept promising himself he'd get Michelle in it before the night was over. But his lover kept distracting him.

After the episode against the piano, they'd gone upstairs for a shower in his large master bath, the only room he'd had completely remodeled after buying the place.

He'd made love to her again under the water's spray, unable to stop touching her, kissing her. They'd dried off and, after he'd rewrapped her wound, they'd chased each other down into the kitchen to grab some of the leftover étouffée he'd brought home last night.

Ben smiled. They'd christened that room, too, and then come back to the music room to snuggle on the couch, whispering about Isabel's treasure. Plotting, as they had when they were children, what they would do when they found it.

He looked around the room, noticing his clothes had been folded neatly and were stacked on the floor by the sofa. Hers were gone. "Mimi?"

There were no sounds on the floor above, no smells of coffee brewing in the kitchen. She'd left without saying a word.

"Son of a bitch."

He threw on his jeans and ran his hand through his hair in frustration. Every single time. He was getting sick and tired of her running away from him. Did he have to tie her to his side?

He'd thought last night was a breakthrough. That she was finally opening up, trusting him. His gaze snagged on a tall, crooked cane leaning against the wall. It was beautiful. It also wasn't here last night. Had Michelle left it there for him to find? Did she give presents to all her distractions?

He was such a hopeless fool about Mimi. Where was his line in the sand? When was he going to stop chasing after her?

Ben wrapped his hand around the top knot of the cane and an electric current shocked him, sending him to his knees. The piano started to play and he heard a gruff male voice behind him say, "Never, boy. The answer is never."

Ben turned to the grand piano to see an elderly black man, his beard stark white against his dark skin, his face kind. "I love music. There's something so soothing about it. Magical. Don't you think?"

"Who are you?" Ben lifted himself up to his feet, still reeling from the power of the zap that had felled him. "What are you?"

The old man smiled, shaking his head. "Who and what I am is

not your question. Your question is where is your woman, and how can you find her in time to save her."

"Michelle? Is she in danger? Where the hell is she?"

Ben watched the stranger push himself up from the piano bench, the music still playing without him, and walk to the fireplace to look up at Michelle's childhood drawing.

"Passion is good. You'll need it. But before I tell you, I need you to promise me something." He turned to pin Ben with his sparkling ebony gaze. "You love each other, and it's what will give her strength. This particular *djab* feeds off fear, not love. But succeed or not, you must find Isabel's treasure. Everything depends on it."

Ben rubbed his temple. The *djab*? The treasure? Was he dreaming? And why did this man look so familiar?

He laughed, shuffling past Ben to grab his cane before patting the younger man on his shoulder. "You've seen me before. And you will again. There's a note for you on the piano. She didn't run away from you, Benjamin. Not this time. Now hurry. She needs you." He stopped in the doorway, placing his straw hat firmly on his head. "A Toussaint woman's soul is made to care for the world, but her heart is made for just one man. If he's strong enough."

Ben didn't know why, but he couldn't stop the words that came out of his mouth. "Thank you."

"Don't thank me. Thank the Marassa twins. Those Loa are partial to Michelle. So is—what is it you call him? Ah, yes, BD. Be nice to that one. He's got a rough road ahead."

Ben blinked, and the old man was gone, the echo of music still rippling through the room. The piano. He rushed over and found a note from Michelle. She'd gotten a phone call, and she hadn't wanted to wake him. It was something she thought she had to do on her own.

"Oh, Mimi. You need a keeper, baby."

He knew just the man for the job.

"WHY DO YOU STAY HERE? THIS CITY USED TO BE BEAUTIFUL. Now it's a seedy, musty memory of its former self. I've seen so many wonders around this world. Maybe I'll show you a few."

Michelle smiled sardonically. "You're welcome to go at any time. This is where I belong."

Nothing like being tied to the bed in your long-lost brother's hotel room to bring to light what was truly important. She may have come home to escape her nightmares, but she was staying because it was her home. And the home of everyone she loved.

Gabriel turned away from the French doors that led out to the balcony and sneered. "Where you belong? But I don't, isn't that what you're saying? Do you know what memories I have up here?" He banged the side of his head with his hand. "You were the special one. You were the *bon ange*. I was an accident, powerless, something Mambo Toussaint had no trouble sending away, along with the man who loved her."

Michelle rolled her eyes. "You know I can see you. Why do you persist in pretending you're my brother?"

Gabriel lowered himself with a playful bounce to the bed beside her, her tied ankles protecting him from getting his head kicked in. She saw the red energy, the menacing face of the *djab* beside him, *in* him, as he answered her. "Because it's so much fun. He's so full of anger, this one. Anger at you. At your mother. But more important, he is feeding me with all this delicious pain."

He pointed his finger at her and shook his head, scolding. "You have no idea what this poor boy has suffered because of you. To think he actually missed you as a child. The priests soon beat *that* out of him. They prayed over him, studied him, starved him—all so his father could make sure he wasn't possessed by the same demon hiding inside you, his twin sister."

She clenched her fingers, wishing she could get her hands on him.

The *djab* laughed until tears streamed out of Gabriel's eyes. "I love human irony. His father's latest wife is Wiccan! Can you believe it? And she convinced him to admit to his son that he was wrong, that you weren't possessed, you were just special. Boy, did the news throw ol' Gabe here over the edge."

Oh dear God. She'd had no idea. How could she? She was too busy feeling abandoned by him. By their father. Too busy refusing to trust too much in anyone, to love, because they might leave her, just like Gabe had.

"Poor Gabriel. Didn't his father tell him that he was the one who left? That my mother wanted to keep Gabriel with us? That I wanted him to stay?"

The possessed man whirled toward her, straddling her waist while he gripped her cheeks in rough hands. "He hasn't changed that much. And don't feel sorry for your brother, beauty. He had plans for you. He wanted to fight fire with fire. He'd gathered hair from you and your mother on his visit, thinking he could make a *gris-gris* to protect him from you long enough to convince his mother that it was *he* who was the special one, *he* who deserved to be loved." The *djab* shook his head. "The boy is a little confused. And he truly knows nothing of voodoo. It's sad really. He is a Toussaint after all."

He cackled, his eyes bloodshot and wild as he gazed down at Michelle's prone figure. "You know what I think would drive him completely over the edge? If I fucked you in his body. Surely only a demon could arouse her own brother enough to make him do something so forbidden. The pain would be succulent."

"No."

"Why not, Michelle? It isn't like you have a problem having sex with a spirit present. And please, don't try to tell me you have limits to what you're willing to do in the pursuit of pleasure."

She tried to keep her face blank, her heart rate normal. Bone Daddy said he fed off fear and pain. She wouldn't satisfy him. She couldn't let him know that she was terrified, and so heartbroken for her brother, for herself, that she was having a hard time not screaming bloody murder.

"You disgust me. You bore me. And I have no intention of letting you touch me."

"Strong words from someone who is tied to my bed. I knew you would be fun to play with. Knew it four years ago. And you are. How do you plan to stop me all by yourself?"

"She isn't all by herself. She never has been."

"The boyfriend? I'm impressed, Michelle. You must be really good in bed." The *djab* pulled Gabriel's body off of her, turning to face Ben.

Now she was truly afraid. Ben knew Bone Daddy, he had to know how strong spirits were when they possessed a body. They used the energy to supercharge their abilities. He would kill Ben. Why had he come?

She met his gaze, panicked, but he just smiled.

"I love you, Mimi. I'll always come for you."

The first punch knocked Ben into the wall, and Michelle cried out. "No!"

A powerful tingling, different from the feeling she got when Ben touched her, wrapped around her body.

Michelle, cher, *you need to let me in. Accept me, and I can help you.*
Bone Daddy?

No. She didn't want to be taken over, didn't want to give up control of her body. Look at the damage the *djab* was doing, had done.

I would never hurt you or those you love, cher. *I can help you. I can save Ben. But you have to accept me.*

Ben. He loved her. And she loved him. Had always loved him. If she could save him, nothing else mattered. "I accept you."

Good girl.

It was a little like drowning, falling into the energy as his spirit rose from the bed and into her body. She resisted instinctively for a moment, then she saw Ben crumple to the floor once more, his body still. She opened the door to the Loa, feeling her *ti bon ange* separate from her body, and letting his consciousness take over the reins.

She watched from a distance as her body easily released itself from the ropes that bound it, leaping from the bed to tackle Gabriel and his *djab* rider.

"These people belong to me. Under my protection. You are not welcome here." Bone Daddy reached into the energy surrounding Gabriel, and Michelle felt the violent, magical tug-of-war that ensued between them. For a moment it seemed that the rest of her soul was going to be forcibly ripped from her body.

The *djab* snarled, struggling in Bone Daddy's grip. "You can't control me. You're not even a true Loa. You're a nothing."

Michelle felt her lips form a smile as Bone Daddy, with one impossible push of power, unseated Gabriel's *djab* and held the neck of the limp spirit in his hands. "I'm the nothing who's sending you back to where you belong."

Bone Daddy wasn't surprised by the knock on the door, or the

masked man in the top hat who pushed it open. The strange man
looked dressed for Mardi Gras, with feathers lining the shoulders
of his old tuxedo. He opened a large pouch and Michelle looked
on as Bone Daddy dropped the *djab* inside, closing the drawstrings
tight. "Look out for this one, he was stalking a Toussaint."

The masked figure nodded, turning to leave without uttering
a word.

What now? she wondered. She heard Ben moan and roll onto
his side, and knew that whatever happened next would be worth
it. Ben was alive.

Cher, *I'm not a monster. You're giving me a complex. Have a little
faith.*

She smiled even as the darkness swirled around her, pulling her
into unconsciousness. He really was growing on her.

CHAPTER 10

SHE WAS ALMOST AFRAID TO OPEN HER EYES. SHE WAS dreaming she was in her old twin bed. The air smelled like her favorite bread pudding, the sweet cinnamon-flavored treat her mother always made for her when she was sad. It felt like she was home.

"I know you're awake, Mimi. Open those pretty green eyes for me, baby. I need to see them."

Ben. Her eyes popped open and she jackknifed to a sitting position at the sight that met her gaze. She reached out to pull him closer with a gasp, and a wave of dizziness nearly knocked her back down, but Ben's hands gripped her shoulders gently.

"Are you okay?"

She rolled her eyes. "Am *I* okay? You're the one who looks like you went to tryouts for the WWE."

Ben grimaced, wincing as the expression tugged on his split lip and swollen right eye. "Feels a little like it, too. Although I think my vanity hurts more than anything else. So much for charging in on that white horse to save the day."

"More like a white jackass," she huffed. "You could have been killed taking that thing on." She whacked him lightly on his shoulder.

He laughed, making him groan once more. "Don't go laying on that sympathy too thick, Florence Nightingale. I might start thinking you care."

Her heart raced as she looked at him. She took his hand, drawing his gaze to hers. He stilled at the expression he saw on her face. "I care, Ben Adair. I—"

"Am I interrupting?"

"Gabriel."

Her brother wasn't looking too good. Dark circles deepened the green of his eyes, and his skin was unnaturally pale.

Ben tensed beside her. "Gabe, do you think you should be up right now? Your mother wants you to take it slow."

He smiled weakly and his attention focused on Michelle. "I know. She's been hovering over me like a worried mother hen. And she keeps bringing me trays of food."

Michelle could hear the confusion in his voice. "Of course she does, Gabriel. She loves you. You're her son."

He flinched. "About what happened. I heard what he said, what you said. I know—"

"I wrote to you. Did you know that? Every day for three years after you left." She leaned over on the bed, reaching beneath it until she found an old hatbox. "They all came back unopened. Mom's, too. I thought you didn't want to be a part of our family anymore."

She opened the box and picked up two stacks of envelopes, slightly yellowed with age and wrapped in blue yarn.

Gabriel's jaw worked, his eyes shining as he stepped closer, holding out his hand. "May I read them now?"

She nodded, handing them over solemnly. A hole inside her that she had never completely acknowledged started to close when she saw him look at the letters. He hadn't known about them. Her father was a bastard, but her brother had been just as lonely as she had without his twin.

"Gabriel? Gabriel, honey, where you at?"

She and Gabriel shared a laugh. He lifted his voice to reach her down the hallway. "I'm talking to Michelle."

"You should be lying down! I have bread pudding almost ready and I made you some of my special tea."

Ben smirked. "When one of The Mamas calls, son, you'd better run."

"Apparently." He turned back to Michelle. "Thank you for these."

"Anytime, Gabriel."

He turned to go, then stopped to look over his shoulder at Ben and Michelle. "I'm glad she wasn't alone, Ben. Glad you were here." He closed the door with a firm click behind him.

Michelle quickly wiped a tear that had escaped down her cheek, knowing Ben had sensed all that had gone on in that hotel room while she was talking to Gabriel.

"I can ruin him if you like."

Michelle frowned in confusion and Ben elaborated. "Your father. Say the word and I can make sure his family's business takes a sudden turn for the worse."

She smiled. "Not that I don't like this bloodthirsty side of you, Adair, but it isn't necessary." She glanced toward the door. "He doesn't have anything I want anymore." A sudden thought occurred to her. "How did we get here? Where's—"

Ben chuckled. "Bone Daddy? According to The Mamas, they opened the door a few hours ago to you, carrying Gabriel and me on each of your shoulders. You laid us down, flirted with your mother, then passed out. You don't see him?"

"Flirted with . . . ? No, I don't see him. He saved us, Ben. I just can't believe it."

"I think there's more to our randy Loa friend than meets the eye."

Ben told her about his unusual visitor, how the old black man had mentioned Bone Daddy, and the treasure.

"Isabel's treasure? Really? Are you sure you weren't dreaming?"

Ben raised his eyebrow sardonically. "Let's recap, shall we? You and your brother were just possessed by dueling spirits, one of them responsible for helping to get our two friends together. I can touch people and sense what they're feeling, and you can see ghosties and supernatural spirits. And you're asking me if that was just a dream?"

She made a face at him. "You have a point. But what does it mean? Emmanuel said he and his sister were the only ones who knew about it. Who was that old man?"

"I don't know, Mimi. But I think, since he did warn me you were in danger, we should start looking for that secret panel right away."

She smiled at his earnest expression, even more endearing with the marks on his face. Marks he'd suffered to protect her. "Right away? Couldn't it wait a few more hours?"

He did a double take, trying hard not to grin too widely. "What will we do to pass the time?"

She dropped the covers and pulled off the old T-shirt her mother had, no doubt, dressed her in when she'd gotten her to bed. "I can think of a few things."

Ben stood up and unbuckled his pants, walked over to slip the little metal latch on the door and locked it. "I wonder if your mama knows what a bad girl she raised."

She slipped off her panties and tossed them at his feet. "The longer you talk, the closer that bread pudding is to being ready."

He stripped at lightning speed, making Michelle inhale sharply yet again.

"Oh, Ben."

His beautiful torso was peppered with bruises. "I think my mother has a poultice or something. Maybe we shouldn't—"

"Oh no, you don't." Ben ripped the mosaic-patterned coverlet off the bed and pinned her to the mattress. "You can't promise me heaven then back away. I don't care if you *do* have a black belt."

He kissed her gently, carefully, and Michelle's giggling became moans. She'd been so afraid for him. So afraid she wouldn't make it out of her encounter with the rogue *djab* alive. And now she was here, in his arms.

He pulled his mouth away with a disappointed moan. "I don't have anything. Protection."

"Then we'll just have to be creative." She wiggled against his hips, feeling his erection press against her.

He kissed her again, his mouth caressing her temple, her chin, the base of her neck. When he reached her breasts, she arched into his mouth. Loving the sensation. Loving him.

He lifted his lips. "Say it out loud, Mimi. Please, baby. Don't torture me."

"I love you, Ben."

"Mo laime toi, Mimi." I love you. I've always loved you.

He pressed passionate kisses against her belly, careful of the bandage still covering one side. He nibbled on her thighs, lowering himself between her legs, the lower half of his body hanging off her childhood bed.

Michelle started to chuckle, covering her mouth with her hand. He looked up and narrowed his gaze. "It's not nice to laugh at a man when he's trying to seduce you."

"I was just thinking."

"Also not a good thing to tell the man who's supposed to be your distraction."

Michelle smiled softly. "You're so much more than that. And you know it, Adair."

"What were you thinking?" He pressed his mouth over her piercing, tongue slipping out to circle the tiny silver bar.

"*Ah*. Oh. Yes, well. I was just thinking . . . this is the first time we've actually, um, done anything in a bed."

"I don't really consider this a bed. I'll show you a real bed as soon as I get you back home."

She lifted her hips as his fingers sought out her heat. "After we look for the treasure, you mean."

"I have all the treasure I want, right here."

❧ REDEEM ME ❧

CHAPTER 1

"THAT'S RIGHT. SHE WANTS YOU. SEE THE WAY SHE SIFTS her hair through her fingers, lifting it away from the kissable nape of her neck? How she's leaning closer, so close you can smell the sun on her skin? Her heat? She doesn't care about securities and paperwork. She wants you to stand up and take her in your arms. She is ripe and ready for a good, hard fu—"

"Thank you, Ms. Dane," the man interrupted abruptly as he glanced at his watch. "This was a very productive lunch. But I have a three o'clock so . . ."

Bone Daddy grunted in frustration. "Bah! Did you hear nothing I said?"

"Of course, Mr. Bonneville. I'll have the report in your inbox by morning."

The man stood and turned away from his coworker, already on his portable phone before he'd even left the outdoor café.

Bone Daddy sighed as the man in the suit and tie walked right through him. Of course he couldn't hear him, couldn't see him; the poor bastard didn't even know when a delicious woman was offering herself like a five-course meal at his feet.

He watched the blonde's shoulders fall on a disappointed sigh and leaned closer to her. She couldn't see him either, but maybe she could feel him. He blew against her temple, focusing all his energy on ruffling the tendrils that had curled in the damp heat of the day. "You deserve better, *cher*. If I were in his body, any body at all, I would prove to you just how desirable you truly are."

She shivered, looking around suspiciously. Grumbling to herself about stupid men and vibrators, she grabbed up her briefcase, left a tip on the table, and rushed off in the direction of the blockheaded male she wanted, leaving Bone Daddy behind.

That had been happening a lot lately.

First Rousseau had found the perfect match with Allegra, sending Bone Daddy packing after years of pleasure, and then Ben had swept Michelle away to his crumbly old mansion.

Bone Daddy hated that house. He wasn't sure why. He would almost swear some sorcerer had cursed the ground beneath it, to keep good spirits away. Otherwise, wouldn't he have been pinned to the side of Michelle Toussaint these last few weeks? Not only did she have a sweet ass and a penchant for exhibitionism, she was also the only woman who could see him in his noncorporeal form.

Seven years. Seven years he'd been on this side of the Gate, reveling in the instant gratification, the passion of humanity. He loved mortals. Everything about them. Their resilience, their decadence, the sensations and heights they were capable of achieving.

He was surprised he'd been allowed to stay so long this time, even though the open-ended deal Rousseau's father had made for his own selfish reasons was something Bone Daddy had no problem taking advantage of. Perhaps he'd been left alone because in his world, time had no meaning. What *was* and what *is* occasionally got jumbled about.

It sounded more interesting than it was, in his opinion. The tapestry of that life seemed to pale in comparison to the rich textures and brilliant colors of New Orleans. He wanted to stay.

In that desire lay a twisted path, as his old mentor often told him—as the keeper of the crossroads, he should know. Bone Daddy himself understood that staying too long as a shadow in the human realm, without a purpose or a body, would turn you into something dark and perverse. Something like the *djab*, the rogue spirit who'd gone after Michelle. He never wanted that. He loved pleasing people; he didn't want to cause pain.

So he'd made a bargain with the higher echelon of Loa. In exchange for getting him to Michelle on time, to save her from her possessed brother, Bone Daddy would have to leave the human realm. He would be allowed to remain in New Orleans until All Saints' Day.

It would be the first time he was able to be in physical form without possessing a human. His last chance to "get his desires out of his system," or so his mentor put it. As if that could happen. Afterward he would pass through the Gate of Guinee—the gate to the other side. There he would have to remain regardless of the pleas of the needy voodoo practitioners. It was a difficult term to accept. What was he if not the Love Doctor of the Big Easy? Merely a specter, a wraith.

Unseen and unsatisfied.

But he had All Saints' Day. The day the Ghede family, and a few of the other Loa, could walk the earth in human form. Their own human form. How long before his unique agreement with the Rousseau males had he longed to be allowed to roam free that one special day? As long as he could remember. But his name never came up. Until now.

He'd take it, even as a consolation prize. What Loa wouldn't walk through fire for the chance to be in a body all his or her own? No struggles with a mortal's soul, being able to *feel* everything. No thoughts in his head but his own. Paradise from the first rays of one dawn until the next.

Bone Daddy unchained.

He smiled as he watched the bustling crowd. The locals would be preparing soon. It was nothing like the grand spectacles of the past. The whole city was a bit more somber of late. But it was still All Saints', the Day of the Dead. Cultures and beliefs united to celebrate and remember those who had come before, those who had moved on. Mambo Toussaint was sure to have a grand gathering. Wouldn't she be surprised to see her favorite Loa join in the festivities as a human male? He grinned, impatient for the time to pass.

He could suffer a few more days of hunger. Soon enough he would feast.

"I'M SO GLAD YOU DECIDED TO COME, BETHANY." MICHELLE wove in and out of the late-afternoon New Orleans traffic like a member of the Andretti family. "You were the first person I thought of when we found Isabel's treasure. And I admit, it's a great excuse to get you down here. I didn't think you'd ever leave New York City to come to visit me."

Bethany clutched her seat belt, smiling weakly at her animated friend. She'd never thought she would leave the safety of her East Coast apartment either. But Michelle had targeted her Achilles' heel—history. In particular, the history of Spanish colonization in the Americas. With Michelle's recent find dangling like a carrot, Bethany had taken a few anti-anxiety meds and something for motion sickness, hopped on a plane, and here she was. Groggy, but here. New Orleans. A city with enough history to keep her in geek heaven for years.

She'd always meant to come here, had read everything she could get her hands on about the Crescent City. The parades and bead-throwing she could do without, but the mystery, the magical allure of New Orleans, still called to her. Unfortunately planes made her panicky and airsick, and trains were too crowded and, well . . . made her panicky.

Bethany sighed. She was a bit of an isolationist. But Michelle had always refused to accept that fact. From the moment she'd moved into the New York apartment across the hall from Bethany all those years ago, the beautiful social butterfly had been determined to make friends.

It was an unlikely relationship. Bethany worked from home as a textbook editor, surrounded by her books and her research. The convenience of living in the City That Never Sleeps meant everything she needed was brought to her door, so much so that she was a veritable recluse. Michelle, on the other hand, had loved the glamour of the Big Apple, working in one of the most prestigious art galleries in the city. Men had come to her door with flowers every weekend, and if there was a place to be in town, Bethany could be sure Michelle had been there.

She was ashamed to say she'd rebuffed her energetic neighbor once or twice, and it wasn't until she'd come up to find Michelle admiring her rooftop garden that they'd had their first real conversation. When her exotic neighbor had admitted where she was from, Beth had been fascinated.

Thankfully, Michelle had always been patient with her, trying to answer all her questions, though it was obvious she'd been uncomfortable talking about her past. It was Bethany who had picked her up from the hospital after the mugging, who'd made sure she iced her eye and took her medicine. But she could tell it had shaken Michelle, more than she was willing to admit.

When she'd gone home to Louisiana, Beth had missed her terribly. Their phone calls and monthly video chats were the only thing that kept her sane. She hadn't realized how much she'd come to depend on Michelle's friendship until it was gone. And now, four years later, she was here.

She gave Michelle a teasing look. "So, Benjamin Adair, childhood nemesis, is more than your latest distraction, I take it?"

When Michelle blushed, Beth did a comedic double take. "As I live and breathe," she drawled in a fake Southern accent, "I do declare I have never seen Michelle Toussaint blush over a *man*."

Bethany batted her eyelashes and Michelle burst out laughing. "You in N'awlins now, chile," she sassed back, exaggerating her own natural twang. "Don't go pokin' fun at how we talk."

Leaning back against the headrest, Bethany studied her friend. "This place looks good on you." And it did. Michelle had changed so much. Gone from curvaceous to finely honed. Her arms were lean and defined—strong. Her hair was left down to fall in wild spirals to her shoulders, where she used to keep it straight or slicked back. Her face was free of makeup, yet still glowing. She looked healthy. Happy. In love.

"Yeah? Well, it isn't the big city, but we certainly have our fair share of excitement." Michelle smiled sardonically. "And I'm not talking about Mardi Gras."

Before Beth could prod her for details, they turned into a circular driveway and she felt her jaw drop. "Beautiful."

It was a gorgeous example of antebellum architecture, with white columns reminiscent of the Greek revivalists and wrought-iron weaving around the upper balcony like thriving metal vines. It was a grand old place. Stunning really. Imposing. She wanted to run inside and run away at the same time.

The old live oaks haven't always been in the yard.

At the absent thought, her heart started to pound so hard against her breastbone she thought it might be trying to escape. How did she know that? She must have come across a photograph of this mansion in one of her books on New Orleans architecture. Surely she'd seen it before.

"I knew you'd love it. I tease Ben about owning such a huge white elephant, and Mama says she can't think with so much space, but I told him I was bringing home the one person who would truly appreciate it."

The door opened as Michelle was speaking, and Bethany found herself distracted by the South's answer for Adonis striding toward the car with a wide easy smile. "Good grief."

Michelle chuckled low, turning off the engine. "Honey, you have no idea."

Bethany watched the golden god yank open Michelle's door and pull her into his arms, kissing her passionately.

"Can we all say 'awkward?'" she mumbled as she tried to unbuckle herself with suddenly sweaty palms. When she was finally free, she fumbled for her door.

It opened before she could wrap her fingers around the handle.

"You must be Ms. Bethany Sorelle. Michelle has nothing but good to say about you."

Her eyes widened as they followed the outstretched hand up a long, lean arm to yet another vision of divine masculinity. *Help!* She'd fallen into a porn movie and she couldn't get up.

Bethany felt her face heating, and even though it was the end of October, she blamed it on the weather. She just wasn't used to the humidity. It couldn't have anything to do with the man currently curling his massive hand around hers to help her out of Michelle's tiny deathtrap of a car.

If Benjamin Adair was Adonis, this man was a fallen angel. A beautiful golden angel with a heart-stopping body, full lips, and long, flowing dreadlocks. And tattoos. She couldn't forget the tattoos. But his hazel eyes were kind. And his smile told her she had nothing to fear from him.

Fallen angels were tricky that way.

"Bethany. I feel like I know you already. I'm so happy you've come!" A slender woman with strawberry blonde hair, freckles, and sparkling blue eyes wrapped her up in a surprisingly strong embrace as soon as her feet touched the ground.

Allegra Jarrod. It had to be. Michelle's college friend and, up until the last few months, her roommate. "It's nice to finally meet you, Ms. Jarrod."

"Oh, call me Allegra, please. Besides," she pulled back and smiled lovingly at the man beside them. "It will be Mrs. Rousseau in a few more days."

Ah, so this was Celestin Rousseau. Michelle had told her the two were engaged. A few more days? "You're getting married on Halloween?"

"All Saints'." The gorgeous Ben had stopped ravaging Michelle and come to join them, Bethany's small red suitcase in his hand. "The first day of November, when we honor those who have crossed over."

Creepy. "That's, um, wonderful."

Michelle's laugh was loud, making Bethany smile. "Don't go getting shy on me now, Miss Sass. It doesn't suit you. It is an unusual date, but Allegra is a true romantic. She wants to pay homage to the ... *man* that brought them together."

Beth eyed her curiously at the obvious significance of this mysterious *man* but Michelle didn't elaborate.

"Let's get her inside before we scare her back to New York, *bebe*." The fallen angel slid his arm around Allegra, leading her back into the house while Ben followed close behind.

As she ambled along with Michelle, Beth took in the spectacular surroundings. The lawn was immaculately groomed and a large oak tree in the front yard dripped with Spanish moss. The aroma of gardenias and damp earth embraced her, and she suddenly wanted nothing more than to sit beneath the tree and soak it all in. She was here.

At last.

Bethany allowed Michelle to lead her to the kitchen, where Rousseau was putting the finishing touches on something that smelled delicious.

It was a warm kitchen, lovingly restored, though much to Bethany's dismay, someone had added modern appliances along the way. And a marble countertop. She understood why—she'd just expected to see something different. A large hearth kitchen and the bustling of cooks and servants perhaps.

She'd been reading too many historicals.

Beth suddenly felt self-conscious. The others were gathering bowls and silverware, or dipping their finger into Rousseau's pot, all of them gazing at her with different levels of curiosity and apprehension. Maybe they were responding to her own rising nerves. She wasn't comfortable around people. Never had been.

She pulled her waist-long braid, her only nod to vanity, over her shoulder and fiddled with it, searching for something to say. "So, um, Allegra, Michelle tells me you're writing a book about voodoo spirits. I always enjoyed your magazine articles. You have a way of making people feel like they're on the adventure with you. I look forward to reading the book. I've always found that particular subject fascinating."

Allegra grinned gratefully, her arms coming up as she placed her hair in a sloppy knot on top of her head. The movement showed off the scars running down both arms. That was the only visible sign that the lively woman had been in that horrible accident a few years before.

"I'm glad someone read them," she said. "This story is a little different. A lot different. I'm not sure it would be up your alley."

Bethany felt her shoulders relax at the mention of her favorite topic. "All books are up my alley. Didn't Michelle tell you? Other people fill their apartments with furniture. I fill mine with books. Old, new, on any topic, and in several different languages. What's the title? Is it fiction or non?"

Ben grinned as a blush darkened Allegra's freckles. "It's called *Bone Daddy*," he answered for her. "And according to my Mimi, it's a rather *educational* read. Legs and Rousseau have been researching for months now."

The man at the large stove sent a mock glare in his friend's direction. "That's quite enough, Adair. I'm sure Bethany will find out about that subject soon enough. Your guest looks hungry, and the jambalaya is ready."

They all took their bowls out to the main dining room and sat down, and Bethany marveled at how casual they were in such a grand place. This room was meant for linen and lace, for silver tureens and folded hands. But Ben had grabbed the ornate wooden chair Michelle was sitting on and dragged it closer, until she was nearly sitting on his lap, and Allegra and Rousseau were leaning against each other as they ate.

She was happy for her friend, though she had to admit, she was also jealous. Reason number one hundred and twenty-two why books were better than people: Happy endings were basically guaranteed, but in the end you knew it was fiction, so you felt better going to bed alone. Michelle's happy ending—and Allegra's—was real. They'd each found their Mr. Right. And Bethany was the fifth wheel.

But to be honest, it wasn't like she was actively looking. She was thirty-seven, a creature of habit, and far too set in her ways to change now. Some people were just destined to be alone. It was better than loving someone who would never love you in return. And it was better than settling for anything less than what these two couples clearly had.

She was just scooping another delicious bite of Rousseau's rich, spicy concoction into her mouth when she felt a cool breeze shimmy up her spine. Something tugged on her braid and she turned, her brow furrowing when she couldn't find the source of the tug. "Do you have cats?"

Michelle's bright green gaze focused on the space behind her. "No, we don't have any cats. Bethany, you believe in ghosts, right?"

"We've had this conversation before, only a few dozen times. You know I do. 'There are more things in heaven and earth' et cetera. Especially in this city. It's hard to believe New Orleans isn't full of spirits." She realized everyone was staring at her and lowered her voice. "Maybe I've read too much paranormal fiction. I believe in fairies, too, but don't let that get around. The people I work for wouldn't understand. They're stuffy that way."

The men chuckled at her humorous tone, but Michelle just smiled. "You and your fairies."

"What? I'm telling you, those pesky buggers steal my reading glasses all the time."

Michelle laughed, falling into their old comfortable banter as though no time had passed. "And then conveniently set them on your head when you aren't paying attention?"

Bethany made a face and everyone laughed again. She couldn't believe it, but she was actually having fun. Maybe her anti-anxiety medication was still working. She couldn't remember the last time she'd bantered with someone who wasn't on the phone or the occasional taxi driver. And living, breathing, gorgeous men usually turned her into a mute with an eye tic.

When Bethany felt another tug on her braid she pulled it over her shoulder protectively, looking around once more in confusion. "You don't have cats. Is it ferrets? Gnomes? Something keeps tugging on my hair."

Michelle raised one brow tellingly.

No way. "Michelle, are you saying . . . ?"

She nodded. "He kind of came with the house. Although he's not stuck here—he can go where he wants. But Ben and I have known him since we were young."

"There's a ghost behind my chair? He's a little short, isn't he?"

The cool air on Bethany's back grew stronger, and Michelle laughed.

"He's a bit sensitive about his height. Especially since we've gotten so much bigger. Bethany, meet Emmanuel. Our resident ghost."

"Oh, hell."

CHAPTER 2

BETHANY BRUSHED HER HAIR ABSENTLY IN FRONT OF THE antique bathroom vanity, thinking about the day's revelations. Her inner agoraphobic was screaming at the top of her lungs that she should pack up her suitcase and grab the nearest plane home. Only there could she be safely surrounded by her books and four plain white walls. No ghost whisperers, no telepaths, and no one who claimed to have been possessed by a voodoo spirit for the last seven years. She liked to read about all those things; she wasn't too sure she enjoyed being *in* the story.

Forget porn movie, she'd landed in an episode of *The Outer Limits*.

The strangest part of the evening? She'd believed every word they said. Especially after Ben held her hand and told her a few things about herself that no one else could know. Not even Michelle. And by the somber looks he threw her way the rest of the evening, she knew he'd seen more than he'd shared. She was thankful that he'd kept it to himself.

After a few glasses of wine, Allegra had opened up about the story she was writing. And the fact that though the masses would believe they were reading erotic fiction they would be wrong.

Bethany was fascinated. This Bone Daddy really existed? A spirit who fed off climax, who knew more about sex than she knew about anything—knew how to bring you to the brink with a touch or a word? Who wouldn't be tempted by someone—or something—like that? Although she couldn't imagine having to give herself over long enough for a voodoo ritual, let alone the years Rousseau had been ridden by the Loa.

The bond between Allegra and Rousseau was clear, made even more so by the knowledge that it was she who'd helped the handsome café owner get control over his life once again.

Over the course of the evening, Michelle had told Beth about her abilities, her childhood adventures with Ben and the ghost Emmanuel, and what he'd told them of his sister Isabel's treasure. Ben admitted he'd bought the mansion while Michelle was in New York, because it reminded him of her.

Bethany smiled at herself in the mirror. He was a charming scoundrel. She couldn't help but like him. They were all very nice, for beautiful people.

She stuck out her tongue at her own average visage. No freckled fairy like Allegra, no exotic siren like Michelle . . . just plain Bethany. Her eyes were blue, but not ice blue or indigo, just blue. Her lips were uneven, the top one fuller than the bottom. She touched her cheek; her skin was smooth, but pale. No distinctive mark or feature that made her stand out in a crowd. Even her body was average. Not too plump, certainly not skinny, but it still did what she asked it to, so she couldn't complain.

Her hair was the one thing she'd always liked. Thick, with a natural wave, it shined from her brushing and hung all the way down her back like a curtain of ebony silk. Her aunt, her mother's sister and the woman who had raised her, once told her that the hair came from *her* side, the Spanish side of the family, but her stubbornness was obviously from her father's Scottish side.

Bethany, nine years old at the time, had spoke with a Scots brogue every night for a week after that, but though she would have loved to spite her aunt more thoroughly, it was Spain's history that always held her in thrall. Spanish was the language she'd studied in school, and Spain's empire the topic of her history thesis. Why couldn't her aunt have been Scottish?

A noise in the corner brought her back to her awareness of the room beyond the unusual private bath, with its own vanity table and small, cushioned chair.

Isabel's room. The reason she was here.

The young woman must have been the apple of her parents' eye, if the room was any indication. It wasn't the master suite, but it may as well have been. It was a large room with walls the color of the Caribbean Sea. A room with its own bath and a door leading out onto the balcony. A room fit for a princess.

That noise again.

"Who's there?" She walked into the bedroom and looked around. No one. "Emmanuel? Great. My first night and I'm already talking to a ghost."

Had the books she'd set on the nightstand been moved? She walked over to the bed. "Michelle told me you were a bit of an imp. But she said you were a good friend, and I shouldn't be nervous that blood would leak from the walls or you'd toss my bed around while I'm sleeping. She also said Isabel's hidden panel was in this room, and she'd kept everything there for safekeeping until

I arrived. I wonder if you can help me find it. Not that I'm snooping or anything."

She was babbling to herself. Lovely.

One of the books had fallen to the floor. That must have been the noise she'd heard. She knelt down, her legs tangling in her nightgown as she reached for the book. A cool breeze rode up her spine once more, and she took a deep, calming breath. "Okay, so you're trying to tell me something. Or this is a very drafty old house."

She looked at the wooden floor where the book had fallen. There was a board that looked more worn then the others. "She said panel, not floorboard." The air grew colder, and Bethany shrugged. "All right, I'll look. But if you make me break the rich man's house for no reason, I'm totally blaming you."

It was loose, but not loose enough to have been moved recently. This was *not* the secret hiding place Michelle had been talking about. It couldn't be.

She lifted the board and reached up for her small book light, flipping it on and lowering it into the small space she'd uncovered. Letters. It looked like there were three of them. Folded carefully, yellowed with age, they were tied together with a ribbon of lace. She lifted them gently and then her light caught something glinting beneath them.

A locket? She reached for the chain and felt a zap of electricity. Strange. "Michelle is going to be mad you didn't tell her about this, Manuel. I hope you don't mind me calling you that. Emmanuel just seems like such a big name for such a little boy."

She waited for the breeze that signified his presence but felt nothing. Had he left now that she'd found what he wanted her to find? "Hey, Shorty."

Nothing. He had to be gone. She would have gotten a tug on her hair for sure after that remark.

Adrenaline raced through her system. Letters. She gathered up her treasure and hopped onto the bed, lowering the blankets and fluffing the pillows to get comfortable. Were they invitations? Letters from suitors? They must be something special for Isabel, or whoever had lived in this room after her, to have been tucked away so stealthily.

She wrapped the old-fashioned locket around her neck, pinning it to her nightgown. Somehow it felt right to wear it as she carefully untied the lace and unfolded the first letter. She would be the first person to read these since they'd been hidden! The thrill of discovery made her giddy. She slipped on her black-framed reading glasses.

Eighteen twenty-seven. That was the date at the top of the letter. The month of September. Nearly two hundred years ago.

"Good grief."

There was no formal address at the beginning. No indication of who it was at the bottom. Was it a journal entry? She started to read, biting her cheek to hold back her squeak of excitement.

Other suitors would speak of your beauty, call you "my darling, my dearest." Others may compare you to a cold and distant goddess. You are far from cold, fiery Isabel. You are passion incarnate, sent to tempt me . . .

"Oh my." Bethany caressed the brass locket as she read. Her body heated, her mouth forming the words that detailed how well this man knew Isabel's body. About the night he'd come to her room, how he'd climbed up to her balcony. How she'd let him in.

1827
New Orleans

"You shouldn't be here, Marcel." Isabel knew herself to be a hypocrite. If he had any inkling of how desperately she'd wanted him to come, how she'd paced her rooms praying that he would, it would make a mockery of her protest. And now . . . what if someone found them?

"Isabel, my fire. How could I stay away?"

Dios mio, how could one man be so beautiful? She couldn't tear her gaze away as he shut the balcony doors, turned the lock, and started to undress.

She raised a hand to cover her breasts, easily visible beneath the thin white nightgown, and he bit his lower lip, then spoke, his voice rasping and low. "Don't cover yourself, Isabel. Not from me. I've seen those perfect breasts, held them in my hands, though not long enough for my liking. Our first time was too short. I need more."

Oh, she did, too. Some of her friends, recently wed, told horror stories about the honeymoon night. Perhaps she was of lesser moral fiber. Or maybe it was her mother's French blood. Whatever the cause, her desire for Marcel had made their first tryst at her friend's masked ball the most exciting, romantic night of her life, despite her scandalous behavior.

He'd found her in the library, where she'd gone to get away from all the puffed up Creole dandies. Young and old men of fortune or title, sometimes both. All seeking an alliance with her family. Her name. Praising her beauty, as though it was an accomplishment, her *only* accomplishment. All of them left her cold.

Marcel had taken off his mask and she'd recognized him as the handsome rider she'd seen on her walks with Catherine. The one who always seemed to run into them, getting off his horse to talk to Isabel about the book she was holding, or the weather, or the latest news of the town. The man she'd been dreaming of for months.

Catherine had known everything about him and wasted no time in telling her after their first meeting. Their mothers both studied under Marie Laveau, learning to be hairdressers by day and voodoo priestesses by night. Catherine and Marcel traveled in the same circles. The circles her father would have beaten her soundly for being aware of.

According to Catherine, Marcel's mother had been the belle of her quadroon ball, so beautiful everyone wanted her, despite the rumors of her ties to voodoo. His father was a Frenchman Isabel knew well, since his acknowledged heir from his *recognized* marriage had been attempting to court her all season. Their fathers talked business and smoked cigars while their mothers had tea, all of them ignoring the arrangement of *plaçage* he'd made with the Creole woman, and the son that had come from that union. It was a scandalous story of lust and infidelity, one Isabel shouldn't be privy to.

Just as Marcel should not have been allowed to the party that night at all. Yet he had come. For her. And showed her that all the rumors she'd heard about him were true. He was an exquisite lover. She could not resist his advances, did not want to. When he'd set her on the desk and knelt at her feet . . . She'd had no idea a mouth could do such things. It was she who had begged for more, who eagerly bent over her friend's father's desk and lifted her skirts for him. For Marcel.

Perhaps there *was* something wrong with her, for even though she had searched her heart these past few days, she could find no trace of regret.

She lifted her chin defiantly, though it trembled. Her body's reaction to him was frightening. Overwhelming. Perhaps he'd bewitched her.

"You have other lovers. I've heard the women whispering about you. Even Catherine says you dallied with one of her cousins for a time. Why not seek out one of them if you are in need?"

He was naked now, aroused. Her thighs quivered, her skin flushing as she tried not to stare. He stalked her like a jungle predator, backing her up until her thighs hit the bed. "Catherine is no authority on my love life, my sweet. And you should never listen to idle gossip." He caressed her cheek with the backs of his fingers, and she shivered. "I will never lie to you, Isabel. There have been others whom I've pleasured well. Virgins, as you were, who offered themselves to me, and experienced women who craved more than their fat, pale husbands could provide. It is a fact I have taken great pride in."

Isabel flinched and turned her back on him, but he gripped her shoulders firmly, refusing to give her space. "You *will* hear this. The stories are true. But they are all in the past. From the moment I laid eyes on my fire flower, my Isabel, no other would do. I'd risk everything for another taste of you, for one smile from those luscious lips. I need you, only you. Look into my eyes and know I speak the truth."

He turned her back toward him and she found herself lost in his blazing amber gaze. She knew. What was between them was too powerful to be a lie. Too strong for rules to bind. She was his.

"Kiss me, Marcel."

"*Yes.*"

She cupped his jaw with her slender hand, marveling. They were nearly the same color. Light bronze, golden skin. So similar and yet their worlds were never allowed to touch. "Touch me. Please."

"I've been dreaming of you saying those exact words for days, sweet Isabel. Forever."

He slipped off her nightgown and lowered her gently onto the bed. But she didn't want gentle. Everyone treated her as though she were made of porcelain. Cold. But Marcel called to the fire inside her. He knew her need was as great as his own. She wanted to be taken as he took her that first night.

Feeling his hard body pressed against hers, no skirts or ruffles, no buttons between them, was heaven. He lifted his head from her neck and she could see in his expression that he felt the same. Her hands lifted from their lax position by her head, reaching up to run her fingers through his cacao-colored curls. Like warm silk in her palms. She tugged.

Marcel smiled. "Impatient, love? We have all night."

Isabel moaned in frustration. She was unstudied. One of his other lovers may know how to entice him, how to show him that the slow kisses he was peppering her shoulders with, her breasts with . . . *yes, just there* . . . were not enough.

His erection telegraphed his heartbeat against the curve of her hip and she held her breath. Did she dare to touch him as she had so often in her daydreams? To taste him as he had tasted her? Could she be so bold?

One of her hands left his hair and slid down his tensing back. His lips paused on her hard nipple, his body still as he waited to see what she would do. Her fingers tingled as they slid around his hip, feeling the bone and sinew, the fine hairs on his body. Her hand slid between their bodies and curled around his hot shaft, her lashes fluttering at the bolt of electricity that shot up her arm and into her core.

"Oh."

"Oh?" Marcel growled. "Is that all you can say? Grip it tighter, Isabel. Yes, like that. It doesn't hurt. It feels . . . *Merde*, love, it feels so . . ."

"Perfect."

Bethany nearly tumbled out of bed as the masculine groan echoed through the room. No one was there. She noticed the letter, slightly crumpled in her hand, and swore. What had happened? How could she have fallen asleep in the middle of reading such a priceless letter? She should have been more careful.

Marcel.

"What a dream."

Somehow the letter from Isabel's rather descriptive bed partner had become one hell of a realistic sexual fantasy for her. One that had ended too soon. Her body was on fire for her late night lover. For *Isabel's* lover.

"Why Marcel? There are tons of other names to choose from. Jacques. Pierre. Etienne. Okay, not Etienne, but still, Marcel?" She shrugged, pushing back the covers and refolding the letter to set it carefully on top of the others on the bedside table.

Only she would take a simple piece of correspondence and turn it into a saga of star-crossed lovers. That kind of story always ended badly. The reality was no doubt simpler to explain. Sweet, innocent Isabel was not so innocent, and she had a bit too much fun during her coming out. But, according to Michelle, no one knew what happened to her. There were no records of her existence. No paintings. Not even the ghost, Emmanuel, could tell her what had happened to her.

Maybe she'd run away with her lover.

Maybe she was buried in the walls.

Beth got up and shuffled her feet across the smooth wooden floor. She turned on the faucet on the bathroom vanity sink and splashed her face. "I should have brought my toys. Who cares if the security cameras see them? Or guards pull them out in front of everyone at the airport and embarrass me. Am I supposed to buy new ones every time I travel?"

Bethany looked into the mirror and was swept away. She was Isabel. Beautiful, blue-eyed, raven-haired Isabel. Naked and being fucked against the vanity by a lust-crazed Marcel.

"Isabel! It's late. Your papa wishes to know if you are coming down for breakfast."

Marcel's growl rumbled against her back at the voice on the other side of the door, his thrusts increasing in speed and power, filling her, shaking the furniture with his need. "Tell her you'll be down soon. Tell her to go away, Isabel. That you're coming."

"Go now and tell him, um, oh, I'll be down soon. Tell him I'm coming. I'm coming!"

OH GOD, BETHANY WAS COMING. STANDING AT THE SINK IN her friends' house, she was moaning and trembling as though she'd just had the best sex of her life.

"What the hell?"

She hesitated before glancing in the mirror again. Her skin was flushed, her eyes sparkling, and her body trembling from the waves of pleasure rocking through it, but she was still her. Still Bethany Sorelle.

"Good lord, talk about jet lag." Maybe it was the wine. The medicine definitely should have worn off by now. Besides, if one of them had a side effect of spontaneous climax, there'd be a run on the pharmacy.

It was that letter, and the romance in the air. Combined with all their talk of the sexual Loa, Bone Daddy, surely that supplied her fertile imagination with enough fodder for a highly detailed fantasy.

That was her story and she was sticking to it.

She needed to go to sleep. Forget the day and the plane ride and that erotic missive. She would wake up in the morning refreshed and ready to help Michelle study Isabel's treasure. She had to remember to avoid her boyfriend Ben's touch, since the last thing she wanted was for him or anyone else to know about her strong reaction to an old musty love letter. They might think she was a lonely, desperate woman.

They might be right.

Bethany snuggled back into the four-poster bed, staring at the folded letter as though it would come alive at any moment. The man's masculine scrawl was burned into her brain. Bold, strong, confident.

He had seduced Isabel—that much was obvious. His words made it clear he wasn't about to let her forget what they'd done together. That explained the sexuality of her dream. But where had the other parts come from? The friend, the servant, her concerns about the difference in their stations, not to mention her internal conflict about her own desires. It was so detailed. So real.

Maybe because she desperately wanted it to be. Wanted to be Isabel, just for a moment. To have that kind of passion directed at her.

She rolled onto her side and heard the jangle of the locket chain. She'd forgotten she was wearing it. She reached up to take it off and then hesitated. She didn't want to. Her fingers stroked the intricate flower engraved in the brass of the locket and it soothed her, lulled her.

She'd take it off in the morning. Take it off and show Michelle, adding it to the other things her friend had found of Isabel's. But she wasn't sure she wanted to show her the letters. Not just yet. Not until she'd had a chance to read them first.

"Marcel." She breathed the name on a sleepy sigh, a part of her hoping she'd dream of him again. Even if he wasn't real.

CHAPTER 3

HE WAS IN THE ST. LOUIS CEMETERY NEAR BASIN STREET. Drawn before the first rays of dawn, compelled to this place, though he wasn't sure why. He'd arrived in time to witness the departure of the teenagers in ghoulish masks who'd dared each other to brave Halloween beside the mausoleums and grave sites.

Luckily for them, the Ghede looked after foolish children. In his experience, when humans looked for trouble, they usually found it.

He reached a beautiful marble mausoleum, smaller than the others. The profile of a lovely woman's face was carved into the doorway like a heartbreaking cameo, just above the image of a small boy at play. She looked young. Had she died in childbirth? He searched for a name, but there was none. No family name, nor the years she'd lived and died. Why would someone go to all this trouble to make a remembrance so lovely, only to keep the dead's identity secret?

That was his idea of hell. To be unremembered and unsung.

"You're here."

Bone Daddy whirled around but saw only shadows. Still, he knew the old man's voice.

"I am. I thought All Saints' didn't require me to possess a body. Please don't tell me I must pry open a dead grave and take over a corpse." He shuddered. "I would not enjoy my last day on earth in a state of decay."

The laughter wrapped around him like an embrace, making him smile.

"No, son. You'll have a body all your own, fresh and living, as promised, for the day. I'll tell you why you're here, but first I have to warn you to be careful. You'll be human. No powers. No magnetism other than your own natural charm. You'll feel hot and cold, suffer the pangs you never felt, even when you rode Rousseau. And you'll feel strong emotions, just as humans do. And just as with humans, there will be repercussions for your actions. If you step too far out of line, you may not like the consequences."

Bone Daddy rubbed his hands together in excitement. His mentor was always so ominous. He really needed to lighten up. "Sounds like fun, old man. Want to join me? I know a few spots down the road that you would love."

The deep sigh was a breeze in the damp morning air. "Some of us have to stay behind, to keep the home fires burning. It's time, BD. Time for you to have your day. Use it well. Try not to waste a moment."

"Why aren't the others here? You said you'd tell me why I had to come to this cemetery."

"One journey begins where the last met its end."

He knew the old man was gone, he could feel it. "A riddle. Lovely."

Bone Daddy didn't care. The dawn was coming. The sky had lightened, setting the stage for the new day. His day.

He would seek out his friends, have as much food as he could fit in his stomach, and take as many lovers as he could. Maybe he could convince Rousseau to put the past behind them. He'd grown fond of the boy.

He'd grown rather attached to all of them. Michelle and Ben, Allegra. He'd come to the conclusion over the last few days that the other Loa were right. He'd lost his perspective. He was no family ghost. No pet. He was supposed to help. To guide humans as the others did toward a better life. Or in his case, a better sex life.

Attachment was not wise.

Soft morning light hit the graying stones and monuments around him, and he began to feel it. A shimmer. A tingle. Little ants on his skin.

Skin?

He looked down and saw himself change. Slowly. With every second it hurt more. Everything hurt. Heaviness, like lead in his limbs, dropped him to his knees.

"Damn."

What was going on? The ants on his skin had become a vicious mass of fangs and stingers, piercing him, sending fire racing through his veins. Blood. Blood pumped by a heart beating far too fast to be natural.

Something was wrong. This couldn't be right. Would he be given life just to die? Surely the others didn't willingly go through this year after year. Was this part of his punishment for staying so long?

Dizziness swamped him, and bile rose in his throat as he smelled the stench of garbage and death. Smelled the staleness of sweat. His own?

He gagged, but nothing came out. His stomach began to spasm and he looked up wildly, seeking purchase, balance, in a world gone sideways.

And saw her. The carving in marble. She looked so serene. So lovely.

Familiar.

Why did she look familiar?

He collapsed, looking down in surprise to see a wound carving itself into his side. He cried out, but before the blood could flow the wound healed, a scar forming before his eyes. A raised, ugly slash.

It felt as though he'd been gutted. His hands closed into fists, body curling into a fetal position as the pain overcame him.

This was *not* what he'd been expecting.

The last thought he had before he fell into unconsciousness was of her. The woman in the carving. At least he'd be lying beside her as he died.

The thought was comforting.

"You really didn't have to come, Allegra. You're getting married tonight. You should be relaxing."

Allegra slipped her arm through Bethany's, sending her an impish wink. "Are you kidding? This is perfect. A morning adventure. I've never been here this early, but I love this place."

Michelle rolled her eyes. "You love cemeteries? I should have known. Why do I always befriend the weird ones?"

Bethany noticed how uncomfortable Michelle was, and it took her a minute to realize why. "Is it, um, busy this morning?"

Michelle rubbed her arms briskly, keeping her head down. "It's All Saints' Day. It's like Times Square on New Year's."

Bethany shuddered. "That's more than a little unsettling."

Allegra's eyes were wide as saucers. "I'm so sorry, Michelle. I hadn't even thought about ghosts. Well, other than Emmanuel. Are we sure he knows where we're going?"

"He knows."

Now she felt like a heel. Bethany trudged along beside the two women, her head swimming. She hadn't considered Michelle's ability when she'd asked to come here this morning. Hadn't considered anything but Isabel.

She was obsessed.

She'd spent the last two days immersing herself in Isabel's journal and studying the trinkets she'd saved behind the panel.

Isabel's treasure wasn't what she had expected. An intricate silver hair comb, a smooth river stone, and a puzzle box they still hadn't been able to open had been tucked away in her hiding spot along with her diary.

She was an interesting character, Isabel. Bethany had been learning so much about her. Her father was an ass. That much was clear. He had been using his daughter's beauty to barter, holding her hostage to his own greed. He'd sent his wife away long ago, and the elder Spaniard missed no opportunity to blame her French mother for all his woes and each of Isabel's flaws.

Her only solace was her maid, Millie, Millie's cousin Catherine, and her little brother, Emmanuel. They protected her from her father's abuse as much as they could. Keeping all of her secrets.

She also spoke of a man in her journals. A man she referred to as M. Just M.

I love M. If God is good, he will let us find a way to be together.

M came to me the other night. It was like a dream.

It was like *her* dream, and it was damned eerie. Bethany hadn't told anyone about the letters yet, or about her nightly visits from Marcel. She wasn't afraid they wouldn't believe her. But it was hers. He was hers.

Her secret lover.

She looked forward to going to bed each night, knowing he would come to her again. Sometimes it was a repeat of that first night. Sometimes she was Isabel when he'd found her in the library. Or in their favorite spot in the park. Always passionate, always fiery.

She was falling a little in love with M herself.

Bethany knew it was crazy. But she didn't care. They were just dreams. Though the more she read Isabel's journal, the more she wondered. Was the mysterious M *her* Marcel? If it were true . . . but how could it be?

"The reception will be good for him. I think Rousseau needs to realize that his father's way is not the only way. That people like your mother practice the voodoo religion for positive ends. With faith and love instead of greed. He needs to find peace. Come full circle."

Michelle shook her head at Allegra. "You know my mama. Her celebrations are unique. I'll understand if you and Rousseau don't stay too long after the ceremony. Hell, if Ben wasn't holding it in his backyard, I wouldn't stay long."

Bethany listened to their conversation with only half her attention. Poor Rousseau. Another bad father. Like Isabel's. Like Michelle's. Bethany often wondered about her own parents, but they'd died when she was a baby, leaving her in the care of her less than demonstrative Aunt Sally.

She'd read Allegra's notes and a few chapters of the book she was writing. If it had been fiction, she would have been lost in the eroticism of it, the sensuality of this spirit who mounted a human host, riding him into one decadent experience after another. But she knew it was true. Rousseau had lived it. And in his mind, at least from what Allegra had told her, it had felt more like a punishment than a gift.

Allegra was good for him, though. She wouldn't let him feel sorry for himself. Wouldn't let him forget the good and cling to the bad. She was a joyful person, full of life. Beth hoped they lasted.

Personally she was both dreading and looking forward to the evening's celebrations. Michelle's mother was a mambo, a voodoo priestess. A fact Michelle had neglected to mention until recently.

After the minister married Allegra and Rousseau in the mansion's backyard, which was being beautifully decorated by the team Ben had brought in, the All Saints' celebration would begin. People would bring liquor and food for the Ghede, the Loa family who celebrated the night, and maybe someone would even be taken over, or mounted, by a spirit. Eventually they would all make their way to the cemeteries where their loved ones were entombed, to lay flowers, cards, and food.

As long as she had a good seat for that, and didn't have to talk to too many strangers, it sounded like fun to Bethany. She wondered if Isabel had celebrated the day. Or her M.

"He's pretty excited. I think he's found it." Michelle smiled at

Bethany. "That was really clever of you. I never thought to ask him where he was buried. I wasn't sure he knew."

Bethany felt her heart quicken. Families were usually buried close together. Though there was no record of Isabel, she was sure there would be some clue, something that would help her discover what had happened to the young woman. Emmanuel might be the key.

"You've got to be kidding me." Michelle sounded shocked.

Bethany turned the corner, her eyes on a lovely miniature mausoleum. It was beautifully preserved, but Michelle was looking on the ground beside it, her mouth open.

Allegra shouted in surprise. "Holy hell! Is that guy dead?"

Michelle whirled around. "Wait, *you* can see him? Tell me what you see."

The redhead squinted, looking carefully before she answered. "A hot naked man, hopefully just passed out, lying on the ground."

Michelle looked at Bethany, who was having a hard time lifting her gaze away from the most perfectly formed male ass she'd ever seen. "I see him, too. I think it's safe to say he's not a ghost. Yet."

Michelle knelt beside him, feeling his neck for a pulse. "He's breathing. You don't understand." She rolled him over and the women all gasped. He was beautiful.

"This is Bone Daddy."

"No way." Allegra joined her on the ground, studying the perfectly sculpted face, the full lips, and long, velvet lashes. "This is Bone Daddy? He looks so young. So—"

"Alive?" Michelle rubbed her temple. "I have no idea how this could happen. This is no possession. It's really him, in physical form. I need to talk to my mother. And Ben." She slid her hand into her jeans pocket and pulled out her cell phone with shaking fingers.

Bethany was having a hard time catching her breath. He looked just like the man in her dreams. Marcel. Had the Loa been visiting her in her sleep? Making all her fantasies come true? Fooling her?

She took Michelle's place at his side, needing to get a closer look at his face. Allegra took off her shawl and covered his hips, which helped. How was a woman supposed to concentrate when such a perfect specimen appeared at your feet, naked and hung like a . . . Well, superiorly endowed.

"I know him." She didn't know she'd whispered out loud until Allegra gripped her arm.

Bethany looked up to see Allegra's confusion. "How can you?"

She blushed. "I've dreamt about him."

"Well, damn." Michelle was standing over her, phone in hand. "I was wondering where he'd been keeping himself. Ben's on his way over to help get him into the car, and Mama is coming over to the house right away."

Allegra chuckled, making the other two women turn her way with worried expressions. "Don't you see? It's perfect. He's here. Bone Daddy is human. On mine and Rousseau's wedding day." She clutched Michelle's hand. "It's perfect."

Bethany looked down to watch those long dark lashes flutter open, revealing stunning amber eyes. Oh God, it was him.

He tried to focus, swallowing a moan of pain as he turned his head and caught her gaze with his own. He blinked. His tongue came out to wet his dry lips, and she leaned closer, riveted.

"Not quite ready for three of you yet, *cher*. But if you find me a bed, I will give you a morning to remember." His eyes rolled back in his head and he was gone again.

"Priceless." Allegra fell on her butt as her laughter overtook her. "That is definitely Bone Daddy."

Michelle chuckled at Allegra's mirth. "Without a doubt."

Bethany bit her lip hard, resisting the urge to give that perfect nose of his a good punch. Bone Daddy, huh?

Great.

CHAPTER 4

SOMEONE MUST HAVE GOTTEN DRUNK LAST NIGHT. THE hangover was so bad even *he* could feel it. He tried to separate himself from the pain, as he had in the past, but it wasn't working. In fact, the harder he tried to focus, the more it hurt. The throbbing convinced him that he wasn't in Rousseau or anyone else. He was in his own body. Human.

So far the experience wasn't going exactly as he'd planned.

He shifted his legs beneath the thin sheet that covered him. He was in a bed. That was a step in the right direction. Better than a cemetery for the things he had planned.

Had he only dreamed that Allegra and Michelle had found him? And the other female, who was she? Blue eyes like the deepest ocean. A sharp, stubborn chin he wanted to bite. He hadn't seen the rest of her but he was sure it would be just as delectable.

"He must be thinking good thoughts."

"Very good."

Bone Daddy kept his eyes closed, fighting the urge to smile. Michelle and Blue Eyes. He knew it was her. His erection grew thicker and he breathed out slowly, enjoying the sensation of blood and need filling his cock. It ached, but it was a good ache. He was also enjoying the knowledge that she was watching him, watching his growing arousal push against the sheet toward her.

Come closer, cher. *You know you want to.*

"Are you sure you'll be okay alone? Someone needs to keep an eye on him, but I really want to find out what Mama has to say about this. Plus, Allegra's dress needs—"

"I'll be fine, Michelle. I'll just read. Honestly, I'm not sure what all the Bone Daddy fuss is about."

"What about those dreams you were telling Allegra about?" Michelle sounded amused. *He* was not.

"They were just dreams. Reality is something entirely different. Unfortunately."

"So you're saying you don't find him irresistibly attractive?" Good girl, Michelle. She sounded dubious. As she should, Bone Daddy inwardly huffed, waiting to hear the answer.

Blue Eyes paused, hesitating as though studying him again. "He's too . . . *pretty,* don't you think? I can't imagine wanting to date a man that pretty. Ruggedly handsome, yes, even large and adorable—but truly pretty? You'll always wonder if he'll like your new lace panties more on *you* or on himself."

He held himself totally still through Michelle's sobs of laughter. Didn't move a muscle until he heard the door shut behind her, heard the chair creak as Blue Eyes leaned back with a sigh.

And then he pounced.

He heard her breath rush out of her lungs and felt his own

body throb in pain when her knee jammed into his side, but he got her beneath him. He stared into her shocked bottomless eyes and smiled.

"Too pretty? Blue Eyes, you have no idea what kind of trouble you've gone and gotten yourself in to."

Those blue eyes darkened, pupils dilated, and he knew she was feeling the heat of his erection pressing between her thighs through the sheet and her black cotton pants. He pressed the full weight of his hips against her, his body reacting to her softness beneath him, the smell of her.

"Oh, *cher*. You have no idea how good this feels. Just give me a minute to enjoy it, and then I'll prove to you just how rugged and adorable I can b— *Oomph!*"

He landed between the bed and the chair, the hard drop to the wood floor jarring him from his tailbone to his teeth. "Fuck."

Blue Eyes leapt off the bed to kneel beside him, the concern in her expression slightly gratifying. Slightly.

He smiled through gritted teeth. "Are you always so friendly, *cher*?"

She flipped her long, raven-colored braid over her shoulder and pursed her lips. Damn she was cute. "Only when I'm physically accosted by a sleeping Loa-turned-human with a penchant for canoodling with anything that moves."

His bark of laughter surprised him, along with her wit. "Canoodling? I don't think I've heard anyone use that term in . . . let's see . . . actually, never. At least, not in relation to me. They prefer words like: pleasured, satisfied, fucked like they've never been fucked before."

"And humble. So I've heard."

She jerked to a standing position, crossing her arms over her lovely breasts. She was trying to distract him, but he could tell she was blushing. And trying, unsuccessfully, not to look at his naked body.

"You should get back in bed," she said severely.

"Only if you join me, *cher*."

Her expression wasn't amused. Tempted. But not amused. He started to stand up and cringed, more than he needed to, he admitted to himself, but it *did* hurt. Had he gotten a bad body? It was already mid-morning. He didn't have time for all this laying about.

He cringed again. "Damn."

Small, strong arms wrapped around his waist as Blue Eyes helped him back to bed. She liked him. A little. He could tell.

When he was sitting up, the sheet safely draped across his persistent erection once more, he held out his hand. "Since we have yet to be formally introduced, you can call me BD. And what can I call you, Blue Eyes?"

"Bethany."

"Beautiful name for a beautiful woman."

She smirked at him, and his brow furrowed. What was wrong with her? Wounded, dominant, gallant . . . did nothing work on her?

"Do you like men, Blue Eyes?"

Her laughter stung his pride, but at least she wasn't leaving. She relaxed into the chair beside him, allowing him time to study her. It was subtle, her beauty. As though she worked to hide it. No makeup, hair pulled back in a braid, oversized T-shirt. But she couldn't hide the intelligence in her eyes, or that full, sensual upper lip. He wanted to suck it into his mouth. *Merde*, he hoped she liked men. She did say he was pretty.

"I suppose I'll have to forgive your arrogance. If only because you were there for Michelle when I couldn't be."

The *djab*. Michelle must have told her. And she knew about him as well. This Bethany grew more fascinating by the second.

"You are a friend of Michelle Toussaint? Not from around here. Not with that accent. New York?"

Bethany leaned closer, curiosity making her careless. "Don't you know? Can't you read my mind?"

He shifted carefully, not wanting to startle her, and smiled. "Alas, for today at least, I am without any of my regular abilities. Simply a flesh and blood man."

"So you have no idea what I'm thinking right now?"

He leaned forward until his lips were one breath away from hers. She didn't move away. "No, Blue Eyes. But I'd like to think I can guess."

Bone Daddy held himself back, willing her to cover the small distance between them, to kiss him. He wanted, rather desperately, to feel her lips against his own. Those unusual lips.

She stared into his eyes, her curiosity turning to wonder. "Marcel." She pressed her lips to his and he moaned, so intent on his need for the kiss that it took him a moment to register what she'd said.

Marcel?

1827
New Orleans

She'd come. He hadn't wanted her to come here. Not here. She'd shown up at his door, a cloak covering her tear-stained face from the curious ladies of the evening that were his neighbors.

Shame filled him. He lived in a hotel-cum-brothel, no place for a young lady of social standing. No place for Isabel.

"I told you I'd meet you at our spot in the park tomorrow. Do you know what could happen if anyone found you here? What they would do to me—to you?"

"Catherine said she saw you with one of the Devereaux sisters. I just thought—"

He lifted her off his rickety bed by her shoulders, frustration making him rougher than he usually was. "And I saw you at my father's soiree last eve, Isabel. Dancing every dance with my half brother, Antoine." The man who was determined to run him out of New Orleans and steal Isabel merely because he knew Marcel wanted her. "Yet, *I* trusted *you*. Knew you were acting according to expectations, knew you were faithful to me."

She struggled against his hold, not to pull away but to pull him closer. "I trust you, Marcel. You know that I do. You are my world. I'm just so afraid my father will force me to marry before you say we can go. I couldn't live that way. I couldn't live watching you find another, letting another man touch me. Tell me it will be soon, my love. Please."

He wrapped her in his embrace, pushing off her cloak to bury his face in her sweetly scented hair. He had done this to them. Taken advantage of her innocence and ruined her future, merely because he could not live without her.

He'd asked his mother for advice, but she just pushed him, the way she always had, toward his bastard father. "This town is the only place I know you wouldn't be shot on sight for associating with a non-negro woman," she'd told him. "You need capital. The fancy French school your daddy sent you to don't mean nothin' in this world. Ask him for his help. He still owes me. I let him out of our agreement so he could marry that heiress. He promised he would take care of you. If he says no . . . I will just have to remind him who he is dealing with. Maybe tell him a thing or two about that pasty weasel Antoine."

Marcel was tired of all the double standards. The French and the Spanish men came in, waved their money around and took whatever women pleased them, made rules so they could have more. Women became octoroons, quadroons, anything but black. But a man . . . one drop of blood, one trace, and you were black. And if you were black, you had better not fall in love with anyone who wasn't.

Especially not a half-French, half-Spanish debutante who made him so crazy he knew he'd die if he lost her.

She was waiting for his answer. And he knew what he had to do. "Soon, Isabel. Soon, you and I will be able to walk through town proudly as man and wife. Soon I'll be able to tell everyone you are mine."

She lifted her eyes to his, some of the sparkle returning to the deep, damp blue. "And you are mine."

He turned her, tossing her on his small bed with a smile. "Show me."

His heart raced when she reached down and grabbed the hem of her long, lacy blue day dress, pulling it slowly up to reveal her stockings . . . and nothing else.

"You came all the way here alone, with nothing beneath your skirts?" He didn't know whether to spank her or kiss her. Her mound was so prettily framed, making his mouth water, that he decided the spanking could wait.

He lowered himself between her legs, noticing her mischievous smile. Still so pure. He hoped she never lost her innocent sensuality. "You are a naughty girl, Miss Isabel."

She giggled when he leaned in to kiss her forehead, her nose, her lips, his body wound tight with restraint, determined to make her forget the dingy room and the raucous noises outside his door.

"A naughty, naughty girl. But I love it."

PRESENT

Bone Daddy pulled his lips from hers to drag in a lungful of air. Bethany was on his lap, hips grinding against his through the cotton sheet, her moans making him crazy.

His hands were beneath her T-shirt, inside the cups of her bra, her hard nipples piercing his palms with their heat.

The other images were fading like a strange dream, until all he felt was Bethany. All he saw was Bethany. He needed her. He'd never needed anything this badly. He had to be inside her soon or he would combust. "Blue Eyes, please. Take them off for me."

He tugged sightlessly at her jeans, marveling at how his skills had abandoned him. He wasn't playing her like a violin, controlling her passion, thriving on it. If anything, she was playing him, and he was too caught up in his own desires to care.

He growled in gratitude when her hands left his hair and slid to the waistband of her pants. She rose up on her knees to lower them and he kissed the curve of her belly, willing her to move faster, his hands sliding up her thighs.

Yes. Oh, sweet heaven, yes.

"Rousseau thought when Bone Daddy woke up he might be—"

He made a sound of pained denial when the object of his attention ripped herself from his arms, again, leaping with a speed and height that would have been impressive if he wasn't so frustrated.

Allegra stood in the doorway, a tray full of food in her hands and a comical expression of shock on her face. Not directed at him, he noticed, but at the beet-red Bethany, who looked beyond mortified at the intrusion.

She mumbled her apologies and rushed past the redhead in the doorway, out of his sight.

He didn't like frustration. "Son of a bitch."

The tray rattled as Allegra jumped at his curse. She came to set the tray down on the dresser, her expression apologetic. "I'm so sorry, Bone Daddy. I really am. I thought you were still unconscious. And none of us thought that you and Bethany would . . ."

He stood, letting the sheet drop to his ankles, his stance wide, as if preparing for battle. "Why not Bethany and I? Am I not good enough for her? Am I beneath her?"

Allegra paled. "Of course—that's not what I meant to say at all. Bethany just isn't, um, very social." She shrugged helplessly, looking for all the world like he'd kicked her puppy.

"Oh, *cher*, forgive me. It's been an unusual morning." She sniffled, and he wanted to bang his head against the wall. He wrapped an arm around her. "There now, Allegra. Why would you cry?"

"It's my wedding day."

As if that explained everything. But in a way, it did. "Well, surely that is a reason to celebrate. I should have known Rousseau would waste no time in snapping you up. On All Saints' Day, too, eh? Good for him. The Loa and all your ancestors will dance at your wedding. Your life will be blessed."

"And your life will be over if you don't get your hands off my woman and cover yourself." Rousseau and Ben stood in the doorway. Ben had his hand on Rousseau, restraining him, but Bone Daddy could see from his grim expression he didn't approve of the embrace either.

Ingrates.

He lifted his hands from Allegra and took a step back, smiling. "Good to see you, too, boys. I'd love to get dressed so I can find Bethany and pick up where we left off. *If* one of you would be good enough to loan me a pair of pants, that is. I seem to be lacking in the basic necessities this morning."

"Bethany?" The two men spoke in unison, their matching expressions of bewilderment making him angry.

"If I live to be a thousand years old I will never understand the human male. The butterfly that trembles inside her cocoon owns the brightest pair of wings. And when she soars, it is a sight to behold."

The men looked on as Allegra ignored them and wrapped her arms around the naked Bone Daddy once more, squeezing him tightly. "I'm so glad you're here."

He chuckled, his wary gaze still fixed on Rousseau. He understood his possessive friend. He knew if he'd found someone touching Isabel that way he would kill them.

Isabel? What the hell had happened back there? Was Bethany a witch to send him such illusions, to drive him wild with her kiss and her sharp tongue? The men continued glaring and he sighed.

"You may be the only one, *cher*."

SHE HAD TO LEAVE. IF SHE COULD WORK UP THE COURAGE to leave the bedroom, that is. How could she have behaved that way? And with someone who was tantamount to a spiritual gigolo no less. It was humiliating.

And she wanted to do it again.

It was so much better than the dreams. In the dreams she'd had no control. She was Isabel, submissive and shy, newly coming into her own as a woman. But just now, Bethany was the one kissing him, the one driving him, making him lose control.

She wasn't usually like this. This sexual. She was no virgin, but her experiences had always been with friends, awkward and unsatisfying. Her imagination, her books were her outlet. But with Bone Daddy, she couldn't seem to control herself.

Her mouth curved upward in the start of a grin as she recalled the expression on his face when she'd thrown him off the bed. She wondered if anyone had ever said no to him before. Not that her denial had lasted very long. There was just something about him.

She could no longer doubt that it was him, not the unknown Marcel, who had haunted her dreams. Him she'd made love to in the night for the last few days, in the guise of Isabel. The young lovers' story had consumed so much of her daytime studies that it made sense they would insert themselves into her dreams.

But why would Bone Daddy?

BD. He'd told her to call him BD.

"Bethany? Can I come in?" Michelle pushed open the door to her bedroom and closed it behind her, her green eyes darkening with worry when she noticed the open suitcase on the bed. "Are you okay?"

"Sure. Fine. Couldn't be better. Why do you ask?" Bethany scooted back against the pillows to make room for Michelle, who'd come to sit beside her.

Michelle looked down at her hands on her knees and took a breath. "He has a way of making people do strange things. It's not anything to be ashamed of."

Bethany leaned her head against the wall. "That would make me feel better if I hadn't attacked him *after* he told me he had none of his regular abilities."

"You attacked him? Hold on, are you telling me he's totally human? No powers at all?"

"Not a one." Bethany closed her eyes on a groan. "He just looked so upset that I'd tossed him on his butt, that his smooth talk wasn't working on me, that I wanted to kiss him."

"You tossed him on . . . So, not too pretty for you after all, is he?"

Bethany opened her eyes to catch Michelle's smile and relaxed. She wasn't mad. But she still seemed worried.

"Bethany, I know we've told you about him. About what he is. Even though he looks human now, he is anything but. When Mama found out, she told me something that only a few select of the mambos and houngans, the priestesses and priests of voo-doo, know. On All Saints' Day, some Loa are allowed to walk as mortals, humans. But only from sunrise to sunrise. Tomorrow morning, he'll be a Loa again, a spirit." Michelle put her hand on Bethany's arm. "So just be careful not to get too attached."

One day? He only had one day? Bethany's stomach tightened in reaction. It wasn't enough time. She wasn't sure who she was more upset for, him or herself.

Another knock at the door. "Here comes the bride." Allegra slid inside quickly, slamming the door behind her with a large grin on her face. "What do you think?"

Bethany's heart melted. Allegra looked like a fairy queen. The lacy white creation had an empire waist, short bell sleeves, and a curving neckline. "Allegra, you're beautiful."

Michelle stood up to embrace her friend. "She's right, baby girl. You are the most beautiful bride I've ever seen. Rousseau will be blown away."

Bethany reached into her bedside table, where she'd placed

Isabel's treasures, and pulled out the comb. "I don't think Michelle or Isabel would mind if you made this a part of your something old."

She walked over to Allegra, sliding the comb into her hair with a smile.

Allegra's bright blue eyes sparkled with moisture. "What is wrong with me? I'm like a leaky faucet today." She laughed, wiping at her eyes before wrapping Bethany in her embrace. "Thank you."

Michelle clapped her hands. "Okay, come on. We have to get this off you before the men see it. Mama and Rousseau are in the kitchen, making enough food to feed an army. We'll have an early lunch, and then we need to take you to the hairdresser's, and get Bethany a dress for the occasion."

Allegra nodded. "Bone Daddy, too." The two women looked at her askance, and she shrugged. "What? The man has no clothes. The wedding guests may not mind, but Rousseau will."

She ran out ahead of them, Michelle rolling her eyes as she followed closely behind. Bethany hung back. She turned back to the nightstand, pulling out the brass locket that she'd worn every night since she arrived. She really should have shown that to Allegra—it would have gone perfectly with her outfit.

Her fingers closed over the cool metal, enjoying the zap of electricity she'd come to associate with it. Just like the puzzle box, she couldn't get it open. But she couldn't seem to part with it either.

She slid the chain around her neck, pinning the locket to the strap of her bra, feeling it caress the curve of her breast. For some reason, it made her feel beautiful. Strong. Her own secret talisman. She needed one. Especially if she was going to be spending more time with him. Bone Daddy.

One day. He would only be here one day, and Bethany would be gone before the week was out. Would it be so wrong if she allowed herself a passionate fling before she left New Orleans? If she had one wild adventure all her own?

She'd just have to remember that it was only temporary. She couldn't let herself fall in love with someone who was no more substantial than a dream. A man who would disappear by dawn.

CHAPTER 5

"HOW DO I LOOK?"

The women in the clothing shop turned around and sighed audibly. *All* the women. Even the salesclerk. Bethany looked around at them and shook her head. She wanted to jump in front of him, wielding the hanger in her hand, and tell them to back off, but how could she blame them? The man was utterly edible.

He was dressed in linen pants the color of hemp, and a thin white linen shirt. So thin, Bethany could see the outline of his beautifully muscled torso. It was November, but warm enough here that he wouldn't be cold. Too bad. He might be safer walking the streets if he were wearing a snowsuit. But from the panting women eyeing him around her, she wasn't sure any amount of clothing would help.

He looked her way, a question in his eyes, and she lifted her chin. "You'll do."

The salesclerk sent her a look that questioned her eyesight, as did several of the others, but Bone Daddy chuckled in delight.

"I'm so glad you approve, Blue Eyes. I'll take it." He held up one of Ben's credit cards and waved it enticingly. "Now, it's your turn."

Oh hell. Why had Allegra convinced Michelle to send her shopping with this wicked man while they went to the hairdresser's? And why had she agreed so readily, so aggressively, when Michelle had hesitated?

Because she was a grown woman, and she could handle herself. She could handle him. Even when Bone Daddy paid for his purchases, grabbed her hand, and dragged her out of the store and down the crowded street without a word.

"Where are we going?"

She couldn't help but notice the number of double takes he was receiving. From women. From men. All of them marveling over the renaissance painting come to life. His deep-set golden eyes, his impossibly thick lashes, even his cheekbones were beautiful. Maybe it was a good thing he wasn't usually visible. She wouldn't be able to take him anywhere without drawing a crowd.

"To dress you of course, Bethany. Although, I'd prefer to undress you. I understand how much women love to shop."

"Not me." Bethany caught his disbelieving glance as he pulled her around the corner. He obviously had a destination in mind. "Honestly. Shopping online for things I need, sure. But I hate dressing rooms. The mirrors in there are just too accurate. I'd rather live in ignorance of my wobbly backside. I can't see it, so I don't have to think about it."

He stopped in the middle of the sidewalk and faced her. "I love your backside, Blue Eyes. Besides, mirrors are not accurate. They are what *you* see, not what a man sees when he looks at you. Luckily, I am here. So do not trust the mirrors, trust me." He looked up at the sign that bore a picture of what looked suspiciously like a corset and nodded. "We are here."

She tugged on his hand, but couldn't escape his grip. "I don't need underwear, BD. I need a dress."

"But what is underneath is the most important thing, sweet Bethany." He winked at her as he opened the glass door and yanked her inside.

"That saying is about personality, not thongs," she mumbled under her breath, following behind him unhappily.

"May I help—oh my. Good afternoon, sir. How may I help you?" The tall, stunning woman with short, natural curls and flawless dark skin was obviously knocked breathless at the sight of him.

Join the club, lady. Now back away.

The voice inside her head was getting rather territorial. Before she could say a word, Bone Daddy bowed gallantly, revealing his pearl-white teeth in a charming grin that made the salesclerk flutter.

Flutter, for God's sake.

"I hope so, *cher*. I have come to find the perfect ensemble for this gorgeous creature." He tugged Bethany closer, his arm curving over her shoulders, the warmth of his body making her shiver.

The woman looked Bethany up and down with a disappointed sigh, her smile dimming as she pointed to the far corner. "She should find something in her size over there."

Bethany tensed. Reason number two hundred and twenty-three why books were better than people: The jealous, pretty chicks always got taught a lesson in the end.

"Come on, Blue Eyes. I want to see you in lace and silk." His voice was low and intimate, making her forget about the saleslady's rudeness, about her desire to grab a generic dress off the rack and run home. About everything but him.

She walked directly to her normal cotton panties and bras, thinking she might go a little wild and get a matching set in purple or blue, when he tapped her on the shoulder.

His eyebrows were raised so high they nearly disappeared into his hairline. "What, exactly, do you think you're doing?"

"Buying underwear?"

He made a face. "That is not underwear, Blue Eyes. I've got everything you'll need."

"I'll just bet you do." The salesclerk must have come closer when Bethany wasn't looking. The innuendo-laced comment made her fists clench.

Bone Daddy just smiled innocently. "Where is your dressing room?"

Sales-jerk batted her eyes at him suggestively. "Right through those curtains. Our rooms all have locks for . . . privacy."

He lifted her hand and kissed it. Bethany was sure if she looked in a mirror there would be steam coming out of her ears.

"You are as gracious as you are lovely, *cher*. Which is why I know you'll understand that my Bethany is shy, and I am very . . . particular. I hope you won't disturb us until we are fully satisfied with our probable purchases." He turned away from her, leaving the borrowed credit card in her hand as they walked by her and disappeared behind the curtain.

"I thought you said you didn't have any special abilities today."

He winked at her. "I don't. This is pure, natural talent."

She rolled her eyes. "Show-off."

Bone Daddy led her inside the small mirrored cubicle, and she flinched as he shut the door. Exactly what her ego needed—a three-sixty view of her standing beside her very own Loa centerfold.

She watched him in the reflection as he sat down on the bench behind her, his hands full of black lace. He met her gaze. Confident. Aroused. "I seem to recall a certain feisty blue-eyed bombshell wondering about pretty ol' me and the question of lace panties."

She blushed. "I was hoping you'd forgotten that."

His hands gripped her hips and he turned her toward him. "Not one single word. I also haven't forgotten my desire to see you in nothing but lace panties. Take off your clothes, Bethany." She hesitated and his smile faded, his eyes darkening with need. "Please, Blue Eyes."

Wild adventure. Just this once.

Bethany took a deep breath and pulled off her T-shirt, revealing her comfortable, ugly-as-sin white bra. Bone Daddy licked his lips. She slid her fingers into the elastic waistband of her black stretch pants, slipping out of her tennis shoes before lowering the pants to her ankles and stepping out of them with an insecure whimper.

"Oh, sweet heaven."

She glanced up at Bone Daddy's harsh whisper, but he was looking over her shoulder at the mirror behind her. The mirror that showed a brightly lit, unvarnished view of her not insubstantial ass.

She stood up quickly, trying to glare. "You want to change your mind? Let's just buy this, I'll find a dress, and we can go home."

He was silent until she looked down at him. He spread his legs, adjusting himself in a way that should have been crude, but he managed to make it mouthwateringly sensual. "The rest, Beth. Take off the rest."

She swallowed. There was nothing but desire in his expression. Desire for her. It gave her the courage to reach for the clasps behind her, sliding the bra, with the attached locket, onto the floor beside her pants.

"Magnificent."

She looked up at the ceiling, unable to meet his gaze. "Hardly."

"I believe you need a lesson in sexy, Blue Eyes. You don't seem to know it when you see it."

Oh, she knew it. It was sitting in front of her, studying every curve and imperfection of her body. Her aunt had been a model before she'd had to quit her jet-set life to take care of her dead sister's child. For a while she'd tried to make Bethany care about shoes and clothes and waistlines, but it just wasn't something she cared about. She only wanted to be left alone, to read and reread the dusty old books her father had loved. She walked on her treadmill every day, so she wasn't weak. But she knew she'd never be beautiful or sexy. Not like Michelle or Allegra.

"Turn around and look in the mirror."

She obeyed silently, her mind lost in her own insecurities. She saw Bethany, just Bethany, covering her breasts with her hands, standing awkwardly in her white panties with the stretched out elastic band.

Two large, elegant hands slid around that band, tugging her underwear down until she was forced to step out of them. His breath was hot and heavy against her lower back, and she bit her lip, a shot of need arcing up her spine.

Without a word he ripped the tags off the undergarments, daring her to react as he stood and stared at her over her shoulder. She held her tongue, watching his cheeks flush, his jaw clench as he stared at her sex.

She watched her own eyes widen in surprise when he knelt at her feet behind her, wrapping one hand around her ankle and lifting her foot to slide one leg through the black lace panties.

Her heart was racing, her breath growing shallow as he slowly raised the black lace bikini up her legs, his fingertips caressing her skin as he went. When they were on, he reached behind him for the matching demi-cup bra.

Like a child, she opened her arms, allowing him to dress her. He closed the rosette clasp, his arms around her, body pressed against her back. He pushed her braid to the side, draping it over one shoulder, placing his chin on the other. "Look at yourself, Bethany. See what I see."

The bra made her breasts look bigger, rounder. She could see her hardening nipples poking through the black lace. The color made her skin look more creamy than pale. She inhaled sharply when his hands covered her view, caressing her through the fabric, circling her nipples with unsteady hands.

Bone Daddy pressed a kiss along her jaw. "See how you affect me? One touch and I'm on fire for you."

Bethany's fingers traced the curve of her stomach. The high cut of the underwear made her legs look longer, sleeker. His hands followed hers, covering them before slipping beneath the lace, into her damp curls.

"Beth, oh, sweet baby, feel how hot you are." His hips rocked against her, making her moan when she felt his thick erection press between the cheeks of her ass even through the linen and lace. "How hot you make me."

"Oh God." She couldn't stop her surprised cry when he moved around in front of her and fell to his knees between her and the glass, parting her legs with his shoulders and pulling the lace to one side.

She leaned forward, placing her hands on either side of the mirror to keep her balance as she looked down, watching his fingers spread the lips of her sex, baring her to his gaze.

He growled, burying his face between her thighs, his tongue circling her clit before curling to fill her sex. Bethany's knees jerked, her legs trembling at the intensity of the sensation. So good. So good.

She turned her head, looking into the mirror to her right to see his profile, watching his jaw work, his throat as he swallowed. His eyes closed, long lashes skimming his cheeks as he drank her down. The sight only heightened her need.

His finger joined his tongue inside her and fire licked up her spine. Every nerve of her body was sparking, her blood blazing with heat. She lowered one hand to his curls, pressing his head closer, needing more.

His groan vibrated against her clit, and she tugged on his hair instinctively. She shook her head, a sound of denial escaping her lips as he stood, moving to stand behind her once more.

She heard the rustling of fabric behind her, felt the tear of lace against her skin as he yanked it as far to the side as it would go. And then he was there, stretching her, filling her so completely that she cried out.

He turned her head and bit at her upper lip. "Shhh, Blue Eyes. You don't want anyone coming to see what's wrong, do you?"

She shook her head rapidly. No. No, because then he'd stop. And he couldn't, he wouldn't . . . "Don't you dare stop."

"Never." He kissed her, his hands clutching her hips so tight. *Yes.* He powered against her, fast and hard, as though he'd lost all control.

She loved it.

"Open your eyes, Bethany. Open your eyes and look at the beautiful woman I'm fucking."

Damn, his voice was sexy. She hadn't even realized her eyes had closed. She lifted lids heavy with desire and felt her breath catch in her throat. She felt like a Peeping Tom, looking into a window to catch an intimate moment between lovers.

Tendrils of hair had fallen from the woman's long braid, curling damply around her glowing cheeks; her lips were swollen from her lover's kiss. She was bent over, her curves pressing back against the man greedily, begging for more.

They were beautiful. *They* were beautiful.

"You are a goddess, Bethany. And so tight. So sweet. *Merde*, I don't know how much longer I can last."

She watched his neck arch, head falling back as his hips picked up speed. Deeper. Harder. Faster.

Her vision blurred. All of her awareness focused on reaching that climax she could sense, just a breath away. A heartbeat. A thrust. "Oh God. Oh God."

Marcel.

She turned, sightless, her mouth seeking his when she flew over the edge. Flashes of colored light blinded her, her body a lightning rod of sensation. Passion.

He shouted into her mouth, pressing hard against her as he came. They slid to their knees, still connected, still eating at each other's mouths as the waves of their climax faded.

Her skin cooled and her brain started working again. What was that? She didn't know it could be like that. That good. That unbelievably, amazingly, pinch-me-I-must-be-dreaming good.

Reason number one why people were better than books. That.

He lifted his mouth from hers, his amber eyes filled with as much wonder as she was feeling. "Who are you, Blue Eyes? What kind of spell are you weaving?"

She opened her mouth to answer him, and an impatient knock sounded outside the dressing room. "Don't make me come in there and get you two, because I will. Three minutes, and then this nice saleswoman will make Ben pay her for a broken dressing room door."

Bethany pressed her forehead against the mirror. "Oh, hell."

Bone Daddy chuckled against her back. "Michelle is a feisty one. But then, so are you." He pulled away and she gasped as liquid dripped down her thigh. When he started swearing in French, she knew what it was.

"Bethany, I—"

She held up her hand, trying to process what she'd just done. She'd never had unsafe sex in her life. Not that she had that much sex, but when she did, she was always safe. And always in a bed.

He was the one weaving the spell. And right now, she wasn't liking her reaction to it.

She stood up and grabbed her underwear, wiping the moisture from her inner thighs with a silent groan. She reached for her stretch pants, pulling them on quickly, her mind reeling. When she was fully dressed she grabbed her underwear and bra, balling them up in her fist and turning toward the door.

His hand pressed against it, barring her way.

"What?"

"That's never happened before, Bethany."

She gave him a brittle smile. "I didn't think it had. You may have been having sex for hundreds of years, but you've only been human for a few hours. You haven't had a chance to be irresponsible."

"Yet, you are mad." He sounded hurt.

She sighed, focusing her gaze on her hand curled around the knob. "You're wrong about me. I'm not feisty, or sexy, and I'm certainly not a witch. I'm not . . . cut out for this kind of thing. I thought I could be, but I'm not." She knew he wanted her to look at him, was willing her to, but she refused. "Let me go, Bone Daddy. Your day is passing by."

He lifted his hand and she hurried through the door, passing her friends. Their expressions changed from disbelief to concern when they saw her face. She tried to smile at Allegra, but she felt like bawling her eyes out.

"Your hair looks beautiful," she said in a wobbly voice. "Oh, they used Isabel's comb."

A tear slid down her cheek and Allegra wrapped an arm around her, glaring over her head to where she knew Bone Daddy must be standing.

She heard Michelle's voice through the ringing in her ears. "You two go back home, Allegra. Take the car. We'll meet you there."

She let Allegra lead her outside, feeling like a fool, and even worse, a horrible guest. "I'm sorry."

"Don't you dare be sorry, Bethany. If anyone should be sorry, it's that oversexed Loa." She sounded angry. "You know, Rousseau wasn't happy he'd come, but I thought it would be a great opportunity to mend fences. To heal. But no. He can't stop taking advantage long enough to be a gentleman. To be respectful."

Bethany sniffled. "No. It wasn't like that. We both lost control. He's actually kind of . . . wonderful."

"Wonderful? I'm confused. If he's so wonderful, why are you crying?"

Because Loas didn't wear condoms, and a part of her was desperately hoping he'd left her something to remember him by. And that thought scared her more than anything else.

CHAPTER 6

HE DIDN'T UNDERSTAND WOMEN. SCRATCH THAT. HE UNDER-stood women better than anyone in the history of the world. Except Bethany. He didn't understand her. And he really didn't understand his reaction to her.

He loved women. All women. Loved to see them in the throes of passion, to watch their sated smiles as they fell asleep after he'd pleasured them into exhaustion. He always knew what they were thinking—it was a gift of his kind.

"That's it."

"What's it, BD?" Ben was sitting on his bed, slipping on his socks and shoes. The men had decided to get dressed in his room, giving the master bedroom to Allegra and the women.

Bone Daddy shifted in his chair, thinking of the present he'd left there for Bethany. He hoped she liked it.

"Benjamin, when you marry Michelle Toussaint, and I know

you will, make sure you spank her at least once a day. That woman is a tyrant."

Ben laughed. "I would, my friend. But I think she would enjoy it too much." His brown eyes studied Bone Daddy intently. "She told me about the lingerie shop. I had to promise to buy half their stock just to keep the salesclerk from calling the police. Not that I blame you. In fact, I would buy the shop as-is for the opportunity to get Mimi into one of those mirrored dressing rooms."

Though Bone Daddy maintained a nonchalant pose, he was amazed at his own discomfort at having everyone know about his time with Bethany. She was special. There was something about her that called out to his soul. He knew her. He wanted her. He was happy that he'd arrived in time for Allegra and Rousseau's wedding, but Bethany was the main reason he was still here.

He hadn't planned to spend his one day as a human in emotional turmoil over a stubborn little woman. This was his last chance to indulge in life—food, women, wine. Instead he'd only eaten twice and hadn't had a drop to drink all day. All he could do was pine for Bethany. Wanting to talk to her, to apologize again for losing control. To have another chance to lose control. "Bah. Women."

Rousseau turned away from the mirror where he was tying his tie, an unwilling smile forming on his lips. "I'll be damned. You like her, don't you? You don't just want to fuck her, you actually like her."

He was out of his chair and nose to nose with Rousseau before the words had completely left his mouth. "Am I such a monster then? I am a Loa, not the Devil. I came when I was called, and you were better for it. There is a woman in this house whose love you never have to doubt, who chose you over everything else, and in part, that is because of *me*."

"I know. Thank you."

All the bluster drained out of him at Rousseau's words, leaving a strange feeling of vulnerability. "You're welcome. So you no longer think I am beyond redemption?"

Rousseau gazed at Bone Daddy in silence for a moment. Then he did something unexpected. He wrapped his arms around him and hugged him. Tight. "You are not beyond redemption. You are family. Allegra was right. I'm glad you're here."

Bone Daddy turned to a smiling Ben, who nodded approvingly. "As it should be, my brothers. As it should be."

Rousseau released him, and Bone Daddy ran a hand through his curls. "I don't know what to do. I forget myself when I'm around her. Forget my experience, my control. Forget that I only have a few more hours before I must return through the Gate, perhaps for good."

"For good? What are you talking about, BD?" Ben wasn't smiling now.

"Let's just say that after our adventure with the *djab*, they decided it would be better for me to stay on the other side for a while." Bone Daddy saw the guilty expression on Ben's face and shook his head. "No, Benjamin. It would have happened anyway. And perhaps they are right. I should behave as the other Loa. I've become too attached."

Rousseau looked troubled. "This feels wrong. You need to talk to Mambo Toussaint before the wedding. Ben, go get her, will you?"

Ben rushed to open the door before Bone Daddy could stop him, and laughed. Standing outside, with one hand over their eyes and the other carrying trays of food and drink, were the two women Ben called The Mamas. Elise Adair and Annemarie Toussaint.

"Are you decent?"

"Are you kidding?" Ben was still chuckling. "I was just coming to find you two. We have a situation. Oh. Is that pie?"

Mambo Toussaint dropped her hand in time to smack his. "Benjamin Beauregard Adair, that pie is special. It's for Bone Daddy. You can have a crawfish cake."

Bone Daddy backed up as the two women's energy filled the room, along with the delicious aroma of food. His stomach growled loudly, and Elise Adair smiled.

"Looks like we arrived just in time."

"In more ways than one." Rousseau embraced the two women, smiling as they congratulated him on his day. "Mambo, Bone Daddy has a problem."

"It's not a problem, boy. This is your day, yours and your lovely warrior queen's. That's all you need to be thinking about."

Mambo Toussaint raised her eyebrows, drawing his attention to her head scarf, which was a brilliant purple for the occasion. "Humanity looks good on you, Bone Daddy. Is this your first All Saints'?"

Ben swallowed one fried crawfish cake and reached for two more, handing one to Bone Daddy. "And his last. They think he's too attached to us."

"They may be right. Who are we to question the Loa's wisdom? They are the messengers for the divine." But she studied him closer, as if she saw beyond him, in him. "You saved my daughter's life. My son's as well. He's bought an apartment here, came back home. We're getting to know each other again, and you made that possible. I owe you a boon."

Bone Daddy leaned forward to place a kiss on the older woman's forehead. He'd always liked her. She was a compassionate mambo, a healer. Loyal to her religion and her friends. "You owe me nothing, woman. But perhaps I will have some of that pie."

Elise Adair tilted her head, her silvery blonde bob brushing her shoulder. "You are a beautiful man." Her son made a choking sound, and she pursed her perfectly glossed lips and stuck out her tongue. "What? I'm human, and not so old that I'm immune to masculine charm."

Bone Daddy winked at the elegant woman, making her blush, much to his delight. But then she reached out and took his hand. He knew the Adair magic. Knew what she was. He could feel her energy searching his, and he had to admit, he was worried at what she would find.

"Don't worry. I can see why she's so drawn to you. But there's something else." She pulled her hand back, looking confused. "You shouldn't be what you are."

Mambo Toussaint turned her friend toward her. "Is it what we thought?"

"Yes and no. It's hard to see. But I'm not sure if we can help him."

Rousseau shook his head, downing a shot of liquor he'd taken from the tray and shuddering as the heat of it hit his chest. "Is there any way you could be less confusing and vague? My wedding is a few hours away, and I don't have the ability to solve any puzzles."

Mambo Toussaint hummed thoughtfully. "That's exactly what this is, a puzzle. But power will gather tonight when the others come to honor our ancestors and the Ghede family of Loa. Maybe we can find your answers."

Bone Daddy felt his heart leap. He wished he had Ben and Elise's power for a moment, wished he had his own, so he could understand what Michelle's mother was saying. Was there a chance he could stay? He had been working so hard to resign himself to his fate, he hadn't dared to hope there was another way.

"If you find a loophole, *cher*, you know I will take it. Until then—" His full attention turned toward Elise. "You can see why *who* is drawn to me? Bethany? Have you talked to her, touched her? Is she upset?"

The men beside him laughed and shook their heads, and the women smiled. Elise held up her hands. "Very interesting. But no. You are a human male, at least for the moment. You will have to muddle through just like the rest of them. Figure it out for yourself."

The mambo pointed to the food and bowed her head respectfully before allowing Elise to tug her out of the room. Ben clapped him on the shoulder in masculine commiseration. "Welcome to the club, BD. We didn't think you'd ever get here."

"Bah. Neither of you knows what this feels like. With a touch you can know your woman. And Rousseau knew Allegra's thoughts long enough to know how she felt about him. I am blinded. I have no compass. And Bethany does not behave the way a normal woman should."

"You mean she doesn't follow you around like a puppy dog?" Rousseau grabbed a pecan from his pie before Bone Daddy could pull his plate away.

"She expects more than just the opportunity to gaze adoringly into your beautiful eyes?" Ben batted his lashes, brown eyes sparking with laughter.

"Yes, damn it." And he loved it. Loved her prickly manner, her sharp tongue. Loved her subtle sensuality, her wit, and the feel of her around him, her fire.

He could be in trouble.

SHE WAS DEFINITELY IN TROUBLE. "THERE IS NO WAY I CAN wear this in public."

Michelle and Allegra were beside her in the mirror, their smiles huge. Michelle whistled. "Girl, you look H. O. T. *Hot*. I have to hand it to the man, he knows what looks good. You look like Selma Hayek in that dress. And Allegra, you did a great job on her hair."

This was insane. She could hardly believe the person in the reflection was her. Allegra had made her unbraid her hair, pulling the sides back and curling the long tresses so they spiraled softly down her back.

And the dress—a daring, attention-grabbing dress with a flared bottom that ended mid-thigh. She wore more to bed each night. But the black lace bra did give her fantastic cleavage. And she liked her hair, though she had a feeling she'd be spending the evening snagging it on trees, flower bushes, and random buttons.

She glanced at Allegra. So stunning in white. And Michelle wore a violet summer dress, the purple hue a nod to her mother's beliefs, to honor the Ghede family with their favorite color. She looked amazing. Bethany stood between them in temptress red, feeling as though she'd walked into an alternate universe. "This is not me."

"Are you sure?" Allegra adjusted her handiwork so that a thick, ebony curl fell over Bethany's shoulder, and beamed at her proudly. "Maybe you've just been hiding the real you for so long, you don't recognize her when you see her. You *are* a butterfly. He was right."

Butterfly? "Stop paying attention to me. You're the one getting married. This is your special day. The one day when everyone's eyes are on you. Brides don't spend their last few hours of single-hood matchmaking."

Allegra's chin went up puckishly. "Brides can do whatever they want to on their day. Besides"—she shared a glance with Michelle—"I have the rest of my life with Rousseau."

And Bethany only had one night.

After she'd come home and taken a shower, the panic had subsided. Everything about the day had thrown her. Her feelings, the sexuality he'd called out from her, the total loss of control.

She knew now she wasn't cut out for temporary affairs—it was too difficult to keep her heart out of the equation. But it was already involved. She was already involved. She understood now how Isabel had felt, wanting someone you knew you couldn't have. Although, for all Bethany knew, she had managed to run away with her fabulous Mr. M. But there was no running from what Bone Daddy was.

When the dress had arrived with Michelle, along with a note from Bone Daddy asking her to wear it for him, she'd known that she would. She wanted to please him, even as her inner voice called her a fool.

She set her shoulders back and did her best to smile convincingly. "If Aunt Rosaline could see me now, she'd probably die of shock."

Michelle, who'd met her aunt before, made a face. "That grumpy old woman? Do you know she pulled me aside once and recommended liposuction to minimize my '*unfortunate* rear end'? I had to go out and buy a double scoop of Rocky Road and a new pair of shoes before I felt better about myself."

"I'm sorry. I never knew."

She'd found fault with Michelle? But she was so exotic, so lovely. And in New York she'd been the epitome of high fashion.

A thought struck Bethany for the first time, like a bolt from heaven. Maybe it wasn't just her—maybe Rosaline was like that with everyone.

Allegra grimaced. "Sounds like a gem of a woman—no offense, Bethany," she hurried to add. "Trust me, I understand family issues.

Mine were so intimidated at the engagement dinner that they conveniently 'forgot' they'd booked a cruise during my wedding. I'm glad though. I don't think they'd enjoy the reception."

Allegra looked more relieved than disappointed, which Bethany completely understood.

"You're not upset your father won't be here to walk you down the aisle?" she asked.

Allegra beamed once more, her excitement contagious. "No, because I won't be alone. In fact, I may very well be the first woman in history to be walked down the aisle by an honest to goodness Loa."

Bone Daddy? Bethany recalled Allegra's writing about him. It was hard not to be jealous of the fact that both Allegra and Michelle had, for all intents and purposes, *been* with her new lover.

Allegra must have seen something in her expression. "He brought us together, Bethany. Me with Rousseau, and Michelle with Ben, whether she's willing to give him credit or not. He sacrificed his pleasure, and his freedom, to do it. He is what life made him, a sexual entity. But, today, when he is free to make his own choices, any choice he wants, it's you. Think about it."

"Don't push her, Allegra. Just because you found your prince doesn't mean everyone has to right now." Michelle rubbed her shoulders, looking worried. "Sorry, but I've stuck my nose in other people's love lives enough to know I'm not good at it."

Then she focused on Bethany. "I'm glad you're here, and I want you to have fun. But I don't want to be responsible for your heart getting broken. Allegra's right, he is what life made him. Not human. Not permanent. And usually, not monogamous. I'm not saying he doesn't care about your feelings, because he sure seems to, but . . . just be careful."

For a moment, an image from her dreams, an image of Isabel's friend Catherine, superimposed itself over Michelle's face. A wave of dizziness rolled over Bethany and she reached for her head, weaving.

Catherine had warned her away from Marcel. Catherine had wanted her to marry for security. To marry someone. Who? Why had she pushed her so hard? Didn't she know what it was like to be in love?

"Bethany! Bethany, are you all right? Talk to us, please."

Bethany blinked in confusion. She was suddenly lying on Michelle's bed, and Michelle and Allegra were fanning her face and shaking her shoulders. "What happened?" she asked.

"We were hoping you would tell us." Allegra sat down beside her, patting her hand soothingly.

"I don't know. For a moment everything seemed like a dream I'd had before. Like déjà vu. Then the room started spinning." She pushed herself up and grimaced when her hair snagged on Allegra's bracelet. "I'm sorry about this. Really, I'm fine."

A knock sounded on the door and Allegra paled. "It's time."

As Michelle opened the door to Elise, Bethany scrambled off the bed and grabbed Allegra's hands. "Thank you for letting me be a part of your day. You are a beautiful bride. Rousseau is a very lucky man."

The redhead's happy smile returned. "We're both lucky. Thank you, Bethany." She leaned close and lowered her voice. "I love Michelle, but I have some advice of my own. Don't be *too* careful. Sometimes it's that leap into the darkness that can be the most worthwhile."

Bethany smiled as she followed in the wake of the chattering women. Reason number two why people were better than books: No matter how well you think you know them, people can still surprise you.

She headed out to the garden to sit in one of the white folding chairs that had been set up for the occasion. Ben had done a beautiful job putting this together so quickly. The trees were filled with lights, and gardenias and magnolias were blooming everywhere.

A white runner lay across the grass between the chairs and the altar. The freshly painted gazebo was draped in white silk and lit with small spotlights at the base. The workers had even built a temporary bandstand, where a small jazz band was playing softly for the crowd.

There were two giant tables full of food on either side of the garden, one covered in white, the other in purple. Bethany knew that one table was meant for the living, the other for the dead. Later, the party might turn wild, but for the moment, everyone was quiet, in awe of the magic around them and the perfection of the night. There was even a cool breeze.

She felt a tug on her hair and turned to apologize, sure her loose locks had snagged some poor victim already, but no one was sitting behind her. "Emmanuel? Manuel, is that you?" Another cool breeze. "Wanted to see the wedding, too, did you? Well you're welcome to sit with me. Just don't play any tricks tonight, okay? Allegra deserves everything to be perfect."

Her fingers slipped beneath the halter, adjusting the locket. She couldn't resist. She wanted to wear it one more time. She'd promised herself she would share it, along with the letters and all her research, with Michelle tomorrow.

She'd wanted to know everything, to find out what had happened to Isabel, but she'd reached a dead end. Several love letters, a diary, and a nameless mausoleum were all the woman had left behind. Maybe they'd never know what became of her.

The music changed, and she noticed that Rousseau and Ben were standing on the steps of the gazebo. She turned her head with the other guests and spied Mambo Toussaint and Elise Adair on the other side of the aisle, holding tightly to each other's hands.

Michelle came out first, her bouquet of magnolias held low as she walked toward them, her eyes on Ben. Bethany turned to look at the handsome blond, and sighed. You'd think it was his wedding, with that goofy in-love grin on his face. He even stepped forward when Michelle reached the gazebo, but when several people chuckled, he shrugged and stepped back, allowing her to take her place on the bride's side.

Everyone stood as Allegra and Bone Daddy entered the backyard. Bethany heard the female gasps and knew they weren't for the bride, despite how amazing she looked. They were for *him*.

She sighed. Couldn't he have a disfiguring mark on his face, maybe an eye patch? Maybe then she wouldn't feel so insecure each time he was out in public. But he wouldn't be much longer. She couldn't forget that. Maybe he liked the reaction for once. To be seen.

Then she noticed a man a few rows behind her ogling her cleavage and her eyes widened. Someone was noticing *her*, too.

And Bone Daddy noticed him. He narrowed his eyes on the bearded wedding guest before turning back to meet her smile with a grumpy glare. Was he jealous? The thought delighted her.

As he drew closer with the bride, he got a full view of her in the dress he'd picked out. His jaw tightened, not with irritation this time, but need. She could see it. Bethany had never felt so powerful. For tonight, at this moment, she was the siren, the woman in red that no man could resist. Not even Bone Daddy.

She watched him hand the bride to Rousseau, placing a gentle kiss on her forehead. Her heart pounded as she waited for him to come to her, to sit beside her as they watched the love story's happy ending.

He turned, avoiding her gaze as he walked toward the other side of the aisle, finding a seat beside a gorgeous female in a slinky black dress who, if her expression was anything to go by, was thinking she'd just won the man lottery. The woman immediately placed her arm across the back of his chair, using the excuse of speaking in his ear to press her obviously fake breasts against his side.

Her cheeks on fire, Bethany glanced around to make sure no one had witnessed her epic embarrassment and sat down with a thump. So much for being the siren in red no man could ignore. What an idiot! How could she have imagined she could tempt someone like him, that he would waste even one more minute of his one day in the flesh on her?

Ignoring the small frantic tugs on her hair, she fought to get her ragged breathing under control. It was tempting to slump over and cry but she held herself stiffly, determined not to let him see how badly his public brush-off had hurt her. The bastard!

The tugs got harder.

"Not now, Manuel," she hissed from the corner of her mouth. "I'm busy." Thinking of ways to unman a Loa. Painfully.

CHAPTER 7

MAYBE HE *WAS* A DEVIL.

Here he was, watching a minister join the lives of Celestin Rousseau and Allegra Jarrod, and all he could think about was Bethany. Fucking her. He wanted to bend her over the chairs, press her against the gazebo, a tree, *anything*, and take her hard and fast—damn the audience.

Unfortunately, she didn't look too receptive right now. In fact, she looked like she shouldn't be allowed to handle any sharp objects for a while. And worse, she looked hurt.

Didn't she understand that he couldn't trust himself to sit beside her? That, for Allegra's sake and to keep the tentative peace he now had with Rousseau, the smartest thing for him to do was sit as far away from her as possible?

He tried to catch her eye but she was focused unwaveringly on the bridal couple. Apparently she didn't understand.

"Weddings make me so hot. Do you think they'd miss us if we disappeared for a few hours?"

Bone Daddy sighed. He was broken. That was the only way he could explain it. There was a beautiful woman rubbing against him, offering herself on a platter. Offering to satisfy a need so strong it made his teeth ache. He shifted in his chair, moving away from her and shaking his head. Bethany had ruined his day. She was the only one he wanted.

"Thank you for the generous offer, *cher*. But I belong to another."

The large-breasted female pouted, her darkly stained lips too thin, too symmetrical for him to consider kissable. "She doesn't have to know."

He watched Bethany's head jerk as though someone had yanked it, mumbling under her breath before pulling all that long, lustrous hair over her shoulder. "I would know. That is enough. But I believe there is a bearded man a few rows back who is single. Perhaps he would be willing to bring you to pleasure."

The persistent woman bit her lip and slid her hand between his legs just as Rousseau was slipping a ring on Allegra's finger. "I love the way you talk. 'Bring you to pleasure.' You seem to be ready enough. I admire your loyalty but, if I may say so, if you were truly satisfied you wouldn't be so hard for me right now."

His shock at her boldness turned to anger when he realized that Bethany had chosen that moment to glance in his direction. Her gaze honed in on the woman's hand between his thighs and her jaw dropped.

"I now pronounce you husband and wife. You may kiss the bride."

The minister's voice cued the clapping, and as the musicians began to play a celebratory tune, Bethany got up and rushed through the crowd, heading back toward the house.

"Damn it."

He stood and the woman followed, trying to slip her hand in his, as though she believed her wiles had worked. He pulled away from her touch, meeting her surprised expression with one of disgust. "I am taken by a woman who has enough pride not to throw herself at someone who belongs to another. And I am hard not for you but for her. I was remembering her passion, her cries as I took her. I was wishing I was beside her, touching her. And if she'll let me after what you've done, I will touch her again."

He walked away from the dazed woman, ignoring The Mamas' stares as he pushed through the guests surging forward to congratulate the happy couple. All his attention was focused on one thing: getting to Bethany.

An image popped into his head, an image so real that for a moment he was some other place. Another time. A young woman was crying, racing from his room. He'd just woken up to realize there was a naked woman in his bed. A woman who hadn't been there when he'd fallen asleep.

He'd raced after her but it was too late. She'd never believe him. And maybe that was for the best. Maybe Isabel was better off without him.

"*No.*" Bone Daddy shook his head angrily, coming back to the present and quickening his stride. He didn't know where these visions were coming from, but if they were trying to tell him he had to give Bethany up, they could go to Hell. He still had time. And he was going to spend it with her.

SHE WASN'T GOING TO CRY. SO WHAT IF HE WAS MOVING ON to a new conquest? She still looked good, and there were plenty of men out there, most of them actually human, who would still be there for breakfast in the morning.

Maybe it was a blessing in disguise. She was starting to fall for the Loa, and Michelle was right, she wasn't being careful.

She walked up the stairs, heading to Isabel's room—her room— needing a moment to get her game face on. He'd no doubt leave with his new woman in tow, and she'd be able to go back down and be there for her friends, maybe even witness the mambo's ritual.

She started to close the door, but something was blocking her way. Something big and beautiful and angry. What right did he have to be angry?

"Done with her already? She must be easier than she looked."

He pushed through the door and slammed it shut behind him, turning the lock with a firm click. "You look beautiful in that dress, Blue Eyes."

She took a step back, her body heating from the determined look in his eyes. "Thank you. But this is a dancing dress. I think I'll go back downstairs and see if anyone wants to dance with me."

Bethany tried to move past him toward the door, but he was having none of it. He bent his knees, throwing her over his shoulder and heading toward the bed. He tossed her on the mattress and grabbed her before she could scramble away, pulling her face-down onto his lap.

Her mouth went dry. "What the hell do you think you're doing?"

"Dancing." He lifted her skirt, making a disapproving noise as he noticed her sensible underwear. "This was not what I imagined you would have under here."

"If you recall, my other pair was shredded before I had a chance to buy it." When she remembered why, her breathing grew shallow. His grip on her body tightened, and she knew he was remembering, too.

The sound of tearing fabric filled the room, and Bethany felt the air hit her bare skin. He groaned above her. "Oh, baby, I love your ass. I truly do. But I think it needs something."

Her gasp of indignation turned into one of total shock as she heard the crack of his palm across her left cheek, sending a stinging heat blooming across her backside. He spanked the other cheek, humming in satisfaction at her body's reaction.

"Pink. So pretty."

"What was that for?" She was gasping for air, unsure how she felt about the tingling sensations. Her body knew. She was wet, her limbs trembling, her clit pulsing with her racing heart.

"Let's see. You questioned my manhood and said I was too pretty." *Smack*. "You ran away from me not once." *Smack*. "Not twice." *Smack*. "But three times." She wiggled in his embrace, lifting her ass into the air, craving his touch, and he growled, spanking her again. "Don't distract me. Spread your legs a little."

She shuddered, unable to believe she was so aroused by this, that she wanted more. She spread her legs and felt the air hit her soaking sex. She knew he could see, that he knew how much she wanted him, in spite of her ire.

"Oh, *cher*."

"No."

"No?"

"Don't call me that. You call everyone that." She wanted to be special. She didn't want him to forget her.

"Bethany, you are the only one I see. The only one I want." He slid his hand between her legs, groaning as her arousal coated his fingers. "This is all I want. I can still taste you on my tongue, but I need more. I'm hungry, love." He lifted his hand and lowered it swiftly, spanking the lips of her sex, sending sparks of carnal fire through her body.

"Oh my God."

"You like that don't you?" She heard the smile in his voice, and the passion. "My bad girl. I knew you would. You are full of fire for me." He picked her up and lowered her onto her back on the bed, then his hands went immediately to his pants. "Only for me."

"Wait." She started to roll off the bed but he caught her, his eyes going dark.

"Do I have to spank you again?"

She shivered. "You can if you want to. I was just going to see if there was a condom in the bathroom."

He smiled, reaching into his pocket and pulling out a handful to lay across the bed. "Ben already made sure I was prepared."

"Ben's a good man."

He laughed at her breathless statement. "Yes. But I'm better."

She couldn't resist his cocky grin. She leaned forward, kissing him with all the pent-up passion she'd been holding in, loving the feel of his lips beneath hers. He opened her mouth with his tongue, dominating her mouth while he covered her body.

She reached between them and their hands tangled in their struggle to undo his pants. She pushed them past his perfect ass, gripping it in her hands to pull him closer, and he shouted into her mouth.

Tearing his lips from hers, he looked into her eyes. "You're trying to distract me again. You drive me insane, Blue Eyes."

She wrapped her legs around his waist. "Good. Then we're even."

The tearing of foil broke through her daze, and she couldn't help but feel a pang of disappointment that anything would be between them, keeping them apart. But then she was there, helping him roll it onto his thick erection and loving the way he bit down on his lip at her touch.

He slipped his shirt, still buttoned, over his head and looked down at her dress. "I want you to keep it on this first time, love. Want to see your face as you come, wearing the dress I picked for you."

She used her feet to push his pants down past his ankles and to the floor. "As long as you're naked, I'm good."

His chuckle turned into a groan as she took him in her hand. "Bethany, please, baby. I don't want it to be over before it's begun."

"I can't wait, BD. *Please*. I want you now."

He was kissing her again. Kissing her as she guided him inside. He was so big, so thick. Her body was stretching for him, pulling him in greedily. She wanted everything, wanted to burn every sensation, every thrust, every breath into her brain. So she'd never forget.

As if she could.

He leaned on his elbow, wrapping her hair in his fist. "I love your hair, Bethany. Like black silk in my hands. That's right, love, lock your legs around me. *Tighter*. Take it all. Take all of me."

When she thought he was in her as far as he could go, he rolled onto his back, taking her with him. "Ride me, baby."

With her dress floating around their hips and his hands still in her hair, she leaned down to kiss him, suddenly unsure. "I don't think I've ever done this before. I thought you were the 'rider.'"

His smile tightened at her reference to what he was, but he shook his head. "Not this time. It's your turn, Bethany. Lift your skirts and ride me."

She sat up, crying out as the position pushed him even deeper inside her. "Good lord." She lifted her skirt, gathering the flouncing folds in her arms so he could see where they were joined, and rocked experimentally. "Oh my."

"That's right, Blue Eyes. Take me. I've got you." He let go of her hair and gripped her hips with his hands, his neck muscles straining as he watched her take him inside her again and again. "I wish you could see this, love. See your hungry little pussy take me deep. It's beautiful."

He lifted and lowered her against him, helping her find the perfect rhythm. She threw her head back, crying out as each thrust sent a new current of pleasure through her body. She placed her hands on his chest, fingers curling as she rocked against him, her body wild as her need grew.

"Fuck, yeah. That's right, love. It's never been like this. Never. I need . . ." His grip turned bruising and she felt his hips arch off the bed as he lost control. Over and over again he brought her down against him, his thrusts so powerful that they rocked the bed.

They came together, their shouts mingling, rising over the din of the music and laughter down below.

Bethany collapsed on his chest, her body shuddering as she tried to catch her breath. Her shallow pants turned to giggles. She tried to hold them back but she couldn't. Each giggle made him groan as her inner muscles clenched around his still-hard cock.

"Are you by any chance wanting another spanking?" His voice sounded curious, husky.

"Not right this minute. I can't help it—I think its endorphins. You know I read about some very interesting reactions to the release of neuro-hormo—"

He covered her lips with his fingers and pressed a kiss to the top of her head. "You are an adorable and sexy bookworm. But if you giggle anymore you won't get a chance to catch your breath and enjoy your endorphins before I have to have you again."

She giggled.

He sighed against her temple. "Work. Work. Work." He sat up, lifting her off his lap with a groan. He slid off the bed, giving her a wonderful view of his rear end before turning to gather her in his arms.

"Where are we going?"

"To the shower. Grab one of those condoms for me, love. There's a good girl."

She stood silently, watching as he moved about the bathroom removing his condom, turning on the water, and pulling the shower curtain closed. All the while she was studying every finely sculpted inch of his body. Flawless, but for that one jagged scar on his side. "How old are you?"

He didn't turn around. "It's rude to ask an older person his age."

"Only women." She was dying of curiosity. "You look about twenty-three."

"I remember the First and Second World Wars, so I'm fairly certain I'm older than that."

She gasped. "That's amazing. So Loas are immortal then?"

"I think so."

There was a strange note in his voice. She frowned. "You *think* so? You aren't sure how old you are, and you don't know if you're immortal or not. How can you not know?"

He shrugged. "I just don't. I know only that I come when I'm called, and I help those in need of my particular talents."

"Your sex talents."

He turned around and put his hands on his hips, his patience obviously at an end. "Yes, my sex talents, as you call them. Without good sex, there would be no romantic weddings or welcome babies. Without good sex, women would be miserable and men would be more barbaric than they are."

She held up her hands. "I'm not against sex, BD, in case you hadn't noticed. I'm just curious about you. I want—I want to know you."

He ran a hand through his hair. "I should not be so sensitive. He said I needed to be wary of human emotions today."

"He?"

"My mentor. The Loa who met me at the crossroads when I first arrived. Who told me what would be expected of me. And no, I don't know when that was. Only that he was there for me."

The crossroads. She'd read about that, but before she could open her mouth to ask another question, he was kissing her into submission. Into silence.

He unhooked her dress and lowered it to the bathroom floor, then made short work of the front clasp of her bra. She heard the clang of the locket against the tile as he threw her bra on the floor but she was too wrapped up in his kiss to care.

He helped her into the large tub, unwilling to lift his mouth from hers for a moment until they were beneath the hot spray. "No more questions now, Bethany. They'll come looking for you soon, come to take you away from me. And I need you again."

She felt tears building up behind her eyes at his words. No. It was him who was going to be taken away from her. She was the one running out of time. She pressed her bare breasts against his chest, reaching up to wrap her arms around his neck.

He moaned, lowering his head to kiss her throat, her shoulder, anywhere he could reach. "I am addicted to you, love. The feel of you against me, your taste. I can't seem to get enough."

Hearing the lost tone in his voice, she looked up at him and melted. He needed her. For whatever reason, for tonight, he needed her.

"Speaking of tasting." She let go of his neck and slid down his body, her breasts caressing his smooth torso as she dropped to her knees. "I think it's my turn."

His broad shoulders blocked the water's spray and he looked down at her upturned face, surprise tensing his muscles. "Sweet heaven."

"You took the words right out of my mouth." She leaned closer, breathing in the scent of him. He smelled amazing. Soap and sin and pure, animal male. A shiver ran through her as she knelt in front of him. The position was potent. Powerful.

She'd never wanted to do this before. Never had any desire. But as she stared at his long, thick shaft, the head dark and flushed with passion, her mouth watered.

"You've decided to torture me?" His gruff voice brought her gaze back up to his. His hands slid into her hair, thumbs caressing her temples.

"I'm just admiring the view."

He grunted. "Admire it from a little closer, *merci*. I find I haven't the patience for teasing. Not with you."

She was impatient, too. She braced her hands on his hips, licking the head of his cock with a tentative tongue. She moaned, loving the taste, and opened her mouth to take him in.

"Fuck, Bethany." His hands tightened in her hair, but he didn't push, didn't pull her closer. His body was nearly vibrating against her from holding back.

She tried to take more, her lips stretching, throat closing at the large intrusion. She took a deep breath and relaxed her throat muscles, wanting to drive him wild. Wanting to please him the way he'd pleased her.

He was swearing in French, praising her with a voice broken with passion as she learned what he liked. She swirled her tongue around his shaft, beneath the head of his cock, and he swore through gritted teeth, pleading for more. One hand left his hip to caress the balls stretched tight beneath his erection and he shouted his pleasure.

She couldn't believe how exciting it was to please him. Recalling something she'd read from Allegra's notes, she slid her fingertips along the skin between his legs, between the cheeks of his ass, and pressed.

He jerked against her then, unable to hold himself back. He tugged her head back by her hair, his eyes wild, shocked. "Where did you learn how to do that?"

She pressed harder, feeling the muscles part for her touch. "Why? Do you like it?" Where had her boldness come from? She'd always been bold in her head, but it was as if a dam had been broken by him. And behind it was the woman she'd always wanted to be. Strong. Daring. Provocative.

"Are you curious, Blue Eyes? Do you want to know how it feels? To know what my cock will feel like inside your sweet ass?"

She licked her lips, amazed that she was. She did want to know. "Will you show me?"

He closed his eyes, his expression pained. He dropped to his knees beside her, turning her around until she was on all fours. "I want to. God only knows how I want to."

He spread her cheeks and she gasped when she felt the wet pressure of his tongue. He was kissing her, licking her—*there*. And it felt incredible. Indescribable.

"*Yes.*"

He moaned at her sound of approval, spreading her wider, almost painfully, his tongue greedy as it lapped every drop of water off her skin. He lifted his head, reaching for the new condom on the rim of the tub and tearing the foil with his teeth. "I can't, Bethany. Not this time. I can't wait, can't be gentle. I need to fuck you. *Now*."

She scrambled for purchase as he lifted her hips high and thrust inside her. No waiting, no slow thrusts. She cried out and he growled. He reached up to wrap her hair around his fist again, using the other to grip her shoulder tight, pulling her back into him as he thrust.

"I can't get enough, love. Every time I think I will, but I only want you more. Want you so much, baby. So much."

She moaned, pressing back against him, reveling in the wildness of his pumping hips. His hand tightened on her hair and the sharp tug made her cry out. She was close. She could feel her climax waiting, ready to overwhelm her. Just. One. More.

"Oh, *yes!*"

Her internal muscles tightened around him again and again as her orgasm pounded against her like a summer storm. He called out to her, shouting her name as his release carried him away.

By the time their breathing had slowed and the water cooled, she could almost convince herself that he hadn't said what she thought he had.

Isabel.

CHAPTER 8

BY THE TIME THEY MADE IT BACK OUTSIDE, THE REVELRY was in full swing. With the minister gone, the gazebo had turned into a different type of altar, lined with candles, flowers, even what looked to be miniature skulls.

The people who weren't already dressed in black and purple had been given purple shawls to wrap around their shoulders. To honor Papa Ghede, and welcome him to the gathering.

Bethany watched as a man stood at the base of the altar and lifted his glass. "To my beloved Tamara. Wild at heart, free of spirit, and always ready to laugh."

The crowd cheered for the missing Tamara and drank. A woman came forward next. "For Shelly, who never let the cancer kill her spirit."

The cheering and drinking resumed as Bethany felt a shawl fall over her shoulders. She hadn't noticed until he'd returned that

Bone Daddy had gone to get her one, to help her blend in with the others. His hands were warm on her skin.

He spoke softly in her ear. "They are honoring the dead, now when the veil is thin between worlds. Telling stories and jokes about their friends and family, celebrating life."

"I never understood why the celebration of life always seems to include death and skulls." Bethany pulled the shawl closer, unable to stop the feeling of foreboding that fluttered in her stomach.

He wrapped an arm around her and pulled her back against him. "By acknowledging how temporary life is, you appreciate it that much more." His tone grew thoughtful, somber. "Humans are fragile. Plagues, war, even a bad storm can take them away. Yet as long as you breathe, you build and strive and grow. Even amidst tragedy you find ways to laugh, dance, and remember things to celebrate. That is one of the things that attracts the Loa. The passion of humanity. The life you pack into the short time you have."

She leaned her head on his shoulder. "Is it what attracts you?"

"You attract me, Bethany Sorelle. I cannot think beyond that right now. Are you sure you don't want to go back inside before someone sees us?"

"Too late." Bethany chuckled as she saw Allegra and Michelle heading in their direction.

"You came. I thought you might miss it." Allegra's freckled cheeks were flushed, her eyes bright from love and rum punch.

"Yes. Poor you. You might miss it." Michelle smiled, but her green eyes were flickering all around, telegraphing her discomfort.

Bone Daddy reached around Bethany and took Michelle's hand. "Don't fear your gift, Michelle Toussaint. Revel in it. You can see them. Think of the comfort you could bring on this night."

Michelle tilted her head, her smile growing. "You're kind of a softy, BD. Who saw that coming?"

"I did." Allegra singsonged, gasping as she came closer to Bethany. "You braided your beautiful hair again. And it's wet. Oh. Well. Okay then." She giggled. "You started the honeymoon without us."

Rousseau appeared beside her and pulled her into his arms. "*I'm* going to start the honeymoon without you if you don't stop letting Ben fill your punch glass."

She kissed his lips sweetly. "Don't worry, I'm not *that* tipsy."

"Don't blame me," Ben said. "Blame The Mamas. Every time I turn around mine is adding more rum to the spice punch."

He smiled, and Michelle rolled her eyes at his innocent expression. "I see the apple doesn't fall far from the tree."

To Bethany the image was bittersweet. Both couples were just starting their lives together. So much time. She could hear the clock ticking on her and Bone Daddy, and it was killing her. How had she gotten so attached to him so quickly?

An answer that she didn't want to consider kept echoing in her mind. Like a remembered dream. Or a memory long forgotten.

But it couldn't be true.

She heard the sound of drums and they all turned toward the gazebo. The beat was hypnotic. One drum joined another and another, each beating like a heartbeat, as one heartbeat. As hers.

They moved closer and a circle developed around the drummers, people swaying and rocking together. Some on the edge of the circle were dancing. Bethany wanted to dance.

She swayed to the rhythm, watching as Michelle's mother, Mambo Annemarie Toussaint, stepped into the center of the circle and called on Papa Legba, invoking his name for permission to begin. He opened and closed the doorway between worlds, looked over the crossroads. A messenger, Bethany had read, like Mercury. He was also synonymous with the Christian Saint Peter, the keeper of the keys.

The drums were making it hard for her to think, to concentrate on Mambo Toussaint's words.

Bending over, the priestess sprinkled cornmeal in a design on the grass. Bethany felt the strongest yank yet on her braid, but, knowing it was Emmanuel, she shrugged it off and moved closer, wanting to see.

The drums were pounding faster, matching her breath.

It was an inspiring ceremony, honoring life, the earth, God. Honoring the Marassa twins, the Loa who looked out for twins like Michelle and her brother, Gabriel. And finally, Papa Ghede and his family. He was the Loa of death and fertility, the taker of the souls of the dead, protector of children who die before their time. She'd read something about him, but . . . the drums . . .

"You are paler than I remembered, and older, but I would know those blue eyes anywhere, Isabel."

She turned and the world spun crazily around her. She shook her head, trying to focus. It was the bearded man who'd smiled at her. The one Bone Daddy had glared at as he'd come down the aisle.

"What?" What had he called her?

"Still such a silly girl, chasing after that trash when you could have been a queen. My queen." He came closer and repulsion filled her. But that didn't make any sense. He was a stranger.

He wrapped his fingers around her wrist, his grip painful, bruising.

"Let me go. I don't know you. I think you have me confused with someone else."

Silver glinted on the edge of her vision and she gasped, seeing the knife in his other hand. "I'll have you confused with a corpse if you don't come with me. Quietly. You and I have some unfinished business, Isabel. And Marcel isn't invited this time."

BONE DADDY WATCHED THE REVELERS WITH A SMILE, ELISE on his arm near the center of the circle. She patted his sleeve. "Thank you for being here. Annemarie is thrilled to have you so close for the ritual, and I know Allegra was overjoyed to have you walk her down the aisle."

"Both are my pleasure, *cher*. I have enjoyed my time with your family and their friends." He thought of Bethany.

"And you don't want to leave." She wasn't asking.

"No. I do not." Now more than ever. He would be happy merely to stay beside Bethany, even if she couldn't see him. Maybe he could get Michelle to convince her to move to New Orleans. If not, he would simply follow her to New York. Loa didn't feel the cold.

"Perhaps Papa Ghede will hear your plea."

She didn't sound hopeful, and neither was he. He was fairly certain he wasn't the most popular Loa right now. Especially after Rousseau. Although he had given them the soul of the *djab*. Perhaps that counted for something.

"Love is a powerful force, Bone Daddy. It can make miracles happen, allow you to stay here on our side of the Gate of Guinee." Her hand jerked on his arm. "It can even save a soul near death in time for a second chance."

"What?" He felt the blood leave his face, somehow knowing that what she'd said was important. "What do you mean, Elise Adair?"

She shook her head, placing her other hand on his arm. "I don't know, it's your memory. It's hidden, deep inside . . . but it is yours."

The scar along his side began to throb painfully, as though the wound were fresh. He looked down but saw no blood, no open wound.

"Mama Elise, BD, there you are." Michelle came rushing up to them, breathless. "Something is wrong. Emmanuel won't stop crying." She looked at Bone Daddy. "He says you need to help her, that you're the only one who can."

"Help who?"

Where was Bethany? He looked around the yard, seeking out her red dress, her long dark braid in the frolicking throng. He didn't see her.

Michelle shook her head in frustration. "That's just it. He keeps saying Isabel. But it doesn't make any sense. Isabel was his sister; even if she hadn't disappeared, she couldn't possibly be alive to save."

Bone Daddy stumbled backward and the only thing keeping him standing was Elise's hands on his arm.

Isabel. Save Isabel.

Memories filled his head. Ugly and cruel. Terrifying and empty. And suddenly he knew. Oh God, he knew.

"Bethany!" He jerked out of the older woman's hold and ran toward Ben, grabbing him by his shoulder. "Bethany is in danger. I need you to take me to the St. Louis Cemetery now."

Ben didn't hesitate. "We'll take my bike."

Michelle, Allegra, and Rousseau were right behind them. "We'll follow in my car. I'll be right behind you, baby," Michelle called out to Ben, running past them and into the house.

Bone Daddy hopped on the large, black motorcycle behind Ben, and seconds later the machine roared swiftly into the night. How could he have forgotten her? Even for a moment?

Isabel.

As they got closer to the cemetery, memories grew clearer in his mind. Blue eyes like the deepest ocean. An unusual upside-down mouth that he longed to kiss. Blood pouring down her flowered dress as she lay with her throat sliced open beside her crying brother.

"Son of a bitch! Can't this thing go any faster?"

"Almost there, BD." Ben revved the vibrating motorcycle, weaving through the pedestrian traffic.

God please let him get there sooner this time.

He saw the decorative iron gates of the cemetery and patted Ben's shoulder to slow down enough for him to jump off. He hit the ground running, weaving his way through the aboveground tombs, his feet knowing exactly where he was going.

Save her. Save Isabel. Save Bethany.

A voice rang out. "You haven't changed a bit, big brother. I knew your mama made a deal with the devil."

He stopped a short distance away from the nondescript man who held Bethany against him, a dirty knife to her throat. His brow wrinkled. He didn't know this man, and yet—

"Antoine?"

"Enough of me to matter. And look who I found, right on our special anniversary. Do you believe in fate, Marcel? I would have said no, but since I realized I would get a second chance to kill the both of you, again, I've decided to rethink my position." He tilted his head, talking to the frightened Bethany. "Perhaps this time I should make sure he is completely dead. Would you like to die last this time? See me in action, so to speak?"

Bethany sneered. "Go to hell."

Bone Daddy was afraid to blink, to take his eyes from his woman as she insulted the man with her life in his hands. "Let her go, Antoine. Please. You never wanted to hurt Isabel, it was me you were after. Besides, that was years ago. This woman is *not* Isabel."

Antoine laughed through the scruffy brown beard. "He thinks me feebleminded, Isabel. We were both sent to the best schools, both given the finest education France had to offer. He says you are not you, yet he stands before me, ready to lay down his life for you. Two and two is still four in this century, is it not?"

Bethany was looking straight at him, and he wanted to cry. He couldn't fail her again. She was still alive and he had to insure she stayed that way. "You never studied, Ant. You would have been sent home if our father hadn't continued to send them funding. I'm surprised you could tie your shoes. Now be a man, let her go, and come and fight me like you're dying to."

"I'm dying to. Ah, the irony." Antoine cackled. "Oh good, more company. Welcome to the show." He narrowed his gaze over Bone Daddy's shoulder. "Is that . . . no, it can't be. I truly do believe I'm dreaming." He cupped Bethany's breast in one hand with a vulgar leer. "The girl who gave me my blushing bride on a silver platter. Yes, I think I do believe in fate. Ms. Toussaint has given you to me again."

Bone Daddy heard the shocked gasp and knew Michelle was behind him, and the others as well. "This is not like last time, Antoine. I trust Bethany, and I know she didn't go with you willingly.

Your mind games will not work on any of us this time. We see you for what you are."

The man's eyes narrowed, the spirit of Antoine clear to see in the fire behind them. "Good. If you can see me, you can clearly see the knife as I slice open *Bethany's* throat."

At first he could have sworn she was blinking back tears. But no. Bethany winked at him. Her hands, which had been clinging weakly to the arm holding the weapon, tightened and pushed out quickly. She ducked, jamming her elbow between his legs before rolling away.

It was the height of foolishness.

But it was a chance.

Bone Daddy rushed the body possessed by his half brother, knocking the knife out of his hands and punching him in the jaw.

"Something different." Antoine cupped his chin, circling Bone Daddy warily as he watched Bethany crawl on the ground toward the knife. "Isabel is more of a fighter now. The last time it was almost a relief to kill her when she refused to marry me. All she did was whimper and cry, and call for you to come for her." He met her gaze and she froze beside the knife. "He never did, by the way. Never came to save you. Not until it was too late to matter."

Shame at the memory burned through Bone Daddy. He'd been too late. "You are a bastard."

Antoine growled, losing all semblance of calm. "No. You are the bastard, Marcel—the shameful stench our father could not wash off his shoe. You ruined everything you touched. Father. Isabel. You should have taken the money and agreed to let me have her. No one would have had to die. And you would have been free to live your own life."

Out of the corner of his eye, Bone Daddy saw Ben grab Bethany and drag her to safety. He was glad. No matter what happened to him now, *this time she lived*.

Bone Daddy shook his head. His brother had never understood. "Without her there was no life."

The average body of the bearded man dove on him with nearly inhuman strength, throwing him against the corner of the small mausoleum that held the bodies of Isabel and her brother.

Pain arced through his limbs and he crumpled to the ground. He pulled himself up to his knees in time for Antoine to kick him in his stomach, knocking the wind out of him. Knocking him to the ground once more.

Antoine wasn't Loa, but a ghost strong enough to possess a body was strong enough to enhance its strength. Without his abilities, Bone Daddy knew he wasn't a match for the angry spirit.

"I see you, spirit." Michelle's voice rang out strong and clear in the night. "I am *bon ange*, a guardian for souls, and I *see* you, and all those who dwell here."

Antoine's eyes widened warily. "*Bon ange?* You, Toussaint?"

Bone Daddy got to his feet. "You look scared, little Ant."

Michelle came closer, and Ben, Rousseau, and Allegra stayed right with her, obviously unwilling to leave her side. "The spirits don't appreciate you disrupting their home with your darkness. I see you. And you will leave that body and never bother us again. Now."

She muttered something Bone Daddy couldn't quite make out through the pain-induced roar of blood pounding in his ears. But he could see Antoine's reaction.

The man fell to the ground, rolling along the narrow walk, hitting the tombs as though someone were beating him. After a few moments, he was still, his shallow breathing the only indication that he lived.

It was over. It was finally over.

He'd gotten his second chance.

And she was still alive.

"Bethany?" She was kneeling by his side, tears streaming down her cheeks as she touched his face, her expression one of relief. And wonder.

"You remember?"

She nodded and shrugged at the same time. "A little. I remember you. I remember loving you."

He lifted her into his lap on the cool ground, rocking her as Rousseau and Ben helped the shaken, bearded man out of the cemetery. Michelle glanced up at the sky, which was already starting to change with the predawn light. She turned a worried look to the couple on the ground. "We'll be waiting outside the gate."

Bone Daddy turned away from Bethany long enough to smile at Michelle. "You see? I told you your gift would help people."

Michelle's laughter was choked by a sob. "I'm just glad it worked this time . . . Marcel?"

He nodded and she sniffled, turning to pass Allegra, and headed toward the gate.

Allegra was crying, too. "Thank you for coming to my wedding."

"Aw, *cher*. Thank *you* for honoring me with such a gift. I will treasure it always." Bethany held him tighter and he slid his hand beneath her chin, lifting her face up to the dim light. "I will treasure this day above all others, Blue Eyes. Because of you."

"If I called you would you come back to me?" Her voice was wavering, and he knew she was hanging on by a thread.

He wished he could comfort her with false hope, but he'd promised he would never lie to her. "I want nothing more, but I don't think I'll be able to. Not for a very long while."

"This isn't fair."

He caressed her face, his finger tracing the full curve of her upper lip. "I disagree. I was here this time. Here in time to stop him. I didn't have to hold your dead body in my arms. Or Emmanuel's."

He remembered finding her, finding Emmanuel crying beside her. The little boy had followed her to the cemetery, trying to protect her, but he'd been far too young. He'd hidden until it was over, too afraid to move. Unfortunately, neither of them had realized that Antoine and his helpers were still there, waiting for their moment to finish Marcel.

"I wish I'd been able to save him. I tried, but I was injured, knocked out and left for dead."

Bethany shook her head at the self-loathing in his voice. "You came for us. In my book, you're a hero. Today, yesterday, and always."

He held her close, kissing her gently, sweetly. He wouldn't pray for more than he'd gotten. But he wished. Wished to someday be given the chance to have a life, a full life, with her spirit by his side.

The light was getting stronger and with it, a strange tingling in his limbs. He gripped her shoulders. "Bethany, listen to me. I love you. I loved you then, as Isabel, and I love you now. With everything that I am, I love you. And I always will."

She reached for him once more, pressing her lips, salty and damp with tears, to his. She wouldn't let go, even when he felt the tingles turn to ants, though this time there was no physical pain. But he ached inside as he faded from her sight.

He stood up, watching her collapse on the ground where he'd been only moments before, crying as though her heart would break. The way his was breaking.

"Time to go." The familiar voice sounded regretful but reso-
lute. There would be no second miracle for Bone Daddy.

He bent down and focused on blowing a tendril on her temple.
"Always."

She lifted her hand as she felt the breeze and he smiled before
stepping through the gate that had appeared beside them.

His day was over.

CHAPTER 9

"She hasn't left the room for three days and she's barely eaten."

"Bethany will come out when she's ready. I don't think you'd be doing any better if it was Rousseau who'd disappeared into thin air."

She smiled at Michelle's protective tone from the hallway that led to the kitchen. What Allegra didn't know was that Michelle had knocked on Bethany's door every few hours, offering food and talking softly in the doorway. Keeping her company.

Michelle was a good friend. However misguided, Catherine had been, too.

It was strange, looking over the diaries again and remembering. There were still a lot of missing parts, a lot of blanks. But she knew who she was. Or who she had been.

Isabel.

She touched the locket she'd kept pinned to her shirt since they'd brought her home. She knew how the latch worked now, but she couldn't bring herself to look inside. He'd given it to her. Along with his promise that he'd find a way for them to be together. A promise that, in the end, he just couldn't keep.

She still couldn't believe he was gone. Or that the Marcel she was remembering had somehow become Bone Daddy, a sexual Loa who would live forever.

A part of her wanted to turn around and hide in her room for a few more days, but that wasn't who she was anymore. No more hiding. She had to celebrate her life. It was too short not to. She owed him that much.

"I smell something cooking. Is there enough for me?" She entered the kitchen and chaos ensued.

Allegra and Mambo Toussaint both came to wrap her in relieved embraces. Even Ben lifted her up in a bear hug that left her feet dangling off the floor. Rousseau rushed to get a bowl for the seafood paella he was making, knowing how she loved all things Spanish, he told her with a gentle smile. And Elise passed by, handing her a glass of mango juice and kissing her cheek. She'd never had so much attention in her entire life.

Michelle hung back. She was smiling, but her eyes were wary. Bethany shook her head. She was still worried about what Antoine had said. About her being identical to the Toussaint who'd put Isabel in danger and about her having done it again by bringing Bethany to New Orleans in the first place.

That was why she had to come downstairs. She jerked her chin toward the dining room, knowing Michelle would follow her. "I have something to show you."

Bethany set the puzzle box down on the table and Michelle looked at her, confused. "Isabel's puzzle box? I've already seen it."

"It wasn't Isabel's. I—she didn't put it in her secret spot." She smiled as the others huddled in the doorway between the kitchen and the dining room, unwilling to put forth the effort to pretend they weren't listening.

Michelle sat down in the chair across from her. "Then who?"

"Only two other people in the world, besides Isabel, knew about the secret panel. Emmanuel." Bethany felt the cool breeze and smiled lovingly. "And Catherine Toussaint, Isabel's very best friend."

Michelle flinched, looking at the box as if it had turned into a poisonous snake.

Bethany sighed. "Isabel had given it to her as a gift. A box they could hide secrets in. One only they could open, because they had to do it together." She raised her eyebrows. "Isabel did love her secrets."

She placed one finger from each hand on two indentations on either side of the box. "Now you."

Michelle studied the remaining sides and then placed one hesitant forefinger on each of the last two indentations. The lid popped up with a click and the others gasped. Bethany slid the lid in a circle, opening it the rest of the way, as curious as everyone else.

"It's a letter." Michelle's voice was hushed.

Bethany was surprised. "Catherine obviously got someone to help her put one last secret inside."

Elise Adair huffed audibly and glided to the table. "I am not a patient woman. The suspense is killing me." No one argued when she picked up the amazingly preserved letter and carefully unfolded it, studying the shaky handwriting. "It's to Isabel from Catherine."

Elise's eyes began to water, and Bethany tapped her fingers

lightly on the table, drawing the older woman's gaze. "Out loud would probably be better."

"Not sure about that. But okay."

They all listened raptly as Elise read Catherine's letter. The young Creole woman was obviously distraught and riddled with guilt over the events she had unwittingly set in motion.

Catherine had been a paid companion to Isabel, instructed by her father to inform him of Isabel's movements, a fact she'd been okay with until they'd become friends. But she still took the money.

When Isabel fell in love with Marcel, Catherine truly believed he would break her heart, leave her as he left the others. But in the letter she wondered if she would have fought as hard to break up their relationship if she hadn't been worried about her own future.

Antoine had tricked her. Used her concern to hatch a plan that would put Isabel in a compromising position, forcing his suit, forcing her to marry him. Catherine found out later that he was known to practice the darker arts of voodoo, about his cruelty and abuse of women. She hadn't known what he'd planned to do to Isabel.

Catherine told Marcel when she realized Isabel wasn't where she was supposed to be, where Antoine had promised she would find them, but she'd believed Marcel either hadn't gotten there on time, or that he didn't believe her. Either way, she'd been grief-stricken when Isabel's body was found.

The group was silent as Ben's mother read the rest of the letter. "Marcel's mother and mine commissioned the tomb for you and Emmanuel. I begged Marie Laveau herself to deliver retribution, and since Antoine was never seen again, I have to believe she answered my prayers.

"I expect no redemption for my crimes. They are too great.

You and your brother slain, Marcel missing, all for my poor judgment and disbelief in the oldest and strongest magic of all—love. Neither I, nor any of my line, shall find lasting happiness in love until this debt is repaid. That is my vow to you. My vow to God. Forever your friend, Catherine Toussaint." Elise was visibly shaken as she read the last line, looking toward Mambo Toussaint with damp eyes. "Oh, Annemarie."

"The last piece of the puzzle." Everyone turned to Allegra, who gestured to Bethany. "Don't you see? If you're Isabel and Michelle is—*was* Catherine, then the debt has been repaid. She got rid of Antoine. She saved you and Bone Daddy."

"And Marcel saved his Isabel." Bethany smiled through her tears. She stood and Michelle rushed into her arms, both of them hugging each other, crying and laughing together.

"Fate is a funny thing." Mambo Toussaint wiped her eyes with a nearby napkin. "Michelle was always obsessed with Isabel's treasure, Ben bought the house for Michelle, and together, they made sure Bethany came back home to fix all that had been broken."

Bethany pulled away from Michelle, feeling the walls closing in on her again. "Not all. Some things can't be fixed."

"What about the Gate of Guinee?"

Bethany looked at Elise with a frown. "The Gate of Whozee?"

Mambo Toussaint shook her head. "It's too dangerous. They could just as easily decide to keep her over there as let him go. Although it does seem more and more like he is one loophole they might be okay with closing. A Loa but not a Loa."

"What. Are. You. Talking. About?" Bethany's teeth were clenched, and her heart was pounding. Was there a way to bring him back? "If I'm the only one in danger, if there's the slimmest chance I could bring him back to me, I say let's do it."

Michelle tilted her head, listening to something only she could hear. "They are talking about the gateway to the other side, Bethany. And Emmanuel says he wants to go with you. So you don't have to be alone."

"OKAY, BETHANY. THIS IS NOT THE WEIRDEST THING YOU'VE ever done."

True, she was wearing a strong-smelling pouch of protection around her neck, held a piece of rum cake in her hand, and was currently walking all over the city looking for a nonexistent cemetery gate while talking to the ghost of her brother from a past life—but surely she'd done worse.

"If you look for the gate, it starts looking for you." That's what the Mambo had said. Every native of the Crescent City knew about it, but it wasn't on any of the tours. It was the gate to the other side. If you were determined to speak to the dead, ask them a question, you could find it. Of course, there was every chance you would die, or be held there as those you loved died, leaving you in a state of purgatory.

"All lovely choices," she mumbled, trudging through the Quarter, trying to build up her nerve.

There'd been no question in her mind that she would do it. For Isabel, who'd loved him helplessly, trapped by her own innocence and the times she lived in. For herself, for the chance to tell him what she hadn't. That she, Bethany, was in love with him, and she didn't want to be without him.

She turned a corner and stopped, looking behind her and back down at her map. There shouldn't be a cemetery on this street, but she was looking directly at it. The map fluttered in the sudden breeze and she folded it up, slipping it in her pocket and holding her hand open at her side. "Take my hand, Emmanuel. Don't be afraid."

She felt her palm cool and smiled. Somehow, she did feel better with him at her side. Isabel had loved her little brother as though he were her own child. She'd wanted to take him with them when she and Marcel ran away. He hadn't deserved his fate. None of them had.

The wrought-iron gate began to open on its own. She saw sparks flying off it, strange lights, and she shivered, recalling something Allegra had told her. "Sometimes it's that leap into the darkness that can be the most worthwhile."

She took a deep breath and began to walk forward, feeling compelled. No turning back now. "Time to leap."

THE AIR HAD CHANGED. THE SKY. AS IF THE COLOR HAD been swept out of the world, leaving in its place a sepia-toned copy. There were tombs lining the road, a few benches here and there, even a shack in the distance. But it wasn't right. It didn't feel real.

"You look lost, little girl."

She whipped around, gasping as she realized the gate had disappeared, leaving the barren road, with another crossing it, heading off into forever. And a man. A kindly old black man with a smile and a curious expression. The hair on his head and face was white, and he was leaning on a cane.

"Where am I?"

He shook his head. "Is that your question? You only get one, I know they told you that. Better make sure it's a good one."

"You look familiar." Bethany squeaked at the young male voice, surprised to feel a tight grip on her hand where before there'd only been a cool breeze. Standing beside her was a ten-year-old boy with raven-black hair and large blue eyes. Emmanuel.

The man's smile broadened at the boy's words. "You've seen me before, Manuel. Isn't that what your sister always called you? I knew I'd see you again. You've been very brave."

The boy puffed his chest out at the male admiration, his expression proud. "Men should take care of the people they love."

"That's right. That's right. Good boy." Sparkling eyes lifted to meet Bethany's gaze, though he was still talking to Emmanuel. "I once knew a man whose heart was pure, who tried to protect the people he loved. A long time ago, on the evening of All Saints' I believe, he nearly died trying to save his dead lover's little brother from being sacrificed along with her."

Bethany held her breath, knowing he was talking about Marcel.

Emmanuel's eyes widened. "What happened to him?"

"Well, boy. You know Papa Ghede protects the innocent, and the very young. It was his night to roam the earth, and when he realized what had happened, he took pity on the man, the son of someone so close to the powerful voodoo queen."

Marie Laveau? It had to be. Marcel's mother had been one of her apprentices. Bethany opened her mouth to ask a question, and the old man's finger came up to silence her. "One question. But wait until I'm done telling this sweet child my story."

She nodded and he continued. "The man was heartsick. Pained in a way that no doctor could heal. The Loa have power, but even if they could have turned back the clock, as they had before, Ghede knew the world was not ready for what this man truly desired. A chance to live, free and in love, with his woman.

"The only thing to do was wait. But Ghede knew the man would go mad with the memories and it would twist him in the in-between time, so he made him forget. Had me watch over the man while we allowed him to spend the years he would have to wait for his chance to come round again doing what he did best."

"Pleasuring women." Bethany nodded. In a way, it made perfect sense.

The old man shushed her. "I wasn't planning on saying that in front of the child, but yes. Okay, I've told my story. You may ask one question now."

Her heart pounded. She understood now. They'd given Marcel a gift, a chance. He'd never actually died. He'd just become Bone Daddy. A temporary Loa. Which explained why he knew so little about his own kind. He wasn't truly one of them. Not completely.

She only had one question. "How can he return to my world, to live out a life with me?"

He chuckled. "That sure he wants to, eh?"

Isabel may have had a doubt. Bethany didn't. "Yes. Yes, I am."

He nodded. "That's good. Much better. Well, I suppose the answer to your question is clear. All he has to do is ask."

"I'm asking. I want to be with Bethany."

She was afraid to turn around. He was here. Right behind her. She shuddered, looking down to see that Emmanuel was beaming, almost glowing with happiness. She watched the old man tilt his head, looking at Bone Daddy over her shoulder.

"You sure? You'll be human. One short, fragile life. With only one woman."

She glared at the smiling man, but he was ignoring her, waiting for Bone Daddy's answer.

"I'm sure. I love her."

A tear slipped down her cheek. He loved her. She'd known, but hearing him say it with no hesitation, choosing her over an immortal life of sensual satisfaction . . . How could she ask for a stronger declaration of his love?

"The only thing left is the toll." The old man stood up straighter, his smile gone, white eyebrow raised.

"But I brought cake." No one had told her about a toll. Had he let them both come all this way, only to keep them here?

"I'll stay."

"Emmanuel, no." Bethany reached for his hand, but he'd slipped away, going to stand beside the older man, expectation and excitement on his face.

The man tapped his pants thoughtfully with his straw hat. "You would certainly work. You think you're ready for what's down the road?"

Emmanuel was nearly hopping with excitement. "What *is* down the road?"

"You know what they say. My father's house has many mansions. Go wait for me by the corner."

Emmanuel turned back to Bethany, wrapping his arms around her in a warm hug, then before she could return the favor, he was sprinting toward the crossroad.

"You've been a good mentor to me. A good friend. Thank you, Papa Legba."

Bone Daddy laid a hand on her shoulder and she gasped at his touch.

"And you're a good boy. Take care of yourself, and don't go being a hero. We may not be around the next time to save your bacon. Bacon. Hah." Papa Legba winked at her and then he was gone. All of it was gone.

But she could still feel him beside her. Where he belonged.

CHAPTER 10

"I told you I wasn't going anywhere, Blue Eyes."

"I'm not taking any chances."

"But, Bethany, if you leave me like this, how can I bring you pleasure?"

Bethany stood at the foot of the bed, smiling in satisfaction at her handiwork. She'd used some of the silk shawls leftover from last week's celebration to tie him to the four-poster bed. Naked.

She licked her lips. "You're bringing me pleasure right now, BD. Trust me."

When they'd come back to the old mansion, after Michelle and the others had welcomed them home, Mambo Toussaint sobbing with relief, they had faded into the woodwork. Food had been set outside their bedroom door, and clean clothes, but other than that, they were left alone.

The last few days had been heaven.

They'd talked until their voices were hoarse. About their memories of the life they'd lived before, about all they'd been through since they were parted. There were some things Bethany didn't want to know. As far as she was concerned, the Love Doctor of the Big Easy had closed his practice to take care of a single patient. Her.

They'd opened the locket together, and the small paintings inside had given her a start. "But Isabel was so sought after, everyone thought she was so beautiful."

BD had winked. "She was. She is."

The image of Isabel in the locket, opposite the image of Marcel, looked exactly like Bethany. A little younger, her Spanish and French heritage showing in her light olive skin tone, but other than that, they were identical. Same lips, same eyes. She'd always thought herself plain.

"If I've learned anything from all the years I was waiting for you, it is that people change. Their ideas about the world, about each other, about beauty. But some things never do. You are beautiful, Bethany. You are timeless."

He remembered everything now, the final gift the Loa had given him, but he still wasn't comfortable being called Marcel. "It was another life. I was a different man. I think I'll be BD for a while. Until I find something better."

She could still see Marcel inside him. The way he looked at her, his desire to take care of her. But there was a confidence, a soul-deep strength that emanated from him that was all Bone Daddy. And nearly irresistible.

He smiled. "Come on, love. Don't make me beg."

"As if you would," she huffed, climbing on top of him and leaning forward to place a soft, teasing kiss on his lips.

"Oh I would, Blue Eyes. For you. Only for you."

She sat up, her fingers tracing the scar that curved around his side and stomach, a reminder of the pain-filled past. He'd gotten this trying to save her brother, Manuel. "Do you think Emmanuel is all right?"

"I've told you, baby. Emmanuel is better than fine. He's no longer trapped in the past, trapped in his childhood. No longer a ghost. And who knows, maybe he'll get another chance at life as well."

"I read a book about reincarnation once. It was fascinating. They said there are these things called soul groups and you all keep coming back together, learning life les—"

"Bethany." His voice was stern.

"Yes, BD?"

"You have a sex slave tied to your bed, naked and hard for you. Are you sure you want to talk about books right now?"

He did look a little pained. She could feel his erection hot against her, and all at once, she didn't think books were all that interesting. Overrated, really. Especially when compared against the real thing.

ABOUT THE AUTHOR

R. G. Alexander has lived all over the country and has studied archaeology and mythology, has been a nurse and a vocalist, and is now a writer. She is married to a talented chef who is her best friend, her research assistant, and the love of her life. Visit her website at www.rgalexander.com.